PRAISE FO

TEA SHOP M

"T tea-shop business in this country to the status of wine bars and bustling coffee houses." —*Buon Gusto* (Minneapolis, MN)

"Engages the audience from the start . . . Laura Childs provides the right combination between tidbits on tea and an amateur sleuth cozy that will send readers seeking a cup of *Death by Darjeeling,* the series' previous novel."

—*Midwest Book Review*

Death by Darjeeling

"Highly recommended" by the Ladies Tea Guild
"Book of Choice" by the Red Hat Society

"Tea lovers, mystery lovers, [this] is for you. Just the right blend of cozy fun and clever plotting."

—Susan Wittig Albert, bestselling author of *Bloodroot*

"It's a delightful book!" —*Tea A Magazine*

"Murder suits [Laura Childs] to a Tea."

—*St. Paul Pioneer Press*

"If you devoured Nancy Drew and Trixie Belden, this new series is right up your alley."

—*The Goose Greek (SC) Gazette*

"*Death by Darjeeling* is a good beginning to a new culinary series that will quickly become a favorite of readers who favor this genre. The cozy and inviting setting will quickly draw readers in and a likable cast of characters will have them eager to return." —*The Mystery Reader*

"Gives the reader a sense of traveling through the streets and environs of the beautiful, historic city of Charleston."

—*Lakeshore Weekly News* (Wayzata, MN)

Tea Shop Mysteries by Laura Childs

Shades of Earl Grey

LAURA CHILDS

BERKLEY PRIME CRIME, NEW YORK

SHADES OF EARL GREY

A Berkley Prime Crime Book / published by arrangement with the author

PRINTING HISTORY
Berkley Prime Crime mass-market edition / January 2003

Cover art by Stephanie Henderson.
Cover design by Leslie Worrell.
Text design by Kristin del Rosario.

For information address: The Berkley Publishing Group,
a division of Penguin Putnam Inc.,
375 Hudson Street, New York, New York 10014.

Visit our website at
www.penguinputnam.com

ISBN: 0-425-18821-3

Berkley Prime Crime Books are published
by The Berkley Publishing Group,
a division of Penguin Putnam Inc.,
375 Hudson Street, New York, New York 10014.
The name BERKLEY PRIME CRIME and
the BERKLEY PRIME CRIME design
are trademarks belonging to Penguin Putnam Inc.

PRINTED IN THE UNITED STATES OF AMERICA

10 9 8 7 6 5 4

ACKNOWLEDGMENTS

Heartfelt thank-you's to Mary Higgins Clark for her kindness and gentle *noodge* into mystery writing; my agent, Sam Pinkus; everyone at Berkley Publishing; friends from Malice Domestic, MWA, and Bouchercon; the wonderful tea hostesses (tireless entrepreneurs, all of them!) at countless tea shops around the country who have embraced my series; all the marvelous booksellers who have kindly recommended my books; the writers and reviewers who have generously featured my books in their magazines, newspapers, newsletters, and web sites. Much gratitude to my husband, Dr. Robert Poor, to Jennie, Mom, and Jim Smith, and the many readers who continue to be charmed by Theodosia and the Indigo Tea Shop. Tea and trouble keep brewing in Charleston because of you!

Find out more about the author,
her Tea Shop Mysteries Series,
and her Scrapbook Mystery Series
at www.laurachilds.com

CHAPTER I

SCURRYING ACROSS THE Italian marble floor of the Lady Goodwood Inn, Theodosia Browning glanced up at the gleaming painting of the inn's venerable founder and matriarch. Harriet Beecher Goodwood gazed down at her guests from her lofty perch. With her glowing porcelain skin, heavy necklace of blue topaz, and pale peach organza gown cinched tightly about her waist, she was the very picture of Southern femininity. A woman with a properly demure manner who also conveyed a fine aristocratic bearing. Yet her watchful eyes seemed to betray a certain wistfulness, as though Lady Goodwood would prefer to step out of her formal portrait and mingle with the carefree throng that milled about below.

In her black satin slacks and figure-skimming smoking jacket, Theodosia breathed a silent prayer of relief that modern-day Charleston women were no longer bound by strict social constraints or uncomfortable, tightly corseted gowns. How on earth would she ever be able to fly about the Indigo Tea Shop, greeting guests and brewing tea, if she were costumed in ankle-length skirts, pantalets, high button boots, and a whale bone corset? Better yet, how would she even draw breath in an outfit like that? Especially when summer's heat and humidity crept in from the low-country and turned the city into a real cooker!

"Theodosia! Over here!" Drayton Conneley, Theodosia's dear friend and right-hand man at the Indigo Tea Shop, gave a casual wave to her from the spot he'd staked out near the potted palms. Sixty-two years old, with a head of grizzled gray hair, Drayton was dashingly attired in a cream-colored cashmere jacket, dove gray slacks, and trademark bow tie. Theodosia noted that, for this late autumn party, Drayton had chosen a muted paisley bow tie. Plu-perfect, of course, and the signature touch that always made Drayton the picture of elegance and charm.

Theodosia grinned at Drayton as she pushed her way through the crowd. What a sport he was to accompany her here tonight in lieu of her usual boyfriend, Jory Davis. Especially when Drayton didn't even know the bride-to-be! But then, Drayton was always a gentleman and a good sport. Intrigued by her vision of starting Charleston's first authentic tea shop in the historic district, Drayton hadn't hesitated to resign his rather lofty position at one of Charleston's major hotels and leap at the opportunity to become her master tea blender and majordomo.

Theodosia had a great admiration for risk takers. Of course, she'd been one herself. Just three years ago, she'd bid a hearty *arrivederci* to job security at one of Charleston's major advertising agencies when she'd resigned *her* job as vice president of client services.

A long-abandoned, dusty little tea shop on Church Street had quietly beckoned. Along with a yearning for a far more independent lifestyle and a desire to chart her own course, make her own business decisions. Theodosia knew she would get out of the tea shop exactly what she put into it, and she was fine with that. More than fine, in fact.

And Drayton and Haley Parker, dear friends and willing accomplices, had been there with her from the very beginning.

Drawing upon his years spent in Amsterdam as a master tea blender, Drayton had immediately set about stocking the Indigo Tea Shop with an enviable selection of loose teas. Pungent, orange-red Assams. Smoky, slightly sweet Ceylon teas. Fragrant Darjeelings from the steep slopes of the Himalayas. There were also sparkling emerald green teas from Japan, gyokos and senchas, that were a touch puckery and a bit of an acquired taste. Plus a robust assortment of Indonesian, Malaysian, Turkish, and African teas, as well as the enticing black tea grown at the Charleston Tea Plantation located some twenty-five miles south of Charleston on Wadmalaw Island in the low-country.

Haley, Theodosia's young pastry chef, was a sometime student who was still trying to determine her way in the world. How lucky for the Indigo Tea Shop, however, that Haley delighted in baking her infamous blackberry scones, cream muffins, gingerbread cakes, and shortbread in the tiny little aromatic kitchen at the back of the tea shop. Lately, Haley had even come up with her own recipe for marvels, those deep-fried cookies so peculiar to South Carolina.

And all the elements had come together. Beautifully. The Indigo Tea Shop had fast become a charming little gem of a shop, one stitch in the elegant tapestry of restaurants, shops, museums, and historic homes that made up Charleston's famed historic district.

The tea shop's interior, stripped of its former cork ceiling panels and indoor/outdoor carpet, now gleamed richly with original pegged wooden floors, exposed beams and red brick walls. Antique hickory tables and chairs, some Theodosia had salvaged from the out-buildings of her Aunt Libby's farm, contributed to an atmosphere that was authentically cozy and inviting. Shelves that weren't laden with copper canisters and sparkling jars filled with tea, were crowded with Yi-Hsing tea pots, tea presses, jars of DuBose Bees Honey and Devonshire cream, and their own house brands of packaged teas such as Cooper River Cranberry and Britannia Breakfast Blend. The Indigo Tea Shop was a setting filled with authenticity and grace, and it tantalized guests. And luckily for Theodosia, those guests descended upon her tea shop in droves. The shopkeepers from up and down Church Street, residents of the historic district who had been anxious to adopt a charming little tea shop as their own, visitors to Charleston who strolled the nearby walkways and hidden cobblestone paths.

Theodosia hurried over to Drayton and grabbed his arm. "So good of you to come," she told him.

He smiled down at her. "You're looking lovely," he told her.

"To be perfectly honest," she said, turning her blue eyes upon him and patting her auburn hair self-consciously, "I feel rather tossed together. Delaine called at the last minute to ask if she could borrow my baroque silver card receiver to use as a stand so she could display Camille's wedding ring. So, of course, I had to scoot over here, where I immediately got roped into helping with a few *more* last-minute details. Then I had to make a mad dash home, give Earl Grey a quick run around the block, and get myself all fixed up. And then it started to pour buckets," Theodosia added breathlessly.

The Delaine that Theodosia was referring to was Delaine Dish, a friend of Theodosia's and Drayton's who owned the clothing boutique, Cotton Duck, just a few doors down from the Indigo Tea Shop. Earl Grey was Theodosia's dog, a mixed breed she'd found cowering in the alley behind the tea shop one rainy night. Theodosia had promptly adopted the bedraggled pup and dubbed him a purebred dalbrador. The very grateful and loving Earl

Grey had been Theodosia's constant companion ever since. He had taken to obedience and agility training like a duck to water and had also earned his Therapy Dog International certificate, which gave both of them the privilege of making regular visits to nursing homes and children's hospital wards.

Tonight's *soiree* was an engagement party for Delaine's niece, Camille Cantroux. Camille was engaged to marry a young Marine captain, Corey Buchanan from Savannah, Georgia. In fact, the wedding was just a few weeks away, set to take place the Saturday after Thanksgiving.

"Here's Haley," said Drayton as a young woman in a swirl of black crepe hurried to join them.

"Hey, you guys," said Haley in a breathless rush, "tell me if this dress looks okay." As she executed a self-conscious little twirl, her long straight hair swirled out in a wedge around her. "I borrowed it from my cousin, Rowena."

"Terrific," piped up Drayton immediately, without so much as a look in her direction.

Haley rolled her eyes.

Theodosia, however, took Haley very seriously and studied her little black cocktail dress with an appraising eye. In her short, fun dress she looked like an updated Audrey Hepburn. Coltish, very much the gamin. Except, of course, for her long, straight hair and slightly impudent nature. That was pure Haley.

"You look adorable," Theodosia reassured her. "Youthful, very fresh. I'm confident every young man here tonight will have his eye on you."

"Do you really think so?" asked Haley. She glanced around quickly at the crowd of young people. "There *are* lots of good-looking guys here, aren't there? Do you think they're all Marines?"

"I'd say there are more than a few good men," said Drayton, who never failed to delight in teasing Haley.

Haley, on the other hand, simply ignored his jibes. "How come Delaine is throwing an engagement party here in Charleston when her niece and her fiancé are getting married in Savannah?" she asked.

"Besides the fact that Delaine lives here, Camille also attended school here at Charleston College," explained Theodosia. "So Camille has loads of friends in the area. You know, she graduated this past summer with a B.A. in English literature."

"Cool," nodded Haley. "I was an English lit major once."

"Haley," said Drayton, "you were also a studio arts major, women's studies major, and . . . let's see . . . what was your most recent foray? Business?"

"Hey, smarty," Haley shot back, "I'm *still* taking classes in business administration. This time I will get my degree."

"Of course you will," Theodosia assured her.

"Thanks, Theo," said Haley. "Hey, your hair looks great tonight," she exclaimed as an afterthought.

"No, not really," said Theodosia, nervously patting her hair again.

"Batten down the hatches," said Drayton under his breath. "Here comes Delaine."

Delaine Dish, proud aunt and planner extraordinaire of tonight's engagement party, came plowing through the throng of guests like an ocean liner entering New York Harbor. Delaine's long, dark hair was swept into an up-do and she wore a midnight blue chiffon dress with a beaded camisole bodice and frothy skirt. With her slightly up-turned eyes, Delaine looked tall, dark, and elegant.

"Delaine, darling," said Drayton, greeting her. "You're looking lovely."

Delaine rubbed a bare shoulder against Drayton. "Such a way with women you have, Mr. Conneley."

Theodosia sighed. Delaine was a sweet soul. No one could touch her fiery zeal when it came to raising money for the Heritage Society, campaigning for the Charleston

Humane Society, or selling tickets for the Lamplighter Tour. But Delaine did have a certain fondness for men.

Delaine finally turned her gaze toward Theodosia and Haley. "Having a good time, you two?"

"Everything is lovely," replied Theodosia. "The Lady Goodwood Inn was a perfect choice."

"So was the string quartet," added Drayton, nodding toward the group of musicians tucked off in the corner.

Theodosia let her gaze wander, taking in the small, elegant ballroom with its color palette of cream and pale blue, the multitude of vases overflowing with fresh flowers, the tuxedo-clad waiters who bore silver trays with crystal flutes of champagne. "It's nice to be a guest for once and not the caterer," she told Delaine.

In the past year, the Indigo Tea Shop had catered a multitude of engagement teas, garden teas, and wedding receptions. So being a guest here tonight really *was* a luxury for Theodosia.

"Tell us about Captain Corey Buchanan," Haley urged Delaine. "I love the idea that he's a captain in the Marines. Just the thought of it is so dashing and romantic."

"Well, I don't know him all *that* well," replied Delaine. "In fact I've really only met the dear fellow twice. But I *can* tell you he's a graduate of Annapolis and the Basic School in Quantico, and that Captain Corey Buchanan is one of *the* Buchanans from Savannah." Delaine's eyes sparkled with excitement. "They're a very old family. Terribly well-to-do."

"I'm sure he's a fine young man," said Theodosia, choosing to ignore Delaine's somewhat tactless implication of wealth and riches. "And that he and Camille are very much in love."

Haley nodded in agreement. "In the scheme of things, that's what really counts."

"Have you seen Camille's ring?" asked Delaine, still in a twitter.

"Gorgeous," replied Drayton.

"Oh, no," Delaine was quick to protest. "Not the *engagement* ring. Of course, that's beautiful. Stunning, really. But wait until you-all get a gander at Camille's *wedding* ring. I just put it on display in the Garden Room a few minutes ago. It's what you'd call a *killer* ring. Estate jewelry, don't you know?"

"Estate jewelry," repeated Haley. "What exactly does that mean?"

Delaine looked pleased at Haley's question. "Honey," she said in a hushed tone, "it means the ring has been in Captain Buchanan's family for *decades!*" She took a quick sip of champagne to fortify herself, then continued. "The ring is an emerald-cut diamond flanked by six smaller round diamonds. The center stone came from a distant relative, Angelique Delacroix, who was a French noblewoman married to a minor Austrian archduke back in the mid-eighteen-hundreds. The archduke reputedly purchased the diamond when one of Marie Antoinette's crowns was sold off!"

"Wow!" said Haley, impressed now. "Sounds like the kind of ring a girl could lose her head over."

"Oh yes," Delaine bubbled on. "Wait until you see it." She glanced around. "Captain Buchanan and the rest of the boys should be here any moment. A couple of the groomsmen had tuxedo fittings this afternoon." She rolled her eyes. "You know how young men are. They probably stopped at Slidell's Oyster Bar for a celebratory drink. I certainly hope they won't be indiscreet."

"Or delayed," added Theodosia. All the guests had been sipping cocktails for the better part of an hour now and there seemed to be a restless hum in the tightly packed room. Probably, Theodosia decided, most of the guests were as ready as she was for dinner in the more spacious Garden Room, which had once been the inn's greenhouse. Delaine had been huddling with the Lady Goodwood's head chef for weeks and had finally decided upon an appetizer of she-crab soup, a salad of baby field greens, and an entrée of smoked duck breast, cranberry relish, and fried squash blossoms.

"So when do we get a peek at this show-stopper of a ring?" asked Haley, looking around in great anticipation.

Delaine glanced nervously at her watch again, a jewel-encrusted Chopard. "Hopefully we'll be going in for dinner any minute now. We're really just waiting for Captain Buchanan." Delaine drained the last of her champagne. "Until this afternoon," she explained, "Brooke had been storing the ring in her vault at Heart's Desire. For safe-keeping, of course."

Located on Water Street in the historic district, Heart's Desire was one of Charleston's premier estate jewelry shops. It was owned and lovingly operated by Brooke Carter Crockett, a woman who could trace her ancestry all the way back to the famous frontiersman, Davy Crockett.

Over the years, Heart's Desire had become the premier jeweler for buying and selling estate jewelry. So much fine jewelry was still available in Charleston, owing to the many French and English families who had settled in and around the area during the seventeen- and eighteen-hundreds. And over the years, their rice, indigo, and cotton plantations had yielded enormous wealth and all the trappings that came with it.

"Camille and Captain Buchanan have even agreed to allow the wedding ring to be displayed in the Heritage Society's Treasures Show," Delaine prattled on.

"That starts this weekend?" asked Haley.

"The members-only part is this Saturday evening," explained Drayton, who currently served on the board of directors of the Heritage Society as parliamentarian. "Then the grand opening for the public will be the following weekend."

"Of course," said Delaine, "the wedding ring is not

quite as showy as some of the pieces in the European Jewel Collection, but it's a quality piece, just the same." The European Jewel Collection was a special traveling show that was being brought in to augment the Heritage Society's own pieces.

"It was a lovely and generous gesture on the part of Camille and Captain Buchanan to allow their ring to be displayed," said Drayton.

"Oh, Coop, over here!" chirped Delaine. She waved at a tall, lanky man, beckoning him to come join their foursome. "You-all know Cooper Hobcaw, don't you?" she asked.

"Hello, Mr. Hobcaw," said Theodosia, shaking hands with the silver-haired, hawk-nosed Hobcaw.

"Coop. Just Coop," he told her. Glancing at Drayton and Haley, Cooper Hobcaw nodded hello.

Cooper Hobcaw was a senior partner at Hobcaw McCormick and one of Charleston's premier criminal attorneys. He was smart and tough and wily and had a reputation for playing hardball. Last year he'd defended an accused murderer and had succeeded in getting him acquitted. That had made Cooper Hobcaw slightly unpopular among Charleston's more politically correct set and had greatly rankled Burt Tidwell, the homicide detective who was an on-again off-again friend of Theodosia's.

But a person shouldn't be defined by what they do, decided Theodosia. Cooper Hobcaw had been squiring Delaine around for quite a few months now, and Delaine seemed completely and utterly charmed by him.

"Would you like another drink, honey?" Cooper Hobcaw asked Delaine solicitously.

"Please," she said, handing over her empty glass. "But this time . . . maybe a cosmopolitan?"

"Ladies?" Hobcaw threw a questioning glance at Theodosia and Haley, who both shook their heads. Their champagne glasses were still half-full.

"I'll come with you," offered Drayton.

"No, no, please. Allow me," said Cooper Hobcaw. "You stay with the ladies and keep them amused. I'll bring you a . . . what is it you've got there? Bourbon?"

"Right," nodded Drayton.

"Good man," said Hobcaw with a crooked grin. "I can't stand that bubbly stuff either."

"Okay," said Haley after Cooper Hobcaw had moved off, "tell me which one is Camille Cantroux. There are so many pretty girls here, I don't know one from the other."

"Over there," said Theodosia. "Standing by the baby grand piano. With the short blond hair." She indicated a young woman in a champagne-colored slip dress whose tones just happened to perfectly match her short-cropped and ever-so-slightly-spiked hair.

"The one who's about a size *two?*" said Haley. "My, she *is* pretty, isn't she."

"Camille's adorable," gushed Delaine, who was fairly ga-ga over her young niece.

"Did you help pick out her wedding gown?" asked Drayton, who had finally assumed an *if you can't beat 'em, join 'em* attitude about the wedding discussion.

"Of course," said Delaine. "But being that Camille is so tiny, I suggested breaking from traditional style. Instead of her being overpowered by a big flouncy dress and flowing veil that would make her look like a human wedding cake, I found the most adorable little French creation. It has a bodice with just the tiniest bit of rouching, and a tulle ballerina skirt. *Très elegant*—but, of course, not in white."

"Not in white?" said Drayton. "Then what . . . ?"

"*Ivory,*" said Delaine, as though she'd single-handedly invented the color. "Ivory is so much more elegant than white. White has become awfully" she paused, searching for the word "passé."

"I'm particularly fond of ecru myself," said Haley. "On the other hand, I wouldn't entirely rule out alabaster . . ." Haley suddenly stopped short as a deafening crash echoed through the room. At the exact same moment, a flash of lightning strobed in the tall, cathedral-style windows that lined one end of the ballroom, illuminating the night sky.

Startled, Theodosia took a step backward and turned toward the nearest waiter, fully expecting to see an entire tray of champagne glasses dumped on the floor. But no, the waiter was still clutching his tray, looking around in alarm.

The string quartet had stopped mid-note and the musicians were also glancing about with nervous looks. A strange hush had fallen over the room as the guests milled about, mumbling quietly and looking profoundly unsettled.

As if on cue, a second crash suddenly rocked the room. This time, the noise was louder still. And there was no mistaking the direction from which it came.

Camille Cantroux broke from the crowd and ran to the double doors that led to the Garden Room, where the sit-down dinner was supposed to take place. Grabbing the ornate door handles, Camille tugged at the doors, struggling to pull them open. The heavy doors seemed to resist for a moment, then they suddenly flew open, revealing the interior of the Garden Room.

But instead of elegant linen-draped tables alight with blazing candles, the Garden Room was a disaster! Half of the roof had seemingly collapsed. Rain poured in from above, drenching tablecloths, place settings, floral arrangements, and gifts. Sheets of glass mingled with smaller, dangerously pointed shards. Twisted metal struts, once part of the roof, poked up from the rubble.

And underneath it all lay Captain Corey Buchanan.

Camille's voice rose in a shrill scream. "Corey! Corey!" she cried as she ran to him and threw herself down on the floor, ignoring the shattered glass and jagged metal.

Facedown, arms flung out to his sides like a rag doll, poor Corey Buchanan lay motionless. Camille plucked frantically at the back of his damp uniform as blood gushed from Captain Buchanan's head and rain poured down from above. Desperate, needing to do *something,* Camille struggled to work her arms under and around Captain Buchanan, ignoring the debris that tore at her, wanting only to cradle her fiancé's bloody head in her arms.

Following directly on Camille's heels, Theodosia had raced across the room, covering the short distance in a heartbeat. She'd hesitated in the doorway for a split second, taking in the roof with its gaping hole, the wreckage of glass strewn everywhere, and the one enormous shard of glass that had imbedded itself deep in the back of Captain Buchanan's neck, right near the top of his spine.

And Theodosia knew in her heart there was no hope.

Kneeling gingerly to avoid the needle-like slivers of glass and pointed metal, Theodosia gently placed her index and middle fingers against Corey Buchanan's neck. Hoping against hope, she held her breath and prayed. But there was no pulse, no sign of life in this poor boy.

Captain Corey Buchanan, eldest son and proud warrior of the Savannah, Georgia Buchanans, would never again serve his country as a United States Marine, would never walk with pride down the church aisle in his dress white uniform. Now the only service poor Captain Buchanan would take part in would be his own funeral.

Wailing in helpless despair, Camille rocked her dead fiancé back and forth in her arms. "Now who'll place the wedding ring on my finger?" she sobbed.

Theodosia turned her gaze to the black velvet ring box that was perched atop the silver card receiver she'd brought over earlier. Captain Buchanan had obviously slipped in the back door with the intention of putting the ring on display. But the velvet box sat empty. There was no ring to be seen.

CHAPTER 2

FROM A SCENE that seemed to unfold in slow motion, activity suddenly accelerated with warp speed. Police and paramedics arrived to load Captain Corey Buchanan onto a gurney and hustle him out to a waiting ambulance. A sobbing Camille Cantroux was aided to her feet by Theodosia and Drayton. Then Delaine, shell-shocked and shaking, led her away, presumably to follow the ambulance to the hospital.

The rest of the party goers pressed through the double doors into the Garden Room. They crunched across glass, gaping at the enormous hole in the ceiling and talking in hushed tones about the horrible turn of events.

At one point Theodosia was aware of Cooper Hobcaw arguing with Frederick Welborne, the manager of the Lady Goodwood Inn. Hobcaw's once-elegant suit was now dripping wet. He had apparently run out into the street to flag down the ambulance and guide the paramedics to the nearest entry.

As he loudly harangued poor Frederick Welborne, the

man looked as though he might suffer a heart attack on the spot.

Cooper Hobcaw's slipped into his role as lawyer, Theodosia thought to herself. Probably talking about liability and personal injury suits. She decided she wouldn't want to be in Frederick Welborne's shoes tonight. No way, no how.

"I can't believe this," wailed Haley. She was pale and shivering. "Do you think Captain Buchanan will be okay?"

Theodosia pulled Haley aside and out of the way of the gawkers. "It doesn't look good," she told her in a quiet voice.

Haley bobbed her head rapidly, obviously experiencing more than a little stress. "That's what I was afraid of. Oh, that poor, poor man, did you see the glass sticking out of . . . ?"

Drayton put a hand on Haley's shoulder. "*Shhh* . . . it's okay. Try to calm down."

Haley stared at him with sadness in her eyes. "But it isn't okay," she whispered. "Theo thinks he might be *dead!*"

"We'll phone the hospital later and see what news there is," said Drayton. He kept his voice calm and soothing, and his reassuring tone seemed to work on Haley, seemed to calm her down considerably. "Delaine and Camille went on to the hospital," he added, "so we'll be able to speak with them later and see what's going on."

"We need everyone to exit this room, please!" rang out a loud, authoritarian voice. Cooper Hobcaw stood in the doorway, gazing imperiously at the crowd. When he seemed to command everyone's attention, he clapped his hands together loudly. "Please, we need you-all to leave . . . immediately!"

The crowd seemed to hesitate for a moment, torn between their fascination with the terrible accident that had just occurred and doing what they knew was the proper thing. Then, slowly, people began to depart the room.

Cooper Hobcaw watched as the crowd trickled past him, then strode over to the head table where Theodosia, Drayton, and Haley were still gathered.

What once had been festive and romantic now seemed macabre. The head table had been set with enormous bouquets of white roses and elegant sterling silver candlesticks. Now, one bouquet was knocked over, another completely flattened by a pane of falling glass. Candles had been knocked out of their holders, dishes lay spoiled and broken. Only the large silver teapot and matching cream and saucer pieces seemed to remain unscathed. Set on a matching oval tray, the tea set lent the only hint of normalcy to the entire table.

"Miss Browning, may I have a moment?" Cooper Hobcaw asked. "I . . . I need your help."

Theodosia turned to Cooper Hobcaw, concern on her face. "Of course," she said.

"This may seem a strange thing . . ." Cooper Hobcaw hesitated. ". . . but Delaine is terribly concerned about the wedding ring. Strangely enough, it appears to be . . . missing."

"Yes," said Theodosia. "I noticed that, too." She had immediately seen that the wedding ring was no longer nestled in the black velvet ring box that had been prominently displayed at the head table. *The ring must be . . . where?* she wondered. *Had it been knocked out of the ring box and now it was under one of these tables?* She looked around at the terrible chaos. *Probably.*

"Since you are such a dear friend to Delaine," Hobcaw said, "could I impose upon you to . . ."

"You'd like us to stay here and search for it?" Theodosia finished the sentence for him.

Cooper Hobcaw's face seemed to sag with relief. "Yes," he said. "Would you?"

Drayton suddenly jumped feet-first into the conversation. "Of course we will," he said graciously. "You go on to the hospital and lend what support you can to Delaine and Camille. We'll stay behind and find that ring. Don't worry about a thing."

Cooper Hobcaw clutched Drayton's hand and pumped his arm mightily. "Thank you, thank you so much," he said. Then he grabbed Theodosia's hand and did the same. "You are a dear lady," he told her, then strode quickly out of the room.

Theodosia turned toward Haley. "Haley, why don't you go home now."

"You don't want me to help?" she asked, her eyes still wide with concern. She still seemed rather jumpy.

"No need," said Theodosia. "I'm sure the ring simply rolled under one of these tables." She looked around the Garden Room, noting what an absolute mess it was.

"Okay," said Haley, relief palpable in her face, "but call me the minute you find something out about poor Captain Buchanan, okay?"

"We'll do that," Drayton assured her.

With the Garden Room empty of guests, Theodosia and Drayton stared at each other, unsure of where to begin.

The rain had thankfully let up, but the room was a soggy mess with glass and debris scattered everywhere. In the paramedics' haste to extract Captain Buchanan, they had rolled towels about their hands then shoved the larger hunks of glass aside. Smaller pieces had been ground under the wheels of the gurney and now glistened dangerously.

"The ring must have just rolled out of the box, don't you think?" said Drayton. He sounded positive, but looked a trifle dubious.

"I assume it did," replied Theodosia. "I think if we pull

up the edges of these tablecloths, we'll probably find it soon enough."

But ten minutes of searching high and low, looking under tables, sliding back chairs, revealed nothing. Frustrated, Drayton found a broom and poked through the rubble. Still nothing.

"On top of one of the tables then?" said Drayton. He had removed his jacket and now his shirt was partially untucked and his bow tie hung askew. Theodosia had never seen him looking so frazzled.

"Maybe," Theodosia told him.

This time they sorted through all the table settings, pawed through the damp table linens and wrecked floral centerpieces, and rearranged all the wrapped gifts that lay in a soggy, bedraggled pile on the gift table. Still no ring.

"This is very strange," said Drayton. "I would have sworn the darn thing would turn up. A little thing like that couldn't have rolled all *that* far." He furrowed his brow and scratched his head, the picture of complete bewilderment.

"Do you think one of the guests might have picked it up?" he asked aloud, then gave a mumbled answer to his own question. "No, they were all good friends. Friends of Delaine's, friends of Camille and Captain Buchanan's. If someone found the ring, they surely would have *said* something."

Theodosia, meanwhile, had turned her attention to the gaping hole in the glass ceiling. The rain had completely abated and now there was just darkness and roiling clouds overhead.

Drayton saw her staring up at the ceiling and followed her gaze. "Do you think the roof just gave way?" he asked.

"I suppose it did," she said slowly, still staring upward. "It was an old greenhouse, after all. From before, when the Lady Goodwood used to raise their own orchids and camellias to pretty up the rooms and create centerpieces for the dining room." Theodosia paused, thinking. "Maybe it was hit by lightning. There was that enormous flash."

"It was positively cataclysmic," agreed Drayton.

Theodosia put her hand on the back of a wooden chair, dragged it across the sodden carpet until it was positioned directly beneath the jagged hole in the glass roof. She put one foot on the upholstered seat cushion. "Drayton, give me a boost up, will you?"

Drayton stared at her as though she'd lost her mind. "Good heavens, Theodosia, just what do you think you're going to accomplish?"

"I want to take a look at this greenhouse ceiling."

"Yes, I assumed as much. What I don't understand is *why*."

"Stop acting like a parliamentarian and just help me, would you?"

Drayton steadied the chair with one hand, extended his other hand to help Theodosia as she climbed up. "Don't I always?" he muttered, affecting a slightly pompous attitude.

"Darn," said Theodosia from above.

"What?"

"I can't really see anything. I'm not up high enough."

"Good. Then kindly hop down before you break your neck." Drayton moved to assist her and glass crunched underfoot. "This is dreadful," he declared. "Like walking on the proverbial bed of nails."

"You folks okay?" called a voice from across the room.

Drayton and Theodosia spun on their heels to find an older man in a gray jumpsuit staring at them. By the looks of the man's outfit, he was one of the inn's janitors.

"We're fine," said Theodosia. "You're from maintenance?"

"Yup," he nodded. "Harry Kreider, at your service."

"Would you by any chance have a ladder, Mr. Kreider?" asked Theodosia. "I'd like to take a peek at this ceiling."

"You from the insurance company or something?" he asked.

"No," she replied. "Just very curious. I was a guest here tonight." She raised a hand, indicated Drayton. "We were both guests."

Harry Kreider cocked his head, assessing her request. "Certainly was a terrible thing," he said. "I was sitting home watching reruns of NASCAR racing on TV when they called and told me the roof collapsed on some poor man." He paused. "You ever watch NASCAR?"

"No," said Drayton abruptly and Theodosia rolled her eyes at him.

"Yeah, I s'pose I could get you a ladder," the janitor said slowly, scratching at his jowly cheeks with the back of his hand. "Storage closet's just down the hall. Be back in a moment."

"Thank you," said Theodosia. "We really appreciate it."

"What is this about?" asked Drayton as they waited for the janitor to return with a step ladder. "What exactly are you looking for?"

"Not sure," said Theodosia.

"Well, you're up to *something*."

There was a *clunk* and a *thwack* as the janitor angled a twelve-foot ladder through the double doors, scraping them slightly. He eased the ladder in on its side, then, when he'd caught his breath, set the ladder up directly beneath the gaping hole.

"I'm sorry about this," Drayton said to the janitor.

"No problem. Got to rig up a temporary patch for this hole anyway. Can't have the rain coming in again. Whole place'll be damp by morning otherwise. That darned humidity just steals in and chills you to the bone. Gonna have to seal off this whole wing, I s'pose." The janitor gazed at the mess ahead of him and sucked air through his front teeth. "You two go ahead and take your look up there while I rustle up some tarps. Just don't fall off that darn thing and break your neck. There's been enough trouble here for one night."

"I'll be careful," Theodosia assured him as she scampered up the ladder.

"*Please* be careful," said Drayton as he stood below, clutching the ladder.

Theodosia climbed to within two steps of the top, put a hand gingerly on the metal strut that ran the length of the greenhouse roof. It felt solid and stable. It was the glass that had seemingly crumpled and given way.

She stuck her head up through the hole. The roof, or what was left of it, was still slick and wet from the earlier downpour. Light from below glowed faintly through it. *Okay, no surprises here,* Theodosia decided.

She felt beneath her with her right foot, took a step back down. Now she was eye level with the tangle of glass and metal. She reached out, flicked at a small oval-shaped piece of metal that hung there. It was weathered looking, once silvery, like the rest of the pieces.

"See anything?" Drayton called from below.

"Not really," she said.

"Then kindly come back down."

Theodosia began her climb back down.

"Here," said Drayton, grabbing for her hand once she was in reach, "let's get you back on terra firma."

Theodosia stood next to the ladder, looking thoughtful. "Drayton, let me ask you something. What if someone had their eye on Camille's wedding ring?"

Drayton's eyes widened as he caught the gist of what she was suggesting. "You think someone might have been up there? That this *wasn't* just an accident?"

"I'm not sure," said Theodosia. "Let's just suppose for a moment that a thief was prowling about . . ."

"Camille's ring would make quite a prize," he said slowly.

Theodosia's eyes flicked over the head table, where the

silver tea set gleamed from the wrecked table top. "And the silver?" she asked.

"That's lovely, too," he agreed slowly. "Queen Anne style. Don't quote me, but I believe it was crafted by Jacob Hurd in the mid-seventeen-hundreds. And of course, it's been in the Goodwood family for ages. You see that engraved cartouche on the body of the teapot?"

Theodosia nodded.

"That's the family crest. A heraldic shield on a bed of roses."

"So besides Camille's ring, which I believe Delaine told me had been valued at something like seventy grand . . ."

"Seventy grand!" exclaimed Drayton. "Good gracious."

"And all this silver would have been worth a good deal of money, too," ventured Theodosia.

Drayton nodded briskly, far more familiar with appraisals on antiquities than he was with jewelry. "Oh yes. The teapot alone might fetch ten or twenty thousand dollars. To say nothing of the creamer, sugar bowl, and that magnificent tray."

"Okay, then," said Theodosia, "follow my line of thinking for a moment, will you?"

Drayton cocked his head to one side in an acquiescing gesture.

"What if someone was scrambling across the top of the roof . . ." she began.

"It would have to be someone very skillful and limber," he said, gazing upward. "There are only those struts for support, everything else is glass."

"I agree," said Theodosia. "But it can be done. A case in point: the man who cleans my air conditioner does it every spring in my attic."

"Walks across the narrow wooden struts," said Drayton.

"Yes," said Theodosia. "But maybe tonight this person, whoever he was, got caught off balance. The storm, the pouring rain, a nearby lightning strike spooked him or unnerved him. Or maybe it was just terribly treacherous up there. Anyway, somewhere along the way, his foot just happened to slip."

They both gazed up at the gaping hole.

"And he came crashing through into the Garden Room," said Drayton.

Theodosia pointed to the remains of an elaborate pulley system that hung from the ceiling. "You see that chain and pulley right there? This roof was meant to crank open. It was designed that way back when it was a working greenhouse, before they pulled out the old wooden tables and sprinkler system and turned it into the Garden Room. But I imagine the system still works. You could still open the roof . . ."

"Someone scampered across the roof," said Drayton, still trying out the idea. "With the idea of making off with the ring and maybe even the silver. But instead, this person came crashing down on top of poor Captain Buchanan."

"Yes," said Theodosia, "that might explain the first crash we heard."

"And the second crash?" asked Drayton.

Theodosia hesitated. "I'm not entirely sure. But if someone crashed *through* the roof, wouldn't they have to go back up through it?"

"How?" he sputtered.

"I have no clue."

"Folks?" called the janitor. "Is one of you a The-o-dosia?" He pronounced the name slowly and phonetically.

"That's me," said Theodosia.

"Phone call," said the janitor.

Theodosia and Drayton hurried out to the lobby, where Mr. Welborne was talking excitedly with two staff members.

"I have a phone call?" she said.

The woman behind the front desk indicated a small, private phone booth just down the hallway.

Theodosia seated herself on a small round stool that was covered with a needlepoint cushion and picked up the receiver.

It was Cooper Hobcaw calling from the hospital. He spoke clearly but rapidly for a few minutes and Theodosia listened carefully. Afterward, she thanked him, then hung up the phone.

She stood, drew a deep sigh, and turned to Drayton. "He's dead," she told him sadly. "Captain Buchanan is dead."

CHAPTER 3

FRIDAY MORNING AT 9:00 A.M., the Indigo Tea Shop was packed. Besides their Church Street regulars, a tour group led by Dindy Moore, one of Drayton's friends from the Heritage Society, had decided to begin their walking tour of the historic district with a breakfast tea. And now the group easily filled four of the dozen or so tables.

Drayton hustled back and forth, a teapot in each hand, pouring steaming cups of Munnar black tea and English breakfast tea. Haley had come in early, even though she'd been deeply upset by the news of Captain Corey Buchanan's death, and still managed to bake a full complement of pastries. This morning the customers at the Indigo Tea Shop were enjoying steaming apple-ginger muffins, blueberry scones, and cream muffins, which in any other part of the country would rightly be called popovers.

Standing behind the counter, Theodosia busied herself by handling take-out orders, always in big demand first thing in the morning.

After the horror of last night, she felt reassured and

warmed by the atmosphere of the tea shop. A fire crackled in the tiny stone fireplace as copper teapots chirped and whistled. The scent of orange, cinnamon, and ginger perfumed the air around her.

Teas were like aromatherapy, Theodosia had long since decided. The ripe orchid aroma of Keemun tea from Anhui Province in China was always slightly heady and uplifting, the bright, brisk smell of Indian Nilgiri seemed to calm and stabilize, the scent of jasmine always soothed.

Finally, when the morning rush seemed to settle into a more manageable pace, Theodosia slipped through the dark green velvet curtains and into her office at the back of the shop.

This was her private oasis. Big roll-top desk wedged into a small space, wall filled with framed mementos that included photos, opera programs, and tea labels. A cushy green velvet guest chair faced her desk, a chair that Drayton had dubbed "the tuffet."

Sitting at her desk, Theodosia thought about the hellish events of last night. *Did someone actually crash through the roof and steal the antique wedding ring or am I just trying to rationalize a terrible event? When bad things happen to good people, that sort of thing?*

She thought about it, tried to dismiss her somewhat strange theory.

But it wouldn't go away. Stuck in her mind like a burr.

All right, she thought to herself, *then I've got to tell someone. Who, though? The police? Hmm, seems a little alarmist. No,* she decided, *Delaine will come by. She always does. I'll run it by Delaine and then, if it still holds water, Delaine can take it to the police.*

She wasn't about to get pulled into this, was she? No, of course not.

Haley was always kidding her that she liked nothing better than a good mystery to poke her nose into. Well, she was going to leave this incident well enough alone, wasn't she?

Wasn't she?

Theodosia sighed. On the other hand . . . from the moment she'd climbed that ladder last night, she'd felt as if she was being pulled slowly and inexorably into what appeared to be a web of intrigue.

What was this strange fascination she had with murder? Why did she have this dark side?

Enough, she decided as she flipped open her weekly planner and studied her calendar. This weekend looked relatively quiet. Tomorrow, Saturday night, was the members-only party at the Heritage Society to celebrate the opening of next week's big Treasures Show. And then her calendar was fairly clear until the following Thursday afternoon when they were scheduled to have an open house at the tea shop.

The open house. She had to start thinking seriously about that. The Indigo Tea Shop was about to kick off its new line of tea-inspired bath and beauty products and she had to decide exactly what refreshments they'd be serving, what theme this little launch party should follow.

Theodosia had experienced a brainstorm not too long ago about packaging green teas, dried lavender, chamomile, calendula petals, and other tea and herb mixtures into oversized tea bags for use in the bath. She had commissioned a small batch to be manufactured by a highly reputable cosmetics firm and then tested the feasibility of those products on her web site. Much to her delight, the T-Bath products, as she had named them, had sold remarkably well, so she expanded the line to include lotions and oils as well. This coming Thursday, their open house would serve as the official product launch for the new T-Bath line. She'd already been interviewed by the *Charleston Post & Courier* and a fairly in-depth article about her new bath products would be running in their Style Section sometime next week.

"Theodosia?"

Theodosia looked up to find Haley standing in her doorway. She wiggled her fingers, gesturing for Haley to come in.

"Delaine's here," Haley told her. "She'd like to talk to you."

"How is she?" asked Theodosia.

"Sniffly. Subdued," said Haley. "Same as us."

"You're a real trooper for coming in," Theodosia told her. "Last night was pretty rough."

"That's okay," said Haley. "I feel better now. Sad for poor Camille, of course." Haley shook her head as if to clear it. "Strangely enough, Delaine is dressed to the nines. Anyone else would have thrown on a pair of jeans and a sweatshirt. I guess Delaine's brain doesn't operate that way."

"She probably just came from her store," said Theodosia. "So she had to dress up."

Delaine's store, Cotton Duck, was just down the block from Theodosia's tea shop. Over the past ten years, Delaine had built it into one of the premier clothing boutiques in Charleston. Cotton Duck carried casual cotton clothing to take you through the hot, steamy Charleston summers, rich velvets and light wools for the cooler months, and elegant evening fashions for taking in the opera, art gallery openings, or formal parties in the historic district. In just the last year, Delaine had begun carrying several well-known designers and was now featuring trunk shows several times a year.

"Don't think ill of Delaine," added Theodosia. "It's just her way. Whenever there's a crisis, she dresses up for the part."

* * *

Delaine was sitting at the table by the fireplace, wearing a camel-colored cashmere sweater and matching wool slacks, sniffling into her cup of Assam tea. She looked up with red-rimmed eyes as Theodosia approached.

"Delaine," said Theodosia, "how are you?" She sat down across from her and clasped her hands, feeling a bit like a brown wren in her sensible workday gray slacks and turtleneck.

"Holding up," said Delaine. "Of course, last night was an absolute *horror.* First we couldn't find out *anything* from the doctors, then they informed us that Captain Buchanan had actually *died* en route to the hospital." She bit her lip in an attempt to stave back tears. "Apparently, his respiration and spinal cord had been affected."

"Oh, no," exclaimed Drayton. After taking a quick check of customers, who all seemed to be sipping tea and happily munching Haley's fresh-baked muffins and scones, he had joined them at the table. "How awful," he said.

"If Captain Buchanan had lived," said Delaine in a hoarse whisper, "he would have been a quadriplegic."

"Oh, my," said Drayton, shaking his head sadly.

"How's Camille doing?" asked Theodosia.

"Terrible," said Delaine. "She just sat next to Captain Buchanan's poor body and cried and cried all night. She wouldn't leave him, wouldn't even take a sedative when one of the doctors offered it. Poor lamb, she's absolutely heartbroken."

"And Captain Buchanan's family has been notified?" asked Drayton.

"Yes," said Delaine. "Cooper Hobcaw called and spoke with them first. He's not as . . . close . . . to this tragedy as we are, so he was able to maintain a certain calm and decorum. Then Camille got on the line, too." Delaine fumbled in her purse for a handkerchief, unfurled it, blew her nose loudly. "We're all just so sad. Camille is planning to accompany Captain Buchanan's body back to Savannah later today. That's where the funeral will be." Delaine blew her nose again and glanced about helplessly. "I'm sorry," she apologized. "I'm just so very upset."

Drayton reached over and patted her shoulder gently. "We know you are, dear."

"Thank you for staying last night," said Delaine. "I knew I could count on the two of you."

Theodosia and Drayton exchanged quick glances.

"Camille is planning to take the wedding ring back with her today and return it to the family," said Delaine. "Of course it's the only acceptable thing to do. After all, there won't be any . . ." Delaine's voice trailed off and she dissolved into tears once again.

Theodosia threw Drayton a quick *what do we do now?* glance.

He gave a helpless shrug.

Delaine, sensing the subtle exchange between them, suddenly looked up.

"You *did* recover the ring, didn't you?" she asked.

Drayton, usually eloquent, fumbled for a moment. "Actually, Delaine, we . . . uh . . ."

"There was a *problem?*" she asked. Now there was a distinct edge to her voice.

"The problem was," said Theodosia, deciding honesty was the best policy, "we never actually found the ring."

Delaine was incredulous. "But Cooper said you were going to *look* for it. Surely you . . ."

"We *did* look," Drayton assured her. "We searched high and low, practically tore the premises apart. But . . ." He hesitated, steepled his gnarled fingers together, then pulled them apart slowly, as if to indicate a lack of resolution. "Alas, no ring," he said.

One of Delaine's French-manicured hands fluttered to her chest. "My goodness, this *is* quite a shock."

"It was to us, too," said Theodosia. "We really did search everywhere."

"What do you suppose happened to it?" asked Delaine. She frowned, twisted her handkerchief in her hands, stared at the two of them, obviously expecting an answer.

"We think, that is, *Theodosia* thinks . . ." began Drayton.

"Spit it out, Drayton!" said Delaine suddenly. "If something's gone wrong, I have a perfect right to know!"

Theodosia glanced about the tea shop to make sure her guests hadn't overheard Delaine's somewhat indelicate outburst. "Of course you do, Delaine," Theodosia assured her. "It's just that all we're going on right now is a sort of theory."

"Then kindly explain this *theory*," demanded Delaine. She arched her eyebrows, sat back in her chair with an air that was dangerously close to imperious, and waited for an explanation.

"It involves theft," said Drayton delicately.

"Of the *ring?*" said Delaine in a high squeak.

"Well . . . yes," said Theodosia. *Why is it so difficult to just come right out and say it?*

"Oh my goodness," cried Delaine, sinking back in her chair. "You think the ring has been *stolen?*" she said in a whisper.

"We're not positive," said Drayton, "but it looks that way."

Delaine's face crumpled and she was seconds from another outpouring of tears.

"Remember, this is just a wild supposition on our part," said Theodosia, "but from the looks of things, it's possible a thief might have had his eye on Camille's ring. After all, it was rather beautifully displayed on that baroque silver calling card receiver." *Now why did I have to say that?* Theodosia thought to herself. *Darn, this isn't going well at all.*

"And all that beautiful old silver was sitting right next to it," said Drayton. Old silver that'd been in the Goodwood family for generations.

"Crafted by Jacob Hurd," Theodosia added helpfully.

Delaine nodded tightly. "Of course, I remember the silver. It's all very old, very elegant. I specifically requested it for just that reason."

"Anyway," continued Theodosia, "we think someone might have been prowling across the roof top."

"And taken a misstep," said Drayton.

"Which caused him to come crashing down through the roof," added Theodosia.

"On top of poor Captain Buchanan," said Drayton, grimacing. He knew the two of them sounded like they were doing some kind of tag-team routine.

Delaine peered at Theodosia and Drayton in disbelief. "You're not serious," she said in a choked voice.

"And that's when the ring was stolen," said Drayton. "Or *might* have been stolen," he added. "We're still not sure."

Delaine sat stock-still as their words washed across her. She frowned, leaned forward, put a hand to her mouth. "Then Captain Buchanan was *murdered,*" she whispered hoarsely.

"Oh, no, I wouldn't go that far," said Drayton hastily. "After all, the roof could just as easily have collapsed on its own."

"But the ring is gone," said Delaine slowly. "Nowhere to be found, as you say. Doesn't that *prove* your theory?" She leaned back in her chair again. "Oh my," she murmured to herself, "this is simply *awful.* We'll need to contact the *police.*"

"That's probably a good idea," admitted Theodosia. She would have done it herself last night, but the idea of the thief on the roof hadn't completely gelled in her mind. It had been a theory, a decent one at that. But of course, there was no concrete proof.

Delaine suddenly clutched Theodosia's hand. "Theodosia, you've got to help me!"

"Oh, no, . . ." protested Theodosia.

"Yes," said Delaine, clutching Theodosia's hand even more forcefully and digging in with her nails. "We need to get to the bottom of this, figure out what really happened. Like you, I simply don't want to believe this was all just a horrible accident." Delaine's pleading eyes bore into Theodosia. "Oh please, you're so terribly good at this kind of thing. You helped figure out who killed poor Oliver Dixon last summer when that horrible pistol exploded at the picnic."

"She did do a fine job with that, didn't she," said Drayton, admiration apparent in his voice.

Theodosia frowned at Drayton. "That was a very different set of circumstances," she protested. "I was standing right there and had just witnessed a rather strange argument between . . ." She hesitated, decided she'd better shift her line of conversation back to the here and now. "Delaine, I really wouldn't have a clue as to where to begin. If my theory does hold water, it really was a motiveless murder."

Delaine lifted her head and gazed at Theodosia mournfully. "But that's just it. It was murder!"

"No," said Theodosia, trying to back-pedal as best she could. "I stand corrected then. It was an *accident.* The kind of accident the police need to investigate. Let them determine if there were any suspicious people lurking about in the lobby last night. Any cars seen speeding away from the Lady Goodwood Inn. Any clues left on the rooftop. That sort of thing."

"But we've got to get that ring back!" shrilled Delaine. "Camille is my niece. *I'm* responsible."

"I'm sure Captain Buchanan's family won't hold you personally responsible," said Drayton.

"Of course they won't," added Theodosia. "Because there really is nothing to go on," said Theodosia. "No way to get a bead on this mysterious intruder."

"If there even was one in the first place," Drayton added.

Delaine sat there toying with her own ring, a giant moonstone that glimmered enticingly. "But there is a way," she said slowly. "At least, there might be."

Theodosia and Drayton exchanged startled glances.

"What do you mean, honey?" asked Drayton.

"You said the burglar was probably after the ring. Maybe even had his eye on the antique silver," began Delaine.

"*Probably* being the operative word," said Drayton.

"Well, what if this person really is a practiced thief," said Delaine. "Then this wouldn't be the end of it, would it? This person, this thief who prowls about in the night, wouldn't just stop cold turkey, would he? This, whatever-he-is, cat burglar, would keep stealing, wouldn't he?"

"I suppose so," said Theodosia slowly.

Drayton set his teacup down with a loud *clink*. There was a distinctly funny look on his face. "Where are you going with this, Delaine?"

"I was thinking about tomorrow night," she said. Now a sly look lit her face. "You know, the preview party at the Heritage Society. For the Treasures Show. There's going to be that whole cache of European jewelry on display."

"I was hoping you wouldn't go there, Delaine," said Drayton. He pursed his lips and his lined face assumed a pained expression. "*Really* hoping you wouldn't go there."

Delaine continued to toy with her ring. "Well, Drayton, honey, I just did. So there. And you two know exactly what I'm talking about." She looked up in triumph, then glanced back and forth, from Theodosia's face to Drayton's. "Don't tell me the same thought hasn't crossed your minds. You know darn well that any thief who was attempting to steal an heirloom ring might also have his eye on that European Jewel Collection!"

With that, Delaine put her handkerchief to her face and began emitting little sobs.

Theodosia sat back in her chair and studied Delaine. *Are these crocodile tears or genuine tears of sorrow and frustration? Probably a little of both,* she decided. Delaine was genuinely upset over the death of her niece's fiancé as well as the apparent loss of the antique wedding ring.

On the other hand, if Delaine thought she could goad her and Drayton into helping, then she would. She'd use every trick in the book.

Theodosia sighed. Problem was, Delaine's remark about the Treasures Show at the Heritage Society was a point well taken. *Would a cat burglar stop with just one item? No, probably not. Would the European Jewel Collection at the Treasures Show be enough of a lure to bring him out again? Hmm . . . that was the sixty-four-thousand-dollar question, wasn't it?*

"Drayton, what are you *doing?*" shrieked Haley in alarm.

Standing behind the counter, Drayton was dumping teaspoon after heaping teaspoon of Lapsang Souchong into a Victorian-style teapot.

"Hmm?" he asked. It was early afternoon and the luncheon crowd had just departed. Haley had whipped together chicken salad with pecans and served it mounded on lettuce cups with a wedge of banana bread spread with softened cream cheese. Every plate had sold out.

"You've dumped almost a dozen spoonfuls into that pot!" she told him. "Your tea is going to be so strong it'll take the finish off!"

Drayton gazed down in horror. "Good lord! I completely lost track there, didn't I?"

"Here," Haley said as she elbowed Drayton out of the way, ready to take charge. "Let me do this. You get out the step stool and pull a couple jars of DuBose Bees Honey down from the shelf. You see that lady over there in the yellow sweater?"

Drayton scanned the tea room then nodded obediently, still lost in thought.

"Well, she adored the DuBose honey so much on her scone that she wants to take a couple jars home."

"Okay," he agreed.

"Really," huffed Haley, "it seems like everyone's lost their mind today."

"Who's lost their mind?" asked Theodosia as she emerged from the back carrying a fresh plate of scones.

"Drayton has," said Haley. "He was about to make a superstrong pot of tea. As if that stuff isn't strong enough to begin with," she sniffed.

"Look at our little Haley," said Drayton. "Two years ago she didn't know a Darjeeling from a Yunnan. Now she's an expert."

"That's enough sarcasm, Drayton," Haley snapped. "I wasn't the one who was about to send one of our guests into anaphylactic shock with a gigantic overdose of caffeine."

The bell over the door tinkled as a group of tourists pushed their way into the shop. Haley, sensing that Drayton still wasn't himself, immediately hustled over to seat them.

"Still feeling discombobulated?" Theodosia asked Drayton.

He nodded. "I keep thinking about what Delaine said regarding the members-only party tomorrow night at the Heritage Society. Granted, the installation of the entire Treasures Show won't be completed until next weekend when the public opening occurs. But the traveling European Jewel Collection will be there tomorrow night. For all to see."

"Including our so-called cat burglar."

"Right," said Drayton. "And if this thief had his eye on Camille's ring, he might also be honed in on the European Jewel Collection. It certainly has received enough publicity."

Indeed, there had been a splashy write-up in the Arts Section of the *Charleston Post & Courier* and Drayton had even been interviewed on the *Good Morning, Charleston* radio show.

"If it makes you feel any better, Drayton, those same concerns have been bouncing around in my head, too," Theodosia told him.

"Unfortunately, there really isn't much we can do," said Drayton. He assumed a glum expression. "Something like this, you have to wait and see what happens." He paused, reached behind him for a cup of tea he had brewed earlier for himself, took a sip.

"Chamomile?" asked Theodosia. Chamomile was a tried-and-true remedy for nerves.

Drayton nodded. "Do you know if Delaine talked with the police yet?"

"I just got off the phone with her," said Theodosia. "She was on her way over to the Lady Goodwood Inn to meet with two detectives from the Robbery Division."

"Too bad your friend, Detective Tidwell, couldn't be of help."

"I wouldn't go so far as to call him a friend," responded Theodosia.

Burt Tidwell, one of the Homicide Detectives in the Charleston police force, had once insinuated that Bethany Shepherd, one of Theodosia's former employees, had been involved in the poisoning of a slightly shady real estate developer during a historic homes tour. Theodosia had worked with Detective Tidwell, if one could call it that, to resolve the case and bring the true culprit to justice.

"Besides, Tidwell's in the Homicide Division," added

Theodosia. "Last night's event is being assessed as a robbery."

"Right," said Drayton. He set his teacup down, picked up the two jars of honey, balanced them in his hands as though he were weighing something. "Anyway, I'm still worried about tomorrow night."

"What if we spoke with Timothy Neville?" said Theodosia. "Suggest to him that the Heritage Society might want to take some extra precautions?"

Timothy Neville was the president of the Heritage Society and a good friend of Drayton's. Timothy's great-great-grandmother had been one of the original Huguenot settlers in Charleston back in the seventeen-hundreds and her descendants had become wealthy plantation owners, growing rice, indigo, and cotton. Timothy resided in a magnificent Georgian-style mansion over on Archdale Street.

Drayton nodded. "Timothy might go along with the idea. *Should* go along with it, anyway. It would certainly be in his best interests."

"So you'll speak to him?" asked Theodosia. "Share our concern without completely alarming him?"

"Absolutely," said Drayton, making up his mind. "I'll call Timothy this instant."

CHAPTER 4

"THIS," SAID THE enthusiastic manager of Spies Are Us, "is the slickest little device this side of the DOD."

"What's the DOD?" asked Drayton.

"Department of Defense, my friend. And this little baby provides your first *wall* of defense."

Theodosia and Drayton stood in the high-tech electronics store gazing at a device that looked like a second cousin to a video camera. Around them were showy displays that featured motion detectors, security cameras, tiny cameras that fit into pens and lapel pins, as well as miniature microphones.

"How exactly does this work?" inquired Drayton. He had voiced his feelings to Timothy Neville about heightening security at the members-only party tonight and, surprisingly, had received a green light. The problem he and Theodosia now faced was to select the right security device from the hundreds for sale in the store. Security, it would seem, was very big business these days.

"This motion detector functions like the automatic range finder on a camera," said the young store manager whose name tag read RILEY. "Basically, you set the perimeter via this keypad." Riley's fingers tapped lightly on the shiny keypad. "Then, once the device is programmed, it emits sonar pulses and waits for an echo. But if someone breaks the electronic beam, say they walk through it or even pass a hand nearby . . . then *wham!* The alarm goes off!"

"How large an area will this secure?" asked Theodosia.

"What are we talking, warehouse or retail?" Riley asked.

"Think of a smaller retail space," said Drayton. "With glass cases."

"A smaller area, I'd say you should probably go with two," Riley told them. "If you decide later that you need to expand your protected area, you can always add a couple additional modules." Riley smiled and nodded over the top of Theodosia's head toward a customer. "Could you excuse me for a moment? I've got a customer who's here to pick up a security camera. Poor guy owns a couple liquor stores and is constantly getting ripped off."

Theodosia looked askance at the device in Drayton's hand. "How much is this thing?" she asked.

Drayton studied the price tag. "Ninety-nine dollars," he told her. "I'm amazed this stuff is so affordable."

"Me too. But you know how much technology has come down in price. Look at DVD and CD players."

Drayton stared at her blankly. As a self-professed curmudgeon who was scornful of all things technologic, he still preferred his old Philco stereo and vinyl record albums.

"Well, never mind," Theodosia told him, deciding this probably wasn't the best time to illuminate Drayton on the advances that had been made in the past ten years. "You think we'd need two of these?" she asked.

Drayton studied the brochure and did some quick math, figuring square footage while he mumbled to himself. "Two should do it," he decided. "The jewelry will be on display in the small gallery. That's really our key area of concern right now."

"And Timothy approved this expenditure?" Even though Timothy Neville lived in baronial splendor in a huge red brick Georgian mansion, he was notoriously frugal when it came to expenditures for the Heritage Society.

"When I spoke with him yesterday, he certainly agreed there was a potential for trouble. So yes, he did approve this. Tonight's party is members-only, of course, and he didn't seem to feel we should expect any problems. I think Timothy's got more of an eye toward next weekend. That's when there could be a security issue. I suppose he views tonight as a sort of dry run."

"But he's agreed to security guards, too," said Theodosia. She wasn't about to pin all her hopes on two ninety-nine-dollar motion sensors.

"Two security guards will be posted. But realize, we had to employ them anyway," Drayton told her. "For insurance purposes. Anytime you have a traveling show like this European Jewel Collection, you're contractually obligated to provide a certain amount of security."

They stood there silently, eyeing the device.

"Are we overreacting?" asked Theodosia.

"Probably," admitted Drayton. "In the cold, clear light of day, when you stand in this store and see all this tricky-techy stuff that plays right into people's paranoias, our cat burglar theory does seem awfully far-fetched."

"Right," Theodosia nodded. Her hand reached out and touched the motion sensor. It had a black metallic surface with a matte finish. Very gadgety and *Mission Impossible* looking. "This *is* sort of crazy," she admitted. "You turn this little gizmo on and it generates supersonic detector beams."

"It's nuts," agreed Drayton.

"Maybe we shouldn't buy it then," said Theodosia.

"Of course we should," said Drayton.

* * *

Rain swept down in vast sheets, a cold, soaking late October rain that lashed in from the Atlantic. Spanish moss, heavy with water, sagged and swayed in the branches of giant live oaks like flotsam from the sea. Heroic last stands of bougainvillea and tiny white blooms from tea olive trees were mercilessly pounded, their blossoms shredded then pressed into the damp earth as though some careless giant had defiantly strode through and flattened everything in his wake.

Out in Charleston Harbor, waves slapped sharply against channel buoys as the Cooper and Ashley Rivers converged in Charleston Harbor to confront the driving tide from the Atlantic. The mournful sound of the fog horn out on Patriot's Point moaned and groaned, its low sound carrying to the old historic homes that crowded up against the peninsula, shoulder to elegant shoulder, like a receiving line of dowager empresses.

The lights inside the old stone headquarters of the Heritage Society glowed like a beacon in the dark as ladies clad in opera capes and men in tuxedos splashed through puddles in their evening finery and struggled frantically with umbrellas blown inside out.

Standing in the entryway, Theodosia shrugged off her black nylon raincoat, gently shook the rain from it, then handed it off to a young volunteer, who seemed at a complete loss as to what to do with all these wet garments.

Patting her hair and smoothing the skirt of her black taffeta cocktail dress, Theodosia composed her serene face in a natural smile as she made her way down the crowded hallway, trying to push her way through the exuberant throng of Heritage Society members.

"Theo!" cried an excited voice. "Hello there!"

Theodosia turned to see Brooke Carter Crockett, the owner of the estate jewelry store, Heart's Desire, smiling and waving at her.

"Brooke . . . hello," she responded. But then she was

carried along by a crowd of people and eventually found herself at the end of the great hallway in the suite of rooms the Heritage Society used for receptions such as this and as galleries to showcase items pulled from their vast storage vault in the basement.

Making a mental note to get back to Brooke later when some of the initial hubbub had died down, Theodosia gazed around appreciatively at the interior of the building.

The old stone building that housed the Heritage Society was definitely one of Theodosia's favorite edifices. Long ago, well over two hundred years ago, it had been a government building, built by the English. But rather than exuding a residual bureaucratic aura, Theodosia felt that the building seemed more contemplative and medieval in nature. An atmosphere that was undoubtedly helped along by its arched wood beam ceilings, stone walls, heavy leaded windows, and sagging wooden floors.

It was, Theodosia had always thought, the kind of place you could turn into a very grand home. Given the proviso, of course, that you owned tons of leather-bound books, furnished it with acres of Oriental rugs and overstuffed furniture, and had a passel of snoozing hound dogs to keep you company.

It would be a far cry from her small apartment over the tea shop, she decided, which she'd originally decorated in the chintz-and-prints-bordering-on-shabby-chic school of design, and was now veering toward old world antiquities and elegance.

On her way to the bar, which turned out to be an old Jacobean trestle table stocked with dozens of bottles and an enormous cut-glass bowl filled with ice, Theodosia met up with Drayton. He was chatting with Aerin Linley, one of the Heritage Society's volunteer fund-raisers and cochair of the Treasures Show.

"Theo, you know Aerin Linley, don't you?" he asked.

"Of course," said Theodosia as she greeted the pretty

redhead who looked absolutely stunning in a slinky scoop-necked, cream-colored jersey wrap dress and an heirloom emerald necklace that matched her eyes. "Nice to see you again."

"Besides cochairing the Treasures Show, Aerin authored the grant request that helped secure funding to bring in the European Jewel Collection," Drayton told her.

"I'm impressed," said Theodosia as the two women shook hands. "I've tried my hand at writing a few grant requests myself, mostly to try to obtain program support for Big Paws, our Charleston service dog organization, so I know grant writing is a fairly daunting task. Lots of probing questions to answer and hurdles to jump through."

"It's *awfully* tricky," agreed Aerin Linley. "And there does seem to be a language all its own attached to it, one that's slightly stilted and bureaucratic. Not really my style at all," she laughed. "I think I just got lucky with this one."

"You're still working at Heart's Desire?" asked Theodosia. She remembered that Brooke Carter Crockett, the shop's owner, had mentioned something about Aerin being her assistant.

Aerin Linley fingered the emerald necklace that draped around her neck. "Can't you tell?" she said playfully. "This is one of our pieces."

"It's gorgeous," said Theodosia as she peered at it and wondered just how many cups of tea she'd have to sell to finance *that* little piece of extravagance!

"Never hurts to show off the merchandise," laughed Aerin. "You never know when somebody's in the market for a great piece. But to answer your question, yes . . . and I'm absolutely *loving* it there. And now that I'm handling most of the appraisals, Brooke has been freed up to focus more on acquisitions and sales. She just returned from a sales trip to New York, where she made quite a hit with some of the dealers at the Manhattan Antique Center. They went absolutely *crazy* over our Charleston pieces. I think they were thrilled to get some pieces with real history attached to them as opposed to flash-in-the-pan nouveau designer pieces."

"Of course they were," said Drayton, the perennial Charleston booster.

"I also turned Brooke on to some rather prime buying opportunities for heirloom jewelry down in Savannah," said Aerin. "There are so many old families who have jewel boxes just brimming with fine old pieces. To say nothing of all the secret drawers and panels built into the woodwork of those old homes."

"Did you grow up in Savannah?" asked Theodosia. Savannah was just ninety miles south of Charleston. That great, vast swamp known as the low-country was all that separated the two old *grande dame* cities.

"I did," said Aerin. "But I moved here a few months ago after my divorce." She flashed a wicked grin. "Savannah's really an awfully small town when you get right down to it. And it certainly wasn't big enough for the two of us, once we called it quits."

"Then you know the Buchanans," said Theodosia.

"Quite well, actually," Aerin replied. "And such a tragedy about poor Corey Buchanan. Drayton's been filling me in. Brooke, too." She lowered her voice. "I can't say we're thrilled by these whispered allegations of a cat burglar. Heart's Desire has a well-earned reputation for offering a stunning array of estate jewelry, so we do make an awfully broad target," she said, widening her eyes in alarm.

"There you-all are!" Delaine Dish, with Cooper Hobcaw in tow, edged up to the group. "Look, Coop, here's our dear Theo and Drayton. And Miss Linley, too. Hello," she purred.

"Good evening," Cooper Hobcaw said politely. "Hello, Miz Browning, Drayton, Miz Linley." He executed a chivalrous half-bow in their general direction.

Delaine gazed up at Cooper Hobcaw with studied intensity, then actually batted her eyelashes at him. "Don't you just *love* a real Southern gentleman?" she cooed, seemingly entranced by his presence.

Cooper winced and gave a self-deprecating laugh. "Now Delaine, darlin', most Southern gentlemen are gentlemen," he joked and the rest of them laughed politely.

Aerin Linley put a hand on Cooper Hobcaw's arm to get his attention. "It was nice of you to call Lorna and Rex Buchanan the other night," she told him. "According to Drayton here, you handled a very intense situation with a good deal of care and grace."

Cooper Hobcaw bobbed his head modestly. "I'm sure any one of us would have been glad to do the same thing."

"I take it funeral arrangements have been made?" asked Drayton.

"Yes," said Theodosia, "when is the funeral?"

"Monday," replied Delaine. "In Savannah, of course. Apparently it took some time to notify all of Captain Buchanan's military friends. Some of them were out at sea, so they had to be pulled off their ships by helicopter."

"So sad," murmured Theodosia.

"It is," agreed Delaine, who seemed to have gotten some perspective on the death of her niece's fiancé. She was congenial, Theodosia noted, but her mood was tempered by a certain sadness.

"I'll be driving down Sunday night," Delaine told them. "Celerie Stuart is going with me. She was a dear friend of Lorna Buchanan's. They went to school together at Mount Holyoke."

"And what of Camille?" asked Drayton.

"She's down in Savannah now," replied Delaine. "Staying with the Buchanans." Delaine's eyes suddenly glistened as tears seemed to gather in the corners. "It's the best thing for her, really. To be surrounded by people who loved him."

Drayton nodded knowingly, reached out, and patted Delaine's hand.

The Treasures Show, once the installation was finally complete, would be a stunning display of some of the choicer pieces the Heritage Society had amassed over the years. Established as a repository for historical paintings, maps, documents, furniture, and antiques, the Heritage Society had been collecting antiquities for nearly 160 years. More recently, under the careful guidance of its president, Timothy Neville, the Heritage Society had staged several "appeal" campaigns, with subtle requests going out to Charlestonians asking them to kindly donate some of their more important paintings and pieces.

And certain residents of Charleston, especially those with homes filled to the rafters with inherited treasures, had responded generously. Especially those who had a relatively high tax liability and wanted to get that all-important museum tax credit.

That tax deduction loophole was perhaps one of the reasons the Heritage Society now had in its possession a tasty mélange of French empire clocks, eighteenth-century Meissen figurines, Queen Anne "handkerchief" tables, old pewter, fine sterling silver, and Early American paintings.

A hand-picked assortment that included some of those very fine pieces would be installed during the coming week to make up the Heritage Society's much-heralded Treasures Show.

But for now it was the traveling exhibition of exquisite European jewelry that had captured Theodosia's eye. This collection of jewelry was pure ecstasy, the kinds of pieces a woman could truly dream over.

Here, on a mantle of black velvet, was a diamond brooch that had once nestled at the ample breast of Empress Josephine, Napoleon's one true love. And in this next case was a strand of giant baroque pearls that had reputedly been worn by the Duchess Sophia, when Archduke Ferdinand of Austria was assassinated in 1914. And Theodosia was utterly entranced by the jeweled flamingo pin that had been commissioned by the Duke of Windsor and worn by Wallace, his life-long love and the Duchess of Windsor.

All thoughts of burglars and thieves creeping through the night vanished from Theodosia's mind as she gazed in wonder at the radiant treasures that occupied the glass cases in the small, dark room. Lit from above with pinpoint spotlights to highlight the radiance of the gemstones, the jewelry simply dazzled the eye.

As Theodosia gazed in wonderment, she was suddenly aware of Timothy Neville, the venerable old president of the Heritage Society, standing at her side.

At age eighty-one, Timothy was not just the power behind the Heritage Society, but also a denizen of the historic district, first violin of the Charleston Symphony, collector of antique pistols, and proud possessor of a stunning mansion on Archdale Street that was furnished with equally stunning paintings, tapestries, and antiques. And interestingly enough, all that knowledge and power was contained in a small man, barely one hundred forty pounds, who had a bony, simian face, yet possessed the grace and poise of an elder statesman.

"This is an absolutely stunning show, Timothy," said Theodosia.

Timothy Neville smiled, revealing a mouth full of small, pointed teeth. Any compliment directed at the Heritage Society was a personal triumph for Timothy. But it was not just ego that drove him, it was a sense of satisfaction that the Heritage Society had once again fulfilled its mission.

"The show will be even more spectacular once the complete installation is in place," replied Timothy Neville. "As you can see, we've only just utilized this one room. The furniture, decorative arts, and paintings will be displayed in the back two galleries."

Theodosia pointed to a necklace that featured an enormous pear-shaped sapphire accented by smaller sapphires. "This blue sapphire necklace is stunning," she told him.

"And the provenance is absolutely fascinating," replied Timothy.

Intrigued, Theodosia bent forward and read the description for what they were calling the Blue Kashmir necklace. "Originally worn by an Indian maharajah, then purchased in the twenties and made into a necklace by Marjorie Merriweather Post, the breakfast cereal heiress," she read aloud. "Wow."

"Most people take jewelry at face value," said Timothy, smiling faintly at his small joke. "What they don't realize it that jewelry is often an intrinsic part of history as well. Jewelry speaks to us, tells a story."

Timothy pointed to a case that contained a stunning group of black and gold brooches and pins. "Take this mourning jewelry, for example. Belonged to Queen Victoria. After Prince Albert died of typhoid fever in 1861, the old girl was so distraught she went into mourning for the next three decades. In fact, her mourning policy was so strict that she allowed only black stones to be worn in the English court. Jet, onyx, bog oak, that type of thing, set in silver and gold."

"I had no idea," said Theodosia.

"Most people don't," replied Timothy.

Theodosia turned to face him. "I'm sorry if we alarmed you," she said. "About the possibility of a jewel thief."

Timothy grimaced, pulled his slight body to his full height. Dressed in his European-cut tuxedo, he looked like a martinet, but his eyes were kind. "Yes, Drayton was in a bit of a flap over the accident at the Lady Goodwood Inn the other night. Who knows what really happened, eh? The police are investigating, are they not?"

"Yes, they are," said Theodosia. "At least I *hope* they are."

"Then I suppose we'll have to wait and see what their assessment of the situation really is," replied Timothy. "And in the meantime, bolster our security around here. I actually like the idea of having electronic gizmos. We have security devices on our doors and windows, of course, but I never thought to use them in conjunction with our various exhibits. Of course, the Heritage Society doesn't put on all that many blockbuster shows that are advertised widely to the public. Mostly we're a quiet little place. People find their way to us in ones and twos." Timothy hesitated. "Sad about young Buchanan, though. I never met the fellow, but I knew his grandfather. Fine family." Timothy shook his head and the overhead spotlights made his bald pate gleam. "Hell of a thing," he murmured quietly.

"Delaine," gushed Theodosia, "have you seen the jewelry yet?" She gestured over her shoulder at the small gallery she'd just emerged from. "It's absolutely fantastic!"

Delaine smiled wanly. "Not really. I've been gossiping with Hillary Retton and Marianne Petigru. You know, the two ladies who own Popple Hill Interior Design? Did you know they recently worked on the Lady Goodwood Inn? That superb tapestry in the foyer came all the way from France. I think it might have been hand-loomed by cloistered nuns or something."

"Are you okay, Delaine?" asked Theodosia. Delaine was looking decidedly unhappy and her voice had taken on a shrill tone. She was undoubtedly still upset from the other night. The fact that she'd been discussing the decor at the Lady Goodwood probably didn't help matters, either.

"I'm perfectly fine, Theodosia. I've just been trying to get another *drink!*" Delaine held up an empty glass and lifted her chin. "That fellow over there has been no help whatsoever. I've asked him twice now to bring me a Kir Royale and do you think I have *yet* to see my drink? Of course not!"

"Delaine," said Theodosia, "the man's a security guard, not a waiter."

Delaine furrowed her brow and pulled her face into a petulant expression. "Well, he's *dressed* like a waiter."

"That's part of the setup," Theodosia explained patiently. "Remember, we told you the Heritage Society would have extra security on duty tonight?"

"Oh." Delaine bit her lip as Drayton wandered up to join them, alone this time. "Yes, I guess you did mention that."

But from the look on Delaine's face, Theodosia knew she was still unhappy about not getting her drink. It was amazing that just yesterday morning Delaine had been worked up about possible thievery at tonight's event and now she was consumed with trying to get a drink. Theodosia sighed. Delaine *did* tend to be a bit self-centered.

"Where's Cooper?" Theodosia asked as Drayton joined them carrying a goblet half-filled with red wine.

Delaine shrugged helplessly. "Off somewhere. Mingling, I suppose." She turned to Drayton and eyed the goblet in his hand. "What's that?" she asked.

"A marvelous Bordeaux, Haute Emillion, 'ninety-two. Take it," he offered generously. "It's freshly poured and as yet untouched."

"No thanks," said Delaine. "I'm trying to get a *real* drink."

Drayton, sensing the impending onslaught of World War III, suddenly decided to take matters in hand.

"Pardon me," he said, flagging down a waiter who was hustling by with a tray of drinks in his hand. "Could you fetch us a drink?"

The young, ginger-haired waiter stopped in his tracks, bobbed his head. "Of course, sir."

"Here you go, Delaine. This young fellow here . . ." said Drayton.

"Graham, sir," said the waiter.

"Tell Graham what you'd like, Delaine. He'll take care of you." Drayton fumbled in his pocket for a few dollars, pressed them into the waiter's hand. "For your trouble, young man."

"No problem, sir," replied the waiter.

"I'd like a Kir Royale," Delaine told the waiter. "Cassis and champagne?"

The waiter nodded. "Of course, ma'am. Be back in a moment."

"Evening, ladies," boomed a rich male voice.

Jory Davis, Theodosia's on-again off-again boyfriend, grinned at them. Tall, well over six feet, with a square jaw, sun-tanned complexion, and curly brown hair, Jory Davis had a slightly reckless look about him. He didn't look the way a traditional lawyer was supposed to look, all buttoned up and slightly pompous. Instead, Jory Davis had an aura of the outdoors about him. Dressed in casual clothes, he could have passed for a trout fishing guide. Or maybe a wealthy landowner whose life's love was training thoroughbred horses.

Jory Davis snaked an arm around Theodosia's waist and pulled her close to him, touched his chin to the top of her head. Pleased, she snuggled in against him.

The move was not lost on Delaine. "I see you two are still very cozy," she said.

"Mmm," said Jory. "And why not?" He smiled down at Theodosia. "I was thinking about taking *Rubicon* out tomorrow. What do you think? Are you up for an ocean sail?"

Jory Davis's sailboat, *Rubicon,* was a J-24 that he kept

moored at the Charleston Yacht Club. He was an expert yachtsman and regularly competed in the Isle of Palms race as well as the Compass Key yacht race.

"Isn't it still raining?" asked Theodosia.

"Tonight it is," said Jory, "but the weather's supposed to clear by tomorrow. If there's a chop on the water, it'll just make our sail all the more interesting. And challenging," he added.

Clear weather and a chance to clear my head, thought Theodosia. *Truly a heavenly idea.* The past two days had been fairly fraught with tension, what with the terrible accident at the Lady Goodwood and Drayton's fear that something might go wrong here tonight. Jory's suggestion of a sail in Charleston Harbor and the waters beyond would be a perfect way to put it all behind her.

"You're on," she told him.

"Good," he said. "I'll pick you up around nine, then we'll go rig the boat. And bring that goofy dog of yours along. We'll turn him into a sea dog yet."

"Sailing sounds like fun," said Delaine. The note of wistfulness in her voice was not lost on the two of them.

"Say," said Jory, "I'm going to slip across the room and have a word with Leyland Hartwell. He's representing the Tidewater Corporation in a zoning dispute and I'm second chair. Be back in a couple minutes, okay?"

"Sure," said Theodosia as she watched her tall, tanned boyfriend navigate his way through the crowd.

Ligget, Hume, Hartwell, the firm Jory Davis worked for, was also her father's old firm. He had been a senior partner along with Leyland Hartwell before he passed away some fifteen years ago. Her father had become a distant memory now, but he was always in her heart. As was her mother, who had died when Theodosia was just eight.

"What kind of law does Jory Davis practice again?" asked Delaine.

"Mostly corporate and real estate law," said Theodosia. "Deeds, foreclosures, zoning, leases, that sort of thing."

"So he's never faced off against Cooper in a courtroom," said Delaine.

The thought amused Theodosia. She could see Cooper Hobcaw with his arrogant stance arguing torts against a bemused Jory Davis. But no, that would never happen. Cooper Hobcaw was a criminal attorney, Jory Davis a real estate attorney.

"Cooper Hobcaw seems like a nice fellow . . ." began Theodosia when, suddenly, every light in the place went out. *Whoosh.* Extinguished like the flame on a candle.

Oh no, thought Theodosia, her heart in her throat. *Not again!*

Plunged into complete darkness, the room erupted in chaos. Women screamed, a tray of drinks went crashing to the floor. Across the room, something hit the carpet with a muffled thud. Disoriented by the dark, people began to lunge to and fro. Theodosia felt an elbow drill into her back, a sleeve brush roughly against her bare arm.

Suddenly, mercifully, from off to her left, someone flipped on a cigarette lighter and held the flame aloft like a tiny torch. There was a spatter of applause, then a deep hum started from somewhere in the depths of the building.

"Generator," murmured a male voice off to her right. "Emergency lights should kick on soon."

Ten seconds later, four sets of emergency lights sputtered on.

They blazed weakly overhead, yet did little to actually illuminate the room. The lighting felt unnatural and fuzzy, like trying to peer through a bank of fog.

"Hey!" called a voice that Theodosia recognized as belonging to Jory Davis. "Someone's down over here!"

Theodosia quickly elbowed her way through the crowd in the direction of Jory Davis's voice.

Ten feet, fifteen feet of pushing past people brought her

to just outside the small gallery. In the dim light she could see one of the security guards sprawled on the floor. Jory Davis was already on his hands and knees beside the man, making a hasty check of his airways, trying to determine if he was still breathing.

"Is he okay?" asked Theodosia.

"He's still breathing," said Jory, "but he's for sure out cold." Jory put a finger to the top of the security guard's head, came away with a smear of blood. "Looks like he took a nasty bump to the noggin." Jory glanced up at Theodosia. "Somebody sapped this poor guy, but good," he added in a tight, low voice. Then Jory Davis scrambled to his feet. "Can someone please call an ambulance!" he shouted.

With Jory Davis's forceful lawyer voice ringing out across the room, no fewer than twenty people responded instantly. Cell phones were yanked from pockets and evening bags, and twenty fingers punched in the same 911 call, completely swamping the small crew that manned Charleston's central emergency line.

"Theodosia!" Timothy Neville was suddenly at her side and clutching her arm. "It's gone!" he told her in a tremulous voice. "Vanished!"

"What's gone?" she asked, momentarily confused.

"The Blue Kashmir," Timothy hissed. "The sapphire necklace. It's disappeared from its case!" Timothy clapped a wizened hand to the side of his face and seemed to collapse in on himself.

Theodosia stared at Timothy in disbelief. When the power went out, the sensor beams had stopped working, too, she realized. *Oh, no . . . we didn't even consider that possibility. Had someone cut the power deliberately? Or had the storm just knocked it out?*

No, she decided, if a guard's been injured, the power *had* to have been disabled on purpose.

In the dim light Theodosia could see that Timothy was dangerously on the verge of passing out.

"Are you okay, Timothy?" she asked.

"Yes, yes," he said hurriedly, although perspiration had broken out on his face and his breathing had suddenly turned shallow.

Ohmygosh, Theodosia thought to herself. *Heart attack? Not Timothy. Please, Lord, not Timothy. Not now.*

Pushing his way over to them, Drayton took one look at Timothy Neville's face, grabbed him firmly by the arm, and steered him to a nearby chair a few feet away. "Are you all right, Timothy?" he asked as Timothy sat down gingerly, looking paler than ever.

"Yes, I think so . . ." rasped Timothy, ". . . just let me catch my . . ."

Theodosia whirled about and threw herself down next to Jory Davis. He had once again taken up his position next to the fallen security guard and had bunched up his jacket and put it under the poor man's head. A woman whom Theodosia recognized as Dr. Lucy Cornwall, Earl Grey's veterinarian, was administering CPR to the downed security guard, while Jory Davis continued to monitor the man's pulse.

"There's something wrong with Timothy," Theodosia told them in a rush. "I think he's having a heart attack!"

CHAPTER 5

ON THIS LAZY Sunday in late October, autumn was clearly in the air. The wet weather was temporarily held at bay by a warm front that had finally drifted up from the Gulf of Mexico. It seemed like a toss-up as to whether the day would dissipate into scattered thundershowers or weak sunshine would punch through the low-hanging clouds.

Down at Charleston Harbor, people strolled through White Point Gardens and Battery Park, delighted by the huge displays of Civil War cannons and gazing at the magnificent harbor where whitecaps rose like peaks of frosting. Out on the water, sailboats bobbed like corks, tossed about in the boiling froth, masts straining against strong twenty-knot winds.

But Theodosia was not out sailing today. She was not slicing through the waves, enjoying salty breezes and the exhilaration of navigating tricky cross-currents.

Instead, she sat with Drayton and Timothy on the side piazza of Timothy Neville's home. The sun was warm and caressing, the view conducive to Zen-like contemplation since the piazza overlooked the bamboo groves, rocky paths, Chinese lanterns, and trickling fountain of Timothy's Asian-inspired garden. But the mood was not particularly serene.

Timothy hadn't experienced a heart attack last night after all. After rushing him to the hospital along with the security guard, an EKG had been administered, cardiac enzymes monitored, blood pressure taken every fifteen minutes.

Extreme stress, the doctor had ruled, once he'd studied the test results and learned of the strange events that had taken place at the Heritage Society's party. Extreme stress had triggered a rush of adrenaline and a flood of cortisol, which had produced *symptoms* that closely mimicked an all-out heart attack.

A shaken but stoic Timothy had put up with all the tests and ministrations at the hospital, but staunchly vetoed any notion of an overnight stay even if it was intended purely for observation.

The security guard hadn't fared as well. He lay in intensive care, his head swathed in bandages, fluttering in and out of a coma, hooked up to a host of beeping, glowing monitors.

"Have you seen this?" Timothy Neville winced as he held up the front page of the main news section of the Sunday *Post & Courier.*

"We've seen it," said Drayton. He sat in a wicker lounge chair facing Timothy, looking anything but relaxed. In fact, Drayton was wound so tightly it looked as though his bow tie was about ready to spin.

"Jackals," spat Timothy. "How do they get this stuff out so fast?"

A small article, mercifully positioned at the bottom of the page, led off with the headline GEMS NABBED FROM HERITAGE SOCIETY.

"At least it's not in seventy-two-point type," Drayton pointed out.

Timothy stared at him with a mixture of anger and disgust.

Nervously, Drayton crossed his legs then uncrossed them, deciding that perhaps humor *wasn't* the most practical approach here.

"We look like *idiots,*" raged Timothy. "This is going to cost us donors and then some!"

Theodosia knew that Timothy Neville was worried sick that this incident might also cost him his job as president of the Heritage Society. The man was eighty-one, she reasoned, and had done a masterful job for the past twenty-five years. But how long could he continue? Would this be the political scandal that brought about his downfall? She hoped not, but it was certainly possible.

"Timothy," began Drayton, "I know you have serious doubts about opening the Treasures Show to the public next Saturday. Please . . . just take into consideration how much promotion has already been done, how much publicity we've gotten."

Timothy gazed at the front page of the newspaper again. "Publicity," he snorted. "This kind of publicity we don't need. What's important now is damage control. This incident has been the worst kind of *blight* on the Heritage Society." Timothy spat out the word *blight* as though he were discussing manure.

"Which is why we should stay the course," pleaded Drayton. "Open the Treasures Show to the public next weekend as planned. Show everyone that it's business as usual, that we *haven't* been affected!"

Timothy sighed deeply. "I don't know. I'll have to speak with the insurance company. And our executive advisory committee, of course." Timothy sat quietly in his chair, staring out at the garden. "Any word on the poor fellow who got clobbered on the head?" he asked finally.

"The man's name is Harlan Wilson," said Drayton. "He was one of the security guards from Gold Shield who has been employed by us on several other occasions. As far as we know, he's still terribly groggy, in and out of consciousness. He has a rather nasty concussion as well as a hairline skull fracture. The results of his ECG, his encephalogram, looked very positive, however. There are no interruptions in brain activity, which is a very good sign. Doctors, being doctors, are remaining cautious, though. They haven't allowed the police to question Mr. Wilson as yet. They warn that it might be a day or two before he's well enough for that."

Timothy shook his head. "Such a terrible thing. Poor man getting hurt like that."

Theodosia had remained quiet during most of the exchange between Timothy and Drayton. She wasn't on the board of the Heritage Society like Drayton was. And she wasn't a close friend of Timothy's like Drayton was. But she *did* share their anger and frustration. After all, *she'd* also had a nervous rumbling about this. And had thought, mistakenly it would appear, that security guards and some newly purchased gadgets would be enough to ensure safekeeping of the European Jewel Collection.

Did that make her partially responsible for what happened last night?

With Theodosia's sense of fair play, the answer was a resounding yes. Yes, she was partially responsible. So, yes, she was determined to try to help resolve this problem.

Delaine had begged for her help in trying to find the missing wedding ring; now Drayton and Timothy seemed to be in a fairly tight situation as well.

Theodosia also knew that the one issue that desperately needed to be discussed remained unspoken.

"You know what this means, don't you?" began Theodosia quietly.

"Of course," said Timothy with an air of resignation. "It

means our good name has been besmirched. How willing are people going to be to donate a silver tankard or a piece of Chippendale if they think the Heritage Society can't even offer decent security?" He shook his head. "I doubt they'll even trust us with a dog-eared *photo album* now."

"Timothy," Theodosia said slowly, "this second theft gives us a fairly good confirmation that some kind of special thief or cat burglar *is* operating in the historic district."

She watched as Timothy lowered his head in his hands.

"Why, oh why, didn't I take this more seriously?" he lamented. "I assumed that missing wedding ring had just rolled into a corner somewhere and was lying there in a puff of dust. I never thought any kind of serious *theft* would occur at the Heritage Society. Not in my wildest dreams!"

"Don't be so hard on yourself," spoke up Drayton. "I'd say you took our warning very seriously. When I spoke to you about the wedding ring disappearing from the Lady Goodwood Inn, you were *extremely* agreeable about taking precautions. You even approved the expenditure for the electronic equipment. Which means you did *everything* right, Timothy. No one could possibly fault you or hold you responsible."

Timothy grimaced, unwilling to meet Drayton's earnest gaze. "Oh, but I'm afraid they will," he replied, his voice quavering.

"Timothy," said Theodosia, determined to bring him back to the subject at hand, "we've got to face reality. Whoever is responsible for these thefts has to be one of our own."

Timothy's eyebrows rose like two question marks on his pale face as he stared at Theodosia with trepidation. "Explain," he said. One hand gestured at her weakly, urging her to continue.

"If it isn't someone from our own circle," said Theodosia, "then how else would they have known about Camille's wedding ring at the Lady Goodwood? Or the European Jewel Collection?"

"They read the paper? Studied their intended target?" proposed Drayton.

"The European Jewel Collection was written up in the paper, yes," said Theodosia. She thought for a moment. "But there was nothing about Camille Buchanan's wedding ring. That was . . . that was . . ."

"An accident?" proposed Drayton.

"You're not going to like this, but I'd say it's more likely an inside job," said Theodosia. "As far as the Lady Goodwood's silver goes . . . well, you'd just have to know about that."

"So whoever perpetrated the crime was right there," said Timothy slowly. "They were right there among us last night. Probably sipping drinks, chatting with guests."

They all sat in shocked silence for a moment, pondering the implications.

Finally, Theodosia spoke up. "There's something else, too."

"What's that?" asked Drayton.

"If the two thefts are related, and I think we have pretty much come to the very unsettling conclusion that they are, then poor Harlan Wilson could be in danger," said Theodosia. "Because he's probably the only witness we have."

"But he's still in a coma!" exclaimed Drayton.

"Which is very good news for our thief," said Theodosia. "Unless Mr. Wilson suddenly comes to and is able to provide the police with a careful description. Of course, we don't know for certain that Mr. Wilson even saw the robbery take place. Let's assume that he did, however, and act accordingly. Err on the side of caution."

"So what do we do now?" asked Timothy. He suddenly looked terribly defeated.

"Obviously we need reinforcements," said Theodosia. "And protection for Mr. Wilson."

"The police," said Timothy with resignation. "They're already on it. I spoke with two investigators this morning."

"Did you voice your concerns about a connection with the ring disappearing at the Lady Goodwood?" asked Drayton.

"No," said Timothy. "I guess I just didn't want to believe . . ." His voice trailed off.

"Then might I suggest we call in the big guns?" said Theodosia.

"You mean . . ." said Drayton, glancing sharply at her.

Theodosia nodded. "That's right. Detective Tidwell."

Henry Marchand, Timothy's butler and housekeeper for the last forty years, suddenly appeared behind them. For someone who was so advanced in years, Henry moved with amazing stealth. They had heard nary a footstep.

"Sorry to interrupt, sir, but you have a phone call," Henry said in his somber, papery voice.

Theodosia glanced down at Henry's feet. He was wearing a pair of Chinese shoes. Thin-soled slip-ons made of black cotton fabric. No wonder he moved like a Ninja.

Timothy waved a hand as though to dismiss the call. "Tell them to—"

"It's Mr. Bernard," said Henry with a grave face.

Timothy reluctantly pulled himself up from his wicker chair. "You hear that? Vance Bernard is *chairman* of our executive advisory committee. The committee *I* report to. I can assure you, Vance Bernard is not a happy man today. Which can result in just one thing—my head will be placed squarely on the chopping block!"

Timothy took a few steps to the door, hesitated, turned back toward Theodosia and Drayton. "Once you speak with this fellow, Tidwell, you'll let me know, yes?"

"Of course," Theodosia assured him, then watched as Timothy turned back and entered the house. It was the first time she'd seen Timothy Neville walk without a spring in his step. It was the first time she'd really seen him looking old.

CHAPTER 6

THE NOTES FROM Pachelbel's *Cannon* drifted through Theodosia's upstairs apartment, a cozy fire crackled in the bright fireplace, a chapter from a new mystery novel beckoned. But try as she might, Theodosia just couldn't concentrate, couldn't relax.

After that rather jarring meeting with Timothy Neville, she and Drayton had tried to formulate some sort of battle plan. But nothing had seemed to gel. There didn't seem to be any real clues. After all, if no one person stuck in their minds as a potential suspect, what exactly could they do? Nothing. Nothing at all.

Theodosia lay her book facedown on the sofa, kicked off the afghan she'd been snuggled under, and gazed about, a slightly disgruntled look on her usually serene face.

She loved her little place above the tea shop. It was elegant, cozy, and suited her perfectly. This past summer, she'd taken the big plunge and painted the walls. But instead of a conservative palette of eggshell white or cream, she'd opted for a rich ochre base coat, then sponged a second layer of flaxen yellow on top of it. The result was a sun-washed feel reminiscent of a Tuscan villa. Now the cinnamon and gold Oriental rug she'd always had in the living room really came alive. As did the gleaming seascape oil paintings on the walls. Flanking the double doorway that led to her small dining room, she'd installed two antique wooden columns as plant stands for her Boston ferns.

What had once been very shabby chic had suddenly become the picture of Southern elegance.

That's good, she had told herself. *The nature of a home should shift and mature along with its owner.*

But tonight, the upstairs apartment she'd worked so hard and lovingly on just felt confining.

Enough, she decided as she padded into her bedroom, rooted around in the bottom of the closet for her Nikes, and pulled a pair of leggings from a chest of drawers.

When in doubt, go for a jog.

Earl Grey, suddenly alert and convinced something wonderful was about to take place, sprang to his feet. Toenails clicking against hardwood floors, he circled her repeatedly, ears pitched forward, tail beating a doggy rhythm in double time.

"You got it, fella, let's go," said Theodosia as she grabbed his leather leash off the hook in the kitchen.

Ecstatic now, Earl Grey tumbled down the stairs ahead of her, ready to charge out and own the night.

Heading down Church Street past the Chowder Hound Restaurant, Cabbage Patch Needlepoint Shop, and Floradora, her favorite flower shop, Theodosia and Earl Grey cut over on Water Street to East Bay. The night was cool but not cold. The atmosphere, laden with humidity, lent a soft focus to the light that streamed from the old mansions, garden lanterns, portico and street lamps. Charleston, always highly atmospheric to begin with, positively glowed at night.

The first six blocks they kept it down to a fast walk. Theodosia wanted to stretch her legs, ease out the kinks. She loved to run, had been a runner for some ten years now. But she also knew the cardinal sin in running was to skip the warm-up and zoom right into high gear. That was the absolute *wrong* way to do it. That's how muscles got pulled, tendons sprained.

But by the time she and Earl Grey hit Battery Park at the very tip of the peninsula, they were warmed up and ready to blow out the carbon.

Theodosia gave a fast look around, didn't see anyone who remotely resembled the pooch police. *Excellent,* she thought with a tiny stab of guilt as she unclipped Earl Grey's lead. And with that, the two of them bounded down the pathway that snugged the shoreline.

A salty wind whipped Theodosia's hair out in streaming tendrils, oyster shells crunched beneath her feet. They pounded past a trio of Civil War cannons, past a huge stack of old cannon balls, past the bandstand where so many weddings and wedding party photos had taken place. To their left was the surging harbor with its marker buoys and flickering lights, to their right loomed the dark city of Charleston, the Kingdom by the Sea that Edgar Allan Poe had immortalized in his poem *Annabelle Lee.*

Theodosia took a right where Legare Street intersected and Earl Grey bounded along beside her. They flew down the block, the dog maintaining his easy, loping stride in order to stay even with his beloved owner. Now they were deep in the heart of the historic district again. Streets were canopied over with trees, cobblestones paved a warren of narrow walkways and secret alleys, and large, elegant homes butted up against each other. Theodosia cut to the right, down Atlantic, and whistled softly for Earl Grey to follow. He did.

They skimmed past the tiny brick Library Society building with its ornate wrought iron fence, then turned down a narrow, hidden pathway that ran behind the building. Theodosia slowed her pace, then pulled to a stop just outside the Library Society's lush courtyard garden. In the dim light, she could make out the three-tiered fountain, columns of lush oleander, and large camellia bushes.

Time to reel her dog in, she decided. Time to start the cool-down. Theodosia knelt down, clipped the leash back onto Earl Grey's leather collar, and gave him a reassuring pat.

And in the moment of silence that followed, heard footsteps coming up behind her.

Had someone been following her?

She remained kneeling in the back alleyway, her breath coming faster now, her heart pounding.

If someone *had* been following her, she reasoned, they probably hadn't realized she'd stopped. Which meant they'd be coming around that corner any second. Hastily, she unclipped Earl Grey's leash and wound it around her right fist. The leather and metal snap would make a dandy weapon and Earl Grey would be far more effective as a guard dog if he were free to move about on his own.

Earl Grey stood expectantly now, as did Theodosia, listening to rapidly approaching footsteps.

Suddenly, the nighttime runner was upon them. Startled, obviously not expecting to see someone blocking the pathway, the man, a tall man, skidded to a stop and gaped at Theodosia, his breath coming in hard gasps.

"Theodosia?" he said.

Theodosia stared back, relief suddenly flooding her. The mysterious runner was none other than Cooper Hobcaw.

She put a hand to her heart. "Oh my goodness," she laughed, "you startled me."

Cooper Hobcaw looked equally rattled. "Yeah . . . sorry. Are you okay?" he asked.

Theodosia knew he was probably wondering just what

she was doing here, standing in this dark pathway, looking like an idiot.

"I was just putting the leash back on Earl Grey," she explained, "and heard someone coming." When she'd realized who it was, she had quickly loosened the leather leash from around her hand. There was no reason to let Cooper Hobcaw know she'd been prepared to launch an all-out assault on him.

Now Theodosia bent down and clipped the leash onto Earl Grey's collar. "There," she said as it made a satisfying snap. "Sorry we startled you."

"Hey," he breathed, "same here. You can't be too careful after what happened last night."

"Exactly my thought," replied Theodosia.

"Strange goings-on," said Cooper Hobcaw. "Have you heard . . . is the fellow who got knocked on the head, the security guard, going to be okay?"

"I think so."

"Good," he said. Cooper Hobcaw peered at her in the darkness. "I thought I was the only nutcase who went running through the historic district at night."

"No," she said. "There are actually quite a few of us."

Cooper Hobcaw nodded. "The professional's dilemma, right? Work all day, exercise at night."

She nodded back. "'Fraid so."

"I like your buddy here." He reached out and rubbed Earl Grey behind the ears. Earl Grey responded by tossing his elegant head and inviting a scratch under the chin. "Nice dog," said Cooper Hobcaw. "Friendly, too. I like that."

It was only after Cooper Hobcaw had jogged off that Theodosia remembered he lived over on the other side of Calhoun and not in the historic district at all.

CHAPTER 7

"ONCE YOU TASTE this Formosan Oolong," promised Drayton as he poured a steaming brownish-amber liquid into celadon green ceramic teacups for the three women seated at his table, "I think you'll understand why it's been dubbed the champagne of teas."

Heads bobbed forward, and here and there a delicate slurp was emitted.

"Delicious!" declared one of the women.

A second woman held up the small teacup. "Why no handles?" she asked.

"It's simply the convention for Chinese teacups, or tea bowls as they are often called," replied Drayton. "Same for Japanese teacups. Now if we were drinking a nice strong tea in Morocco or Russia, we'd probably be using a glass. And the English teacup, usually slightly fluted and with a delicate handle, is a derivation of the ale tankard which was often used for imbibing the proverbial hot toddy."

The ladies nodded happily, delighted with their tea tasting and with Drayton's fascinating bits of tea lore.

"This oolong does have a slightly sweet flavor," declared one of his tasters.

"Can you pick up a hint of peaches or honey?" he asked.

The three ladies tasted again, then nodded.

"And chestnuts," he added. "Very often an oolong will offer up a delicate nutty taste. That's a result of the shortened withering period. Freshly picked leaves are dried for only about four or five hours, then allowed to partially ferment. Once the outside of the leaves begin to turn greenish-brown, the tea is fired. Remember," he told them, "tea is one thing that *never* improves with age. Freshness does count."

"I'll never go back to orange pekoe again," declared one woman happily.

"Which, as you all know, is really a *grade* of tea, not a flavor at all," said Drayton as a quick aside. "Now if you'll excuse me, ladies," he stood up from the table, "I shall check to see if a certain batch of croissants are out of the oven yet."

The ladies beamed, caught up as they were in the fascinating world of tea. But then, whenever Drayton conducted one of his tea tastings, he was highly instinctive as well as delightfully entertaining. He was sometimes booked weeks in advance, and often, bed-and-breakfasts such as the Featherbed House or the Allister Beene Home would recommend to their guests that tea with Drayton was a "not to be missed" event.

Drayton hustled over to where Theodosia stood at the counter. "Are the croissants ready yet?" he asked.

"Should be just coming out of the oven," she told him.

Drayton stood for a moment and fidgeted.

"You're thinking of the funeral," she said, noting the suddenly somber look on his face.

"Yes," he said, "aren't you?"

"Here you are, Drayton," said Haley as she came

through the curtains and delivered a plate of golden pastries into Drayton's waiting arms. "And some *pain au chocolat,* too. I had extra dough so I sweetened things up a bit." Haley suddenly paused, registering the looks on their faces. "Oh, gosh," she said, "the funeral's today, isn't it? I wonder how they-all are doing down in Savannah."

"Probably awful," said Drayton.

"That's what I figured, too," said Haley. "I mean, I only met Camille that one time but I really liked her a lot. She was a hoot. Well, you know what I mean."

"Of course, we do, dear," said Theodosia. "She's a lovely girl."

"You called Tidwell, right?" said Drayton.

"You're going to talk to *him?*" said Haley. She didn't care for Tidwell, thought him to be a boor and a brute.

"I sent him an e-mail last night," said Theodosia.

"Technology," Drayton said derisively. "It's going to be the downfall of Western civilization."

"You didn't think so the other day when you guys set up those tracker beams," said Haley.

"And they didn't work, did they!" argued Drayton.

"Hold everything," said Theodosia. "We all know the motion sensors didn't work because someone cut the power. It had nothing to do with a technological meltdown."

"Drayton, don't you have a table full of customers waiting for those?" Haley indicated the plate of baked goods in his hand.

"Don't you have today's luncheon to figure out?" he asked her.

"Tea-marinated prawns on Japanese noodles," she told him. "But I don't anticipate there'll be any leftovers."

"Tea-marinated prawns?" he said, suddenly perking up. "My, that *does* sound lovely. May I ask which tea you've chosen as a marinade base?"

Haley grinned. "You may not. But if any of our *cus-*

tomers are interested, you may tell them it is Lapsang Souchong."

"Mmnn," said Drayton, considering. "Nice, rich, black tea from southern China. Smoky flavor. Should be highly complementary with seafood."

"Maybe there'll be a nibble left over," she told him.

"Let's hope so," he said.

Haley's tea-marinated prawns were an enormous hit. Theodosia wasn't sure exactly what seemed to be bringing the customers in these days—the cool, sunny weather, the hint of autumn in the air, or a sudden jump in the number of tourists—but they were packed for lunch once again. Standing room only, in fact. Giselle and Cleo, two regulars from Parsifal, a gift shop down the street, ended up getting their lunches packed to go in one of the Indigo Tea Shop's indigo blue boxes, rather than stand around and wait for a table.

"Maybe we should be putting tables on the sidewalk," Theodosia lamented to Drayton.

"We've talked about outside tables before and never done it," he said. "It would mean a little more work, but it would certainly increase our capacity as well."

"By capacity, you mean profits," she said.

"Of course I mean profits. Profits are the lifeblood of a business," said Drayton, ever mindful of the bottom line.

"What would we need to do?" she asked. "File something with the city for a permit?"

"I think so," he said. "Maybe your friend, Jory Davis, could look into it."

"Good idea," replied Theodosia, then added, "or is it too late in the year? We could get a cold snap any day now."

"Then we'll be well prepared for spring," Drayton assured her.

By two o'clock things had settled down to normal.

Haley was rattling dishes in the kitchen, clearing away lunch, and had already put a couple pans of gingerbread in the oven in anticipation of the afternoon tea crowd. Drayton was seated at the table nearest the counter, munching his prawns and doing a highly adequate job of snaring the slippery Japanese soba noodles with his pair of wooden chopsticks. Theodosia was arranging antique teacups and muffin plates on the high shelf behind the counter where their old brass cash register sat.

She had collected dozens of teacups over the years, a hard-to-find Shelley Apple Blossom, several Limoges, and a pretty fan-handle Russian teacup from the Popov Porcelain Factory, to name just a few. And she'd decided it was a shame to keep so many stored away in boxes. Better to bring them downstairs and create a fanciful display.

"That's a lovely Shelley," called Drayton from his table.

Theodosia held up the Shelley Apple Blossom for him to admire. It was creamy white bone china covered in a riot of pink apple blossoms. It was also one of the cups and saucers that was most prized among the many avid Shelley collectors throughout the world.

"As you probably know," Drayton told her, "I've got the Shelley Dainty White in the Queen Anne style. Setting for eight. Hudgins Antiques offered me fifteen hundred for it just last year."

"Did you consider selling?" she asked.

"Absolutely not, it's worth twice that. Besides, I love those dishes. They were passed down to me by my dear Aunt Cecily."

When the front door fluttered open a few minutes later, it wasn't the first wave of afternoon customers come for tea. Instead, Detective Burt Tidwell strode forcefully into the room.

Burt Tidwell wasn't exactly one of Theodosia's favorite people. But then again, Burt Tidwell wasn't *anyone's* favorite person. An ex-FBI agent, Burt Tidwell lived in

Charleston in what he considered a state of semiretirement. Which, for the driven, results-oriented, obsessive-compulsive man that he was, meant he was employed full-time, working a sixty-hour week as lead homicide detective for the Charleston Police Department.

Brash, bordering on boorish, Tidwell's physical being projected his inner personality. What you saw was what you got. A tall man, way beyond heavyset, Tidwell had a strange bullet-shaped head that seemed to rest directly upon his shoulders. Worse yet, Tidwell was a bulldog with steel jaws, tenacious, slightly ill-tempered, perpetually dubious.

Yet Burt Tidwell did have a certain way about him. When he chose to be, Tidwell could border on courtly, particularly in discussions with women. He was an avid reader and a keen admirer of Sartre, Hemingway, and Octavio Paz. Many years ago, back when FBI agents were also required to have law degrees, Tidwell had attended Harvard and so still had a keen sense of the written word.

Theodosia seated Tidwell at the table with Drayton, then quickly ferried over cups, saucers, a pot of tea, plates, napkins, silverware, and a tray of assorted goodies.

When she finally sat down next to Tidwell, Theodosia didn't mince words.

"What do you know about cat burglars?" she asked him.

But Tidwell wasn't about to let her slip into a prosecutorial mode quite so easily. He took a sip of tea, allowed his eyes to rove across the tray of baked goods. "Pray tell, what is this delightful-looking bread?" he asked with an inquisitive air as he hooked the plate with his index finger and pulled it toward him.

Realizing Tidwell wasn't going to be as forthcoming as she wished, Theodosia slid the butter plate toward Tidwell. "Persimmon bread," she told him.

"And the tea is . . ."

"Assam. Taste the sweetness?"

"I do. As well as a slightly malty flavor."

"Why, Detective Tidwell, I do believe you're becoming a tea connoisseur," said Theodosia as Drayton looked on, pleased.

Tidwell picked up the cloth napkin and daubed at his lips. "You never know, dear lady, you never know."

"Detective Tidwell," began Theodosia, "you received my e-mail and my slightly abbreviated account of the two thefts."

"The wedding ring and the gems at the Heritage Society. Yes, I did," he said. "Additionally, I spoke with the two investigators, Jacob Gallier and Peter Delehanty, who are currently working both cases. They're not convinced the two incidents are at all related."

This was surprising news to Theodosia. "How could they not look at them in the same context?"

Tidwell shifted his eyes from the persimmon bread to Theodosia's face. "What is your interest in this?" he inquired.

"My friends are involved," she said. "I'm worried about them."

"Ah," he said, "assuming the worries of the world again, are we?" Tidwell shook his great head slowly. "Oh, to be young and burning with such inner fire."

"You were saying," prompted Theodosia, "that Mr. Gallier and Delehanty do not think the two thefts are related?"

Tidwell chewed thoughtfully. "From their perspective, the first incident at the Lady Goodwood Inn seems more like an unfortunate accident."

"And the second incident?" asked Drayton, suddenly deciding to join the conversation. "The missing necklace at the Heritage Society?"

"That *is* a clear-cut robbery," said Tidwell. "No one's disputing that." He swiveled his head toward Theodosia and bore into her with small, intense eyes. "But according to the rather rambling e-mail you forwarded to me, *you* believe there is some mysterious cat burglar prowling the historic district."

"I think it's a distinct possibility," Theodosia said. "And I do think the two cases are related." She looked at Drayton, who hovered nearby, for confirmation.

"We both do," he said.

Tidwell sat back in his chair with an air of finality. "And you'd like me to expound on what I know concerning the phenomenon known as the cat burglar," he said with a sigh.

"Could you?" asked Theodosia with an encouraging smile.

Tidwell reached one paw up, absently brushed stray bread crumbs from the lapels of his tweed jacket. "Closest thing you can compare it to is a great white shark," he said.

"What a strange analogy," Theodosia said, looking perplexed.

Tidwell grimaced. "In my experience, which admittedly is quite limited, a cat burglar tends to be a territorial creature. If the feeding is plentiful in one place, he will tend to stay put."

"And the feeding should be mighty plentiful in Charleston," murmured Theodosia. "Think of all the estate jewelry that's here. Or the priceless antiques and oil paintings that grace so many of the homes in the historic district."

Tidwell nodded. "A tasty treasure trove, indeed. Old families, old money. There is a lovely synchronicity at work."

"So we have to just sit around and wait for this cat burglar to strike again?" asked Drayton somewhat peevishly.

Tidwell reached for a second slice of persimmon bread, took a large bite, chewed with great enthusiasm, swallowed. "If he strikes at all," said Tidwell. "Let me again emphasize that my experience is limited. However . . ."

"However what?" asked Drayton.

"There is another breed of cat burglar," said Tidwell. "And that is the migratory kind."

"Versus the territorial kind," said Drayton. Now his lined face betrayed a fair amount of skepticism.

"Exactly," said Tidwell. "This migratory version follows the goods."

Theodosia and Drayton exchanged puzzled looks. "Which means . . ." prompted Theodosia.

Tidwell rocked back in his chair and the ancient wood creaked in protest. "For openers, there's the summer social season in the Hamptons, opera season in New York, then a long stretch of charity balls in Palm Beach."

Drayton's mouth opened then closed. "Oh," he finally said. "I see what you mean."

Theodosia deftly slid the plate of baked goods closer to Tidwell. "If you had a gut feeling, how would you characterize our fellow?" she asked.

"If I listened to my gut, I wouldn't help myself to a third pastry," said Tidwell with a rueful smile. He reached for a croissant, slid it onto his plate. "Alas, dear girl, I can offer you no great insight."

Drayton and Theodosia sat there looking slightly deflated.

Tidwell saw their distress. "What I may be able to parcel out," he added, "is a small amount of information. The robbery division is working up a guest list from both functions. If something strange rears its head, I'll let you know. How would that be?"

"Good enough," said Theodosia. "Thank you."

Tidwell raised a furry eyebrow and cast a warning glance at her. "You can keep your eyes open," he told her, "but I warn you right now, do not make *any* attempt whatsoever to track, trail, or apprehend anyone you deem a potential suspect." He continued to gaze steadily at Theodosia. "Is that clear?"

"Of course," she said.

"Of course," Tidwell repeated. "Miss Browning, your voice carries such a tone of innocence. But why do I sense a certain degree of insincerity in your promise?"

"No, I'll be careful," Theodosia assured him. "Really I will."

"When are we going to talk about the open house?" asked Haley. She'd emerged from the kitchen and now stood hands-on-hips, staring at Theodosia.

Theodosia, standing up on tiptoes with her right arm extended, stopped in mid-stretch. She'd almost finished arranging her display of teacups.

The finished T-Bath products had all arrived, the shipping cartons stacked so high in her office it made it almost impossible to navigate her way to her desk. And the invitations for this Thursday's afternoon reception had been mailed out well over two weeks ago. So far almost three dozen people had responded with RSVPs and she was confident quite a few more people would just spontaneously drop by. But drop by for what? Their big event was now three days away and it still needed to be finalized!

"I'm sure nobody feels like planning this thing," continued Haley in a somewhat plaintive tone of voice, "but it *is* on our schedule."

"You're right," said Theodosia. "And it's not that we don't want to plan it, we've just been caught up in other things." She glanced across the room at Drayton. "Drayton?" she called.

He looked up from where he was pouring a warm-up cup of tea for two women seated near the front door and held up a finger. "Be there in a sec," he answered back.

"What I thought," said Haley moving into her take-charge mode, "was that we'd try for a kind of Zen-like atmosphere. Try to capture the feeling of relaxation and renewal that the T-Bath products are supposed to impart."

Theodosia nodded. "That sounds like a great idea. We could use a stress-free zone around here."

"And if we brought in some of Drayton's Japanese bonsai trees, they'd make cute accent pieces for all of the tables."

"You think he'll let us?" asked Theodosia. "He's awfully protective of those trees of his."

Drayton had joined them now and was nodding enthusiastically. "Only the Fukien tea plant and the jade tree stay at home. They're the most sensitive. As for the others, the maples, junipers, and larches . . . well, you know I never miss a chance to show off my bonsai," he added with a modest grin.

"Great," continued Haley. "Then, what if on the main table, the buffet table, we have a real knockout floral arrangement. Something very Asian looking. I don't know what you call those arrangements, but they're quite artsy and contemporary looking. I was thinking we could do something with orchids surrounded by stalks of bamboo?"

"I believe the correct term is ikebana," said Drayton. "It's Japanese flower arranging at its most fanciful. In fact, *ikebana* literally translated means 'fresh flower.' You might call it the bonsai of flower arranging."

"Okay," said Haley. "Great."

"We'll ask Hattie Boatwright over at Floradora to design something for us," suggested Drayton. "She took an ikebana workshop with me a few years ago and her arrangements turned out far better than mine." He pursed his lips, thinking. "But then, she's a professional."

Haley continued ticking off ideas in rapid-fire succession. "And the refreshments at our main table should include Japanese green tea, some sushi, nothing too exotic, maybe some California rolls, and some of those little kushiyaki sticks. You know grilled chicken and vegetables with teriyaki sauce?"

"Can you make the California rolls?" asked Theodosia, "or should we ask Miyako's Sushi to do the catering?"

"I can do it," said Haley. "Once I cook the rice and season it properly with wine vinegar, the rest should be a snap."

"Listen to her," said Drayton. "She doesn't even need *us*."

"Oh, yes I do," said Haley. "You two have to figure out where to display all our nifty products. Then you should probably make up some gift baskets for sale, probably using those extra sweetgrass baskets we have in back. And—" she looked around "—oh yeah, dig out those tiny little Japanese cups we've got stored around here somewhere."

CHAPTER 8

IN 1929, WITH an eye to the future and their collective hearts set squarely in the past, Charleston's city council passed the nation's very first zoning ordinance to protect many of their city's historic buildings. Two years later, they went a step further and set aside a full twenty-three square blocks of the peninsula—what is known today as the historic district—containing a rich assortment of historic homes as well as significant commercial, religious, and civic buildings.

The result is a breathtaking architectural preserve. The historic district is replete with Colonial, Georgian, Italianate, Greek Revival, and Federal-style buildings, as well as many examples of the ubiquitous Charleston single house, that have remained unchanged for well over a century. And even though the occasional hurricane blows in to rearrange things (such as Hurricane Hugo did in 1989), the streets are still lined with graceful live oaks, enormous mulberry bushes, and flowering magnolias, and the hundreds of hidden, backyard private gardens are nothing short of breathtaking.

As Theodosia stepped across the patio of the Heritage Society, she was delighted to see that some craftsperson had pieced together the beginnings of what would probably be a splendid-looking wrought iron bench.

Based on the design of a Victorian love seat, the bench was fashioned in a graceful S-curve, with one seat facing one way and another seat facing the opposite way.

Theodosia noted the sections where additional scrollwork would be added and decided the new bench was pretty and whimsical and would be a perfect addition to the patio outside the Heritage Society, since so many of their parties seemed to spill outside anyway.

"That's going to be a lovely bench," she told Claire Kitridge, one of the Heritage Society secretaries, who was seated at the massive wood reception desk. Claire had worked at the Heritage Society for several years and always seemed extremely dedicated.

Claire nodded her frizz of grayish hair. "Isn't it?" she responded. "I'm just crazy over anything that's wrought iron?" she said, allowing her voice to rise at the end of her sentence, making her statement sound like a question.

Sitting at the desk with her blue oxford shirt tucked into a plain navy skirt, Claire looked busy and efficient. She wore nary a speck of makeup and had her glasses strung around her neck on a practical silver chain. Theodosia had always thought Claire to be a straightforward, no-nonsense type of woman. But she also knew that Claire was a devotee of antique linens and had amassed a spectacular collection.

"Still sorting through flea markets, Claire?" Theodosia asked.

Claire fixed her with an eager gaze. "You wouldn't believe the luck I've had. I just stumbled upon some spectacular linen napkins? Damask, woven back in the twenties for the ocean liner, the *Queen Mary?* Wonderful," she declared. "So crisp and smart. They certainly don't make them like that anymore." Claire paused expectantly. "I found some old tea towels, too, if you're interested?"

"I am, but I'm going to have to find a bigger house," bemoaned Theodosia. Tea towels were another one of her passions. Just like her collection of teacups.

"Tell me about it," laughed Claire. "Between my linens, eiderdowns, and antique lace, it's *really* getting out of hand. My house looks like a Victorian parlor run amuck. Think I can stop, though? Hah!" She suddenly spun her chair a half-turn, snatched up the phone. "You're here to see Timothy?" Claire asked.

"Yes, would you see if he can spare a few moments?" Theodosia asked.

"Of course," said Claire. She punched a couple buttons. "Mr. Neville? Miss Theodosia Browning is here at the front desk? Could you . . . of course, I'll tell her." Claire hung up the phone and smiled at Theodosia. "Mr. Neville said to come right in. You know which office is his?"

"Yes, thank you," said Theodosia.

"Let me know about those tea towels," called Claire as Theodosia started down the hall.

"What do you think?" Timothy asked Theodosia as she stepped into his office. "An authentic Sully or a very good copy?" His arm made a sweeping gesture to indicate a portrait of a woman framed in gilt.

Theodosia took a few steps forward and studied the portrait that lay on Timothy's desk. She knew that Thomas Sully was a distinguished painter who had lived and worked in Charleston for many years. He had produced a fairly large body of work, but he'd had his imitators, too. Then again, what successful artist didn't?

Theodosia studied the surface of the painting. It was aged and the glaze crackled, that was for sure. So the painting certainly wasn't recent. The signature looked good and the subject, a young woman sitting beside a fireplace, did seem to emit a certain glow from within. Still . . .

"May I?" she asked. Timothy nodded abruptly as Theodosia picked up the portrait and turned it over. It had been painted on canvas, she noted, not just on a wooden board. And the wooden canvas stretchers looked old and weathered, which was often a good giveaway of authenticity.

"I'd say it's real," she told Timothy. "And a fine example, at that."

Timothy Neville beamed at her. "Well done, Miss Browning. May I ask what aspect of this painting most convinced you as to its authenticity?"

"The canvas looks old," she said. "A little dry, in fact. And the stretchers are the slot and groove kind. That usually indicates late-eighteenth or early-nineteenth century."

"Yes, this portrait is absolutely authentic," Timothy told her. "It's a recent donation and a welcome one at that." Timothy rocked back on his heels. "I don't know how popular we're going to be in the future, however. Our recent debacle last Saturday night may have sealed our fate as far as donations go."

He sat down heavily in his chair, as though he'd suddenly run out of energy and enthusiasm. "Sit, please," he told her.

Theodosia moved around his desk and seated herself in one of the oversized leather chairs that faced Timothy's desk.

"I talked with Tidwell," she told him.

"Good. And I spoke with our insurance company." He drew in a breath, held it, then blew out heavily. "But I'm getting ahead of myself. You obviously came here to share some news."

Theodosia nodded. She wasn't sure how pleased Timothy Neville would be with her news, however.

Timothy leaned forward in his chair. "You kept your meeting confidential?"

"It was just Drayton and myself, yes. Tidwell already knew about the two robberies, of course. But we spoke with him about the possibility of a cat burglar at work in Charleston."

"And what was his learned opinion?"

Theodosia gave Timothy a quick rundown of their conversation with Tidwell, including his territorial great white shark analogy.

When she was finished, Timothy grimaced. "Territorial. I don't like the sound of that at all. Especially with the Treasures Show about to open this weekend."

"Is it opening?" she asked.

"For now, yes," replied Timothy. "The decision's just been made." He hesitated. "Actually, truth be known, we arrived at a sort of compromise. The European Jewel Collection won't be part of it. Those pieces are being packed up even as we speak. They'll be shipped back to the organizing museum in New York. So the Treasures Show that the public will see this Saturday evening will consist only of selected pieces from the Heritage Society's collection. A pair of Louis the Fifteenth chairs, some excellent Meisen ware, this portrait by Sully . . . you get the general idea."

Theodosia nodded. "But no headliner pieces."

"Nothing outside the realm of what we already have. Unless you have something utterly spectacular stashed in your attic. No . . ." Timothy shook his head slowly. "We'll have to come up with something else to put in the small gallery. I don't exactly know what yet." Timothy cast his eyes about his office to the shelves that lined the walls. They contained rare books, old maps, some pewter ware. "Maybe our collection of antique sterling silver letter openers?" he offered, but he didn't sound totally convinced.

Theodosia smiled. "That sounds lovely."

"Still . . ." said Timothy. "There's no guarantee that the disaster of last Saturday night won't be repeated."

Timothy looked so bereft that Theodosia's heart went out to him. "I'm sure everything will be fine," she assured him. "On a more personal note, how are *you* feeling? You gave us all quite a scare the other night."

Tapping his chest, Timothy gave her a rueful look. "I didn't even have a regular physician and now it seems I've inherited a team of specialists. A cardiologist and some fellow who studies respiration. Don't need anyone, of course. I'm as healthy as you are."

Theodosia knew that Timothy adhered to a strict daily regimen of vitamins and minerals. Drayton had even told her once about some sort of life extension formula that he imported from Rumania. Considering that he was just past eighty and acted fifty, that formula just might be the real deal.

"Have you heard any more about the security guard who was injured Saturday night?" Timothy asked her.

"He's still in intensive care at Saint Anne's Hospital," said Theodosia. "I thought I'd stop by and visit him tonight. I was scheduled to go to Saint Anne's anyway. Earl Grey is paying a visit to the children's ward." She smiled warmly at Timothy. "I'll let you know."

"Do that," Timothy said. "We've sent flowers and such, but I'm sure he'd be pleased to see an attractive face such as yours."

"Can you help him?" asked Claire as Theodosia darted past the front desk.

Theodosia stopped in her tracks. "Can I . . ."

"Ever since that necklace disappeared Saturday night, Timothy hasn't been the same," said Claire. "He's been quiet and brooding all morning, hasn't looked good. I'm worried about him. Everyone here is." Claire leaned forward and dropped her voice to a whisper. "We're worried about his heart."

"So am I," confided Theodosia as she slipped out the door.

Goodness, she thought to herself as she hurried across the patio. *This really is a mess. Because no matter how valuable that missing necklace is, and the number has to edge up to almost half a million, it's nowhere near as important as Timothy's health. If he worries himself to death over this . . .* Theodosia suddenly stopped in her tracks, freeze-framing that thought. *No, she wasn't going to think like that. Nobody was going to die. She simply wasn't going to let that happen!*

CHAPTER 9

EARL GREY POKED his furry muzzle through the slats of the tiny patient's bed. Wearing his blue vest with his THERAPY DOG INTERNATIONAL insignia, he looked very official, acted very well behaved.

"Do you want to pet the doggy, Katie?" asked Angela Krause. Angela was a nurse and a friend of Theodosia's. She had worked at Saint Anne's Hospital for almost five years and was a fixture on the children's ward.

Katie, a tiny five-year-old who'd just undergone a round of chemotherapy for acute myeloid leukemia, nodded. Blue veins showed through her almost transparent skin and her head was covered by a small red kerchief. But she was still game to meet Earl Grey.

"Okay, then," said Angela, "put your hand out. He won't hurt you."

Katie stuck her hand tentatively through the slats of the crib. Gently, Earl Grey sniffed at the tiny hand.

There was a delighted giggle and then Katie's entire face was pressed up against the slats.

"Do you want to toss the ball?" asked Theodosia.

Katie reached out her small hand and Theodosia placed a red rubber ball in it. Winding up like an all-star pitcher, Katie flung the ball out the door of her room and Earl Grey bounded after it. Within seconds, he returned and gently placed the ball in Katie's hand.

"Good doggy," said Katie.

"His name is Earl Grey," said Theodosia.

"Earl Grey," said Katie, patting his head gently. "Bye bye, Earl Grey."

Out in the hallway, Theodosia and Earl Grey stopped in front of another patient room.

"What about this one?" Theodosia asked Angela.

Angela looked grim. "Billy Foster," she said. "He hasn't spoken since he underwent surgery three days ago to repair a collapsed lung." She shook her head sadly. "Poor little guy. First he gets banged up rather badly in a car accident, then he's traumatized by the ordeal of surgery. Plus both his parents are in the hospital, too." Angela made a rueful face. "Nobody wearing seat belts. Billy wasn't in a children's car seat." Gazing in the door of the little boy's hospital room, she said, "Sometimes these kids are as resilient as a rubber band, other times they're just incredibly fragile." Angela glanced again in Billy's room, where his small body lay immobile under the covers. "This one"—she looked about ready to cry—"just tears my heart out. The doctors say he should be able to take deeper breaths by now, but for some reason he can't. Or won't. His blood oxygen saturation is low and the poor guy is still on a nasal cannula."

Theodosia bit her lip. This was the hard part of volunteering with a therapy dog. Seeing little children who were so very, very ill.

"Maybe a dog would cheer him up?" Theodosia suggested.

Angela nodded. "We've tried just about everything else we could think of to get him to breathe on his own. She pushed open the doors to Billy's room. "Just hang on a minute, though. Let me go in and talk to him first."

Theodosia watched from the doorway as Angela walked quietly over to Billy's bed, knelt down beside him. She could hear her murmuring to him, gently, very quietly.

The little boy must have understood everything Angela had said, because he suddenly turned his head and stared directly at Earl Grey, his soft brown eyes suddenly big with interest. Angela motioned for Theodosia and Earl Grey to enter the boy's room.

Earl Grey entered slightly ahead of Theodosia, restrained by his leash, but still on his best behavior. When they got to Billy's bedside, Theodosia gave Earl Grey the *sit* command. Earl Grey responded immediately, sitting like a perfect gentleman, staring inquisitively at Billy even as the little boy stared back.

Suddenly, just as Billy leaned forward, Earl Grey thrust his head forward, too. Billy's face connected squarely with the tip of Earl Grey's soft muzzle and the dog planted a gentle kiss on the boy's cheek.

Surprised, the boy drew a sudden, swift intake of breath. Which immediately triggered a beep on the machine he was connected to.

"Oh my gosh!" exclaimed Angela.

"Should I run to get help?" asked Theodosia quickly. Her heart suddenly in her throat, she was convinced something had just gone terribly wrong.

"No, no. It's just that . . ." Angela said in a stunned tone of voice. "He took a breath. She knelt down beside the little boy. "Billy, you took a deep breath, didn't you? The doggy surprised you and you took a deep breath!"

Eyes bright, Billy nodded back at her.

"Can you take another one?" she asked.

Billy nodded and the machine at the bedside blipped happily again.

* * *

How could this visit have turned out any better? Theodosia thought to herself as she and Earl Grey strode back through the corridors of Saint Anne's.

Now they were one floor down and about to stop by to visit Harlan Wilson, the security guard who'd been injured at the Heritage Society. He'd been moved from the ICU to a regular patient room this morning. Theodosia figured that was a good thing. Must mean Mr. Wilson was showing real signs of improvement.

"Pardon me," said Theodosia as she approached the nurses' station. "I'm—"

"We know who you are," said a pretty African-American nurse whose name tag read CECILE RANDOLPH. "Angela just called to say you were coming by with your very gifted dog."

"He's just along for the ride now," laughed Theodosia. "Earl Grey's finished with *his* visiting."

Cecile nodded. "Angie said you wanted to look in on Mr. Wilson?"

"Yes, is he awake?"

"He wasn't when I checked ten minutes ago, but that doesn't mean he isn't now. He's been in and out all day."

"But he's getting better?" asked Theodosia.

"Absolutely," Cecile assured her. The phone on the desk in front of Cecile started to ring and she reached for it. "Go ahead on down. He's in room two-oh-seven."

Theodosia and Earl Grey walked down the hallway looking for room two-oh-seven. It was almost eight-thirty and the hospital was quiet, visiting hours almost over for the evening. Lights had been dimmed and the exit sign glowed red above the door to the emergency stairway at the end of the hallway.

Room two-oh-seven turned out to be the second to the last room. But the door was closed.

Should she go in?

Theodosia paused for a moment, wondering if it was

too late for a visit. Glancing down at Earl Grey, trying to decide what to do, she saw that the dog had his head cocked, listening.

Suddenly curious, Theodosia listened herself. It *did* sound as though someone was moving around in there. Good. Probably Harlan Wilson was awake after all. Perhaps trying to manage a glass of water or reach the call button.

Knocking softly, Theodosia didn't wait for an answer. Instead she pushed the door open slowly. But as the door swung inward on its hinges, she could see that Harlan Wilson was still asleep in his bed. A shaft of light from somewhere—the bathroom?—played across his face.

Theodosia was ready to turn around and leave when Earl Grey suddenly gave a low growl.

She stopped in her tracks, still half inside the room. But now her eyes had had a few moments to get accustomed to the dark. And she was able to see that she wasn't alone. Just to her left, someone was pressed up against the wall of Harlan Wilson's room!

Who could it be? she wondered, her brain trying to process this strange information. *Hospital personnel?* No, no, no, her brain flashed a warning to her. *Not a nurse, someone who meant to do him harm!*

Suddenly, whoever it was, dove around the corner into the bathroom and slammed the door.

In a flash, Theodosia was pulling at the bathroom door. It stuck for a moment, then flew open. Nobody there! Too late! It was a shared bathroom and the menacing visitor must have dashed into the room next door.

Theodosia and Earl Grey pushed through to the adjoining room, found it empty. Without hesitation, they charged out into the hallway . . .

. . . And got there just in time to see the door to the stairwell swing shut!

"Cecile, call Security," Theodosia yelled.

"What?" came a startled voice.

"Security!" yelled Theodosia as she dropped Earl Grey's leash and pushed the door to the stairwell open. "C'mon, fella. Downstairs! Follow him!"

As they charged down the stairs, Theodosia could hear the door at the bottom clang shut. *But which door?* Theodosia wondered as they hit the first-floor landing. *The door that led to the lobby or the emergency exit that opened outside?*

Has to be outside. Theodosia decided as she lowered a shoulder and hit that door hard.

Cool air greeted them as they rushed out.

They found themselves in back of the hospital. Dark and deserted, there appeared to be a thin line of trees and what looked like a small garden where patients could go and sit.

That garden was in deep shadows now, but Theodosia could just make out a figure slipping in among the trees.

"Go get him!" she told Earl Grey. "Stop him!" She'd never taught him *those* commands before, but the dog responded like a champion, dashing off toward the small woods.

Theodosia ran after her dog. *Just maybe,* she thought, *Earl Grey can catch him and run him down like a rabbit.* Because whoever had been lurking in Harlan Wilson's room had certainly been up to no good.

Dashing into the thin line of trees, Theodosia leapt over a fallen log, almost stumbled, then broke out of the woods into the parking lot of the Dixie Quick Market.

From somewhere nearby came the cough of a car ignition turning over, then a loud squeal of tires.

Theodosia ran out to the street. Earl Grey was standing there, tail low, hackles up, still growling. Together they watched as red taillights receded in the distance.

CHAPTER 10

DRAYTON FROWNED AS he carefully measured several spoonfuls of dragon's well tea into a blue willow teapot. Haley always chided him for wanting to "match" teas to teapots. *Well, so what if I do?* he thought to himself. *Would you really want to serve this fine sweet tea from central China in a Japanese tetsubin? No, of course not. No tea lover in their right mind would. The traditional metal tetsubin should be reserved for Japanese green tea like bancha or gyokuro. Or even better, a nice first-flush sencha.*

But Haley's good-natured chiding wasn't what was chafing at Drayton this morning. No, he decided, it was Theodosia's visit last evening to Saint Anne's. And the fact that she had chased, actually *pursued,* some strange intruder down the stairwell and into the dark.

He'd always known Theodosia had a wild streak in her. But this last incident seemed positively reckless!

On the other hand, the fact that some lunatic had been lurking in Harlan Wilson's room seemed to confirm the fact that the guard had actually *seen* the thief at the Heritage Society the other night. So maybe they'd really have something to go on now. That would certainly be welcome news to poor Timothy Neville, who seemed to be waiting on pins and needles for the ax to fall on his head.

"I can't believe you actually chased this fellow," Drayton said to Theodosia. "Did you alert the security staff at the hospital, too?"

Theodosia nodded. "I went back afterwards and talked to them."

"And . . ." said Drayton.

"Someone had fiddled with Harlan Wilson's oxygen line."

Drayton's face blanched white. "Good lord! This intruder really did mean to do harm!"

"It looks that way," said Theodosia. "Apparently Mr. Wilson didn't exactly need the oxygen, it was supplemental, but the intruder didn't know that."

"So the intent was still to harm him," persisted Drayton.

"Looks like," said Theodosia. She glanced up from the counter, where she and Drayton had both been fixing pots of tea. Haley seemed to have all the tables under control. All she needed were the fresh pots of dragon's well and English breakfast tea that were now steeping.

"Has Mr. Wilson been able to say much of anything?" asked Drayton.

"I'm afraid not," said Theodosia. "He's still pretty woozy."

"And you didn't get a good look at the intruder?" asked Drayton.

Theodosia shook her head sadly. "Not really."

"Was he tall or short?"

"Not sure."

"Skinny or heavyset?"

Theodosia sighed. "I'm afraid I couldn't say either way. Sorry. I know if I'd been more alert, or a tad faster, we'd have something to go on."

"No, no," said Drayton. "I didn't mean to imply you'd done a poor job of it. You just got caught unawares. Usually when one enters a hospital room, there isn't a malevolent figure lurking in the dark." Drayton gave her a commiserating look. "You really should call Detective Tidwell again," he urged.

"Don't you think he already knows?" said Theodosia. "The hospital is going to put a guard on Mr. Wilson's room."

"But that doesn't mean Tidwell's in the loop," said Drayton. "He told us those two other fellows . . ." Drayton paused, trying to recall the names of the two men from the Robbery Division.

"Gallier and Delehanty," filled in Theodosia.

"Right," said Drayton. "Tidwell said they were handling the alleged robbery at the Lady Goodwood and the disappearance of the sapphire necklace. The various departments don't necessary communicate with each other."

"You're right," agreed Theodosia.

"Is that tea ready yet?" asked Haley.

Theodosia grabbed both teapots and passed them over to her. "Yes, sorry we're taking so long."

"I kind of heard what you guys were whispering about," said Haley. "This is all getting very frightening."

"I know what you mean," said Theodosia. "I was scared out of my wits Sunday night when Cooper Hobcaw came running up behind me in an alley."

"What?" said Drayton. "He must have strayed pretty far from home."

"He's kind of a weird guy," said Haley. "I'm not sure I trust him."

Drayton's eyes sought out Theodosia's. "You don't suppose . . ." he said.

"What?" asked Haley as she stared at the two of them. "You think *he's* somehow involved in all this?"

"Probably not," said Theodosia, although she couldn't

seem to shake the notion from her head that Cooper Hobcaw seemed to conveniently appear in so many different places.

The bell over the door tinkled and all of them turned to look.

Drayton's face broke into a wide grin. "It's Brooke," he said. "From Heart's Desire. Oh quick, Theo, she's a true devotee of Goomtee Estate tea. Brew up one of those two-cup pots while I go and greet her, will you?"

Theodosia nodded even as she pulled a small silver tin down from the shelf and went to work. Goomtee Estate was a classic, smooth Darjeeling, light in color with a delicate, sweet aroma and gentle hint of muscatel flavor. Most people favored it as an afternoon tea, but Brooke was an exception. She liked it in the morning, hot and black, with no milk or sugar.

"This should steep another minute or so," said Theodosia as she delivered the small pot of tea to Brooke's table.

"Aren't you a love," said Brooke. "Drayton said you were brewing a pot of Goomtee just for me."

"And I have the perfect accompaniment," said Drayton as he hovered over her with a plate. "Fresh-baked baps."

"Scottish breakfast bread!" exclaimed Brooke. "My granny used to bake baps."

"Well, these are made according to one of Haley's traditional low-country recipes, or receipts as we South Carolinians like to say. Not too sugary, not too sweet, but always delightful with a pat of butter and some good sourwood honey." And Drayton scampered off to fetch more baps for the rest of the customers.

"Theo," asked Brooke as she pulled her pot of tea toward her. "Do you have a moment?"

Theodosia slipped into the chair opposite Brooke. "Certainly."

Brooke Carter Crockett was a self-reliant woman. She

had owned Heart's Desire for some fifteen years and had seen it thrive as a small business. Brooke had also offered inspiration and invaluable help to Theodosia when she'd first opened the tea shop. It had been wonderful to receive mentoring from a small business owner who'd already endured her baptism by fire.

Now Brooke seemed to be searching for just the right words. She shook her sleek mane of white hair, brushed it back behind her ears, revealing a pair of canary yellow diamond stud earrings.

Have to be three full carats each, thought Theodosia. *And marquis cut at that. Stunning, really stunning.*

"Theodosia," began Brooke, "I'm just going to ask this flat out. Do you think there's a cat burglar at work in the historic district?" Brooke curled a hand delicately around the handle of the small teapot, poured a steaming stream of the golden-red liquor into her teacup, and waited for an answer.

"Honestly," said Theodosia, "I don't know. I *think* there might be, but it's just supposition. A hunch at best."

"Drayton mentioned something strange to my associate, Aerin Linley, the other night. At the Heritage Society's members-only party."

"What did he tell her?" asked Theodosia.

"Just that you didn't think the death of that poor Buchanan boy was any accident. That you suspected someone might have been up there on the roof."

"Well, the whole incident did have a strange feel to it. Not exactly *engineered,* but not a complete accident either." She knew exactly where Brooke was heading with this line of questioning. With Heart's Desire specializing in high-end estate jewelry, Brooke was understandably nervous about being a possible target. Theodosia wondered if she should tell Brooke about the hospital last night. *No,* she decided, *better to keep that little incident to myself.*

"Brooke," Theodosia said, suddenly getting a germ of

an idea. "Do people just walk in off the street with jewelry and offer to sell it to you?"

"Oh, yes. Absolutely," said Brooke. "Dealers, antiquers, just regular folks. Of course, we get lots of locals. You'd be amazed at the people who come in. There are some folks who put on an impeccable appearance, yet are poor as church mice. They've been selling off inherited jewelry and heirlooms for years in order to maintain a certain standard of living. Naturally, Aerin and I try to be extremely discreet. We wouldn't maintain much of a customer base if we blabbed about who sold this or bought that."

"No, you wouldn't," said Theodosia. "But do you ever"—she hesitated, unsure of how to phrase her question—"do you ever get just a tiny bit suspicious of someone who's selling a very expensive piece of jewelry?"

Brooke hesitated. "Well, yes, I suppose I have in a couple instances. I don't really feel I can go into detail, though . . ."

"That's okay," said Theodosia hastily, "it was just a random thought. Forget I even brought it up."

But Brooke continued to pick at the thread of their conversation. "When a seller *does* act a bit nervous or suspicious, I try to get a quick Polaroid of the jewelry they're offering for sale. Then I check with the Police Department to see if anything similar has been reported stolen. Now, of course, there are several Internet web sites that specialize in the recovery of art and high-end jewelry. You can post stolen, suspicious, or recovered items with them."

"And there are also web sites where you can sell goods, no questions asked," said Theodosia.

"Yes," sighed Brooke, "there are *lots* of those. Antique auction sites, sellers' marts, what have you."

"Can I offer you a little more honey?" asked Haley as she deposited a small silver dish on the table filled with the sticky gold liquid.

"Thank you, Haley," said Brooke. "Your biscuits are delicious. Nice and light, and really great with this honey."

"It's from DuBose Bees," responded Haley. "They're one of our best suppliers and specialize in all different flavors of honey. Sourwood honey, apple honey, melon honey . . ."

"How on earth do you get melon honey?" asked Brooke.

Haley wrinkled her button nose and smiled. "It's really kind of neat. The grower puts his beehives right smack dab in the middle of a field of melons. Apparently, once the bees pollinate the flowers, their honey begins to take on this sweet melon flavor. Works the same way with apples and peaches."

"I never dreamed it was done that way," said Brooke, genuinely fascinated. "I always thought they just added flavoring or something."

Haley glanced up as the bell over the door tinkled. "Hey there, Miss Dimple," she said in a chirpy voice.

Short and plump, edging up into her high seventies, Miss Dimple flashed a big smile at Haley and Theodosia as she swished in wearing a purple wool poncho slung over her purple and red dress. She had worked in the building next door to the tea shop, the Peregrine Building, as a personal assistant to old Mr. Dauphine, the building's owner, for many years. When Mr. Dauphine died of a heart attack last year, Miss Dimple, in a state of anxiety and desperately needing a job, was encouraged by Theodosia to pursue freelance bookkeeping. Now Miss Dimple had a new career handling payables and receivables for several small businesses on Church Street such as the Chowder Hound Restaurant and Turtle Creek Antiques. She even worked behind the counter from time to time at Pinckney's Gift Shop.

"Miss Dimple," said Theodosia, popping up from her chair. "How was your vacation in Coral Gables?"

Miss Dimple toddled over to her in a pair of too-tight shoes and grasped Theodosia's arm. "Wonderful," she gushed. "Do you know they *still* have those water skiers? I saw them back in 1958 and they're still doing amazing stunts, standing on each other's shoulders and skiing backwards."

"Guess you're not a Six Flags kind of gal, huh, Miss Dimple?" said Haley with a mischievous grin.

"You're a wicked girl, Haley Parker," scolded Miss Dimple. "You know my brain would be in an absolute spin if I went on one of those topsy-turvy rides. No, just *watching* water skiers is excitement enough when you get to be my age," she said as she followed Theodosia into the back of the shop.

When they had passed through the green velvet curtains and were in Theodosia's private office, Miss Dimple said in a loud whisper, "I hear you've had some excitement around here again." Her old eyes sparkled. "That theft at the Heritage Society must have put Drayton in a dreadful state. Timothy Neville, too. Neither one has what you'd call a tranquil personality."

"They were both pretty upset," agreed Theodosia. "Still are." She rummaged through the stack of papers that had somehow accumulated with amazing speed on top of her desk, searching for the previous week's receipts so Miss Dimple could bring their books up to date.

"I was so sorry to hear about the death of Delaine's niece's fiancé, too." Miss Dimple paused. "That's a mouthful, now isn't it?"

"It was a tragedy," said Theodosia. "His death and the missing ring have us all on edge."

"Missing ring?" asked Miss Dimple, suddenly perking up. "I didn't hear about that."

Theodosia gave up looking for the receipts for a moment. "Camille's heirloom wedding ring is still unaccounted for. But keep that under your hat, will you? The fact that the ring might be related to the disappearance of that sapphire necklace at the Heritage Society is really just a theory we're going on."

"The theory being . . ." said Miss Dimple.

"Well . . . that the two incidents are related," said Theodosia.

Miss Dimple gazed at her with eyes big as saucers. "Do you know Chessie Calvert?" she asked suddenly.

Theodosia shook her head.

"Two weeks ago, just before I went on vacation, somebody broke into Chessie's house and stole her collection of Tiffany Favrile vases," said Miss Dimple. Favrile vases were among the early efforts of Louis Tiffany. Highly colorful and often fancifully shaped like flowers, Tiffany vases were renowned for their jewel-like brilliance.

"No kidding," said Theodosia. This *was* a bit of a bombshell.

"Now when I say collection, I mean a total of three vases," said Miss Dimple. "Still, they were gorgeous pieces. Inherited from her Grand-Aunt Polly and worth a pretty penny. Chessie was heartbroken."

"So there *have* been thefts before," said Theodosia. "Camille's ring wasn't the first."

"Could be a nasty trend," said Miss Dimple.

"Did your friend, Chessie, report this theft to the police?" asked Theodosia.

"Oh yes," said Miss Dimple. "And they sent a—what-do-you-call-it?—an e-mail to the folks at that Art Theft Association in New York. The police theorized that Chessie's pieces might show up at auction somewhere. Apparently there's a huge demand for Tiffany collectibles."

Theodosia drummed her fingers on her desk. "This isn't good."

"No, it's not," said Miss Dimple. She studied Theodosia with a cool, appraising look. "Let me guess," she said, her old eyes narrowing. "In light of the rather bizarre occurrences with Camille's ring and the necklace at the Heritage Society, you've decided to launch your own investigation." She tossed the word *investigation* out as though she were Watson chatting it up with Sherlock Holmes.

"It's more just looking into things than anything," said Theodosia, offering a hasty explanation. "Delaine was awfully upset. And Timothy's worried sick about losing his job."

"Yes, but bully for you, dear," said Miss Dimple. "Besides jumping in to help, you show a real *intuition* for this line of work." She nodded approvingly at Theodosia. "If I were to place a bet, I'd put my money on you instead of the police."

"Thanks for your confidence, Miss Dimple, but like I said, I'm really . . . oh, here they are!" Theodosia grabbed the packet of receipts that had been clipped together and then somehow buried under a mound of tea catalogs, invitations, recipes, and marketing ideas.

Miss Dimple took the receipts from Theodosia and opened her purse to put them in. "I don't know if what I told you about Chessie Calvert's Tiffany vases has helped or hurt," she said.

"Definitely helped," said Theodosia. "It means there's been a pattern. That's not great news, of course, but it means my theory has credence."

"So you're going to keep investigating?" asked Miss Dimple.

"Absolutely," said Theodosia. *Three instances of valuables stolen, maybe more? You better believe I'm going to keep going.*

"Oh!" Miss Dimple suddenly exclaimed. "What's wrong with me? I almost forgot." She plunked herself down in the chair across from Theodosia and rifled through her handbag. "I found this in a darling little shop in Key Largo and thought it would be absolutely *perfect* for you!" Miss Dimple pulled out a gift wrapped in pink tissue paper and handed it to her.

Theodosia accepted the gift, peeled back the paper. It was a wrought iron trivet in the shape of a teapot.

"Thank you," said Theodosia as a smile lit her face. She was touched by Miss Dimple's thoughtfulness. "It's lovely. Perfect for the tea shop, too. We keep setting hot pots down and scorching our nice wooden counter."

"It's you who deserves the thanks," said Miss Dimple. "If you hadn't pushed me into this freelance gig, I'd be just another old gal sitting alone in her house conversing with fifty cats."

"You don't really have fifty cats, do you?" asked Theodosia in mock horror.

"No, just the two. Sampson and Delilah. But loneliness can drive a person to do strange things."

"Here," said Haley after Miss Dimple had left. She placed a tall, frosty glass filled with cinnamon-scented froth in front of Theodosia. "Try this." Pulling a postcard advertising the historic district's upcoming Lamplighter Tour from the mound of papers on Theodosia's desk, she added, "Use this as a coaster."

"And what is this?" asked Theodosia, intrigued by the interesting concoction that now sat before her.

"A tea smoothie," said Haley proudly.

Theodosia couldn't help but grin. Any smoothie she'd ever had usually consisted of fruit, low-fat milk, and yogurt. Trust Haley to come up with a smoothie using tea. "Okay, what's in it?"

"Take a sip and find out," said Haley. She was fairly dancing on the balls of her feet, waiting for Theodosia to taste her new recipe.

Obediently, Theodosia took a sip. "Mmn," she said. "Apples and cinnamon for sure . . ."

"That's Drayton's blend of apple-cinnamon tea," said

Haley in a rush. "I whipped it in a blender with some frozen yogurt then added an extra dash of cinnamon." Her dark eyes sparkled as she gazed at Theodosia. "Like it?"

"It's terrific," said Theodosia. "I'll bet we could even sell these at lunchtime. Or as afternoon pick-me-ups." She took another sip, feeling pleased. This was what running a small business was all about. Everyone pitching in, everyone contributing new ideas. And doing it in an atmosphere that was fun, fluid, and not a bit stuffy or inhibiting.

"Actually," said Haley. "I *was* hoping to add a couple smoothie offerings to our menu. I've got an idea for a Moroccan mint tea smoothie and one with green tea and mango."

"They're a far cry from a little Victorian teapot filled with English breakfast tea, but I love the idea of showing people how versatile tea can be. After all, people all over the world have been improvising with tea for centuries, frothing it with milk, blending it with spices, adding dried fruits and herbs." Theodosia took another sip. "Plus, we'd be extending our product line."

"Kind of like what we're doing with the T-Bath products," said Haley.

"Exactly," agreed Theodosia. "When I worked in marketing, we called it brand extension."

"Okay then," said Haley, "what about chai?"

Chai was black tea with a blend of spices, usually cardamom, cloves, cinnamon, and ginger, steeped in milk, then sweetened and served hot.

"I can get Drayton to blend the spices, the rest is a snap," enthused Haley. "Well, we might have to get a small cappuccino machine to steam and froth the milk—but that would be it."

"Haley," laughed Theodosia, "this is the Indigo Tea Shop, not the International Food Corporation. Let's go with the tea smoothies for now and see what happens, okay?"

"Okay," Haley agreed. "Hey, is that from Miss Dimple?" She'd just noticed the wrought iron tea trivet that sat on Theodosia's desk.

"She brought it back from Florida for me," said Theodosia. "Wasn't that sweet."

"She's a neat old gal," said Haley as a low buzz suddenly issued from the kitchen next door. "Oops! There goes the oven timer. Gotta check my quiche." And Haley zipped out the door like a jackrabbit.

Theodosia took a few more sips of her tea smoothie with the intention of sorting through the stack of papers on her desk. Besides being a compulsive hoarder of junk mail, she found it difficult to toss out the various tea and tea ware catalogs that found their way to her on an almost daily basis. What if, at some point in time, she just *had* to have some of those pedestal mugs to sell in the tea shop? Or some of those neat wooden honey dippers. After all, they sold a tremendous amount of honey along with their packaged teas. And then there was this wonderful little biscotti company in North Carolina that offered dreamy flavors such as chocolate raspberry and lemon almond.

Better save these catalogs, she told herself. And as she gathered them up, her eyes fell once again on the wrought iron trivet Miss Dimple had brought her from Florida. She stared at the black wrought iron that had been heated then formed into a rounded teapot outline.

So Miss Dimple had known of another strange robbery that had a cat-burglar-like MO. *Have there been other robberies of valuables?* She'd have to check with the police.

Deep inside her a warning bell sounded.

She tried to push her unsettled feelings into the back of her mind, but couldn't.

There'll be more robberies to come, she told herself. *This isn't over. Not by a long shot.*

CHAPTER II

HALEY PULLED OPEN the door of the large institutional oven and peered at her quiche. She had three pans of the stuff baking away inside the oven. And right now all of them were bubbling like crazy and turning a nice golden brown on top.

Looking good, Haley murmured to herself as she eased the oven door closed, then slipped the oven mitt off her hand.

The three pans of quiche would hopefully serve today's luncheon crowd. Hopefully. They were all double pans, but then again, their luncheon business had been increasing at an alarming rate.

Haley hummed to herself as she moved a stack of mismatched salad plates onto the serving counter. Plates that she and Theodosia had picked up at flea markets and estate sales. The fact that none of them matched seemed to contribute to the general feeling of cozy and chaos that reigned at the Indigo Tea Shop.

She remembered very well the day Theodosia had first opened her doors. They'd served fifteen customers that first day. Fifteen inquisitive souls who'd made their way down Church Street and ventured into the tea shop, intrigued by the sights, sounds, and smells.

That had been almost three years ago and business had grown in decisive spits and spurts ever since.

Haley turned back to the oven and flipped open the door. *Perfect.* She quickly pulled all three pans from the oven and set them on top of the large, institutional stove.

The aroma wafting from the quiche was heavenly, she decided. But then, her bacon and red pepper quiche was always a thing of pure joy. How did she know? Haley smiled contentedly to herself. Because lots of folks, oodles of folks, had *told* her so. And because she used a secret ingredient—almost a half-pound of cream cheese in every pan—to guarantee that her quiche would turn out extra smooth and creamy.

Why, just this morning, Brooke Carter Crockett had urged her to put together a recipe book. And Brooke hadn't been the first one to make that suggestion, either. Lots of folks, including Drayton and Theodosia, had brought up the idea.

Haley slid a knife through the first pan of steaming quiche, cutting it into even squares. The idea of a recipe book appealed to her. Heck, she decided, restaurants and church groups all over Charleston had put together recipe books. Some featured gorgeous four-color photos and were professionally printed and bound, others were typed on computers, laser-printed at home, then hand-punched and tied with ribbon.

What would mine look like? Hmm. Have to think about that.

"Haley," said Drayton as he stuck his head around the corner. "Our luncheon crowd awaits today's offering with bated breath."

"Then don't just stand there being erudite, Drayton, kindly *help* me. Nestle a small bunch of green grapes on each plate and let's get going." Haley saw him hesitate for a split-second. "Yes, *those* grapes," she snapped. "Right there in the basket." She shook her head good-naturedly, knowing she was a perfectionist and sometimes a little too hard-driving for her own good. For *anyone's* good. "What would you guys do around here without me to keep up my constant barrage of browbeating?" she added.

"Haley," said Drayton, who was now scrambling to place grapes on plates and slide plates onto trays, "I don't mind saying that sometimes you employ the iron-fisted tactics of a Prussian general."

She grinned as she topped each square of quiche with a bright sliver of roasted red pepper. "Why, thank you, Drayton. I'll take that as a compliment."

"Like hotcakes," marveled Theodosia. "Your quiche just went like hotcakes. How many pans did you bake?" she asked Haley.

"Three," said Haley, who was standing behind the counter, ringing up a final take-out order.

"So there were, what? A dozen servings in each pan?" asked Drayton.

"Yup," said Haley as she handed change across the counter. "Thank you so much," she told her customer. "Come back and see us again."

"Three dozen lunches in the course of an hour or so," said Theodosia. "And that's not counting the tea and scone orders. We don't usually do that many."

"Better get that permit for outside tables," chided Drayton.

"You're right," said Theodosia. "I'm definitely liking the way business is shaping up."

"Wait until the T-Bath products go on sale," warned Haley. "Business will be bonkers."

"You really think so?" asked Theodosia. She was hopeful the T-Bath products would take off, but then again, you never know. Business could be a real crap shoot.

"I think you're going to be pleasantly surprised," said Haley. She stretched her arms high above her head, bent slightly to the left. In her rust-colored long-sleeve T-shirt and long, filmy skirt of rust and blue, Haley looked like a ballet dancer, lithe and limber.

"In case you guys haven't noticed, tea is big business these days," pronounced Haley. "Look at all the green tea candles and tea-scented perfumes and lotions out there on the market. And every time you go into a gourmet shop or kitchen boutique, you find tons of teapots and tea infusers and boxed teas."

"She's right," said Drayton. "And while we may not always like some of the bottled teas or premixed jars of chai in the supermarket, *someone* is buying them. Which I guess is good for us."

"Speaking of business and products flying off the shelf," said Theodosia, "how exactly are we going to display the T-Bath products when we launch on Thursday?"

"I've got that covered," replied Drayton. "I found a marvelous old secretary at Tom Wigley's antique shop. Wooden, a little scuffed, but it still retains most of its original shelves. Not too deep, either. I believe it will fit flush to the wall over near the fireplace and work perfectly as a display case."

"Kind of like the wooden cabinet Delaine has in her store," said Theodosia. "The one holding scarves and purses and such."

Drayton furrowed his brow, trying to recall what was in Delaine's shop. "Something like that, yes. Tom said he'd bring the piece round tomorrow."

Much to everyone's surprise, Brooke Carter Crockett and her associate, Aerin Linley, were back in the tea shop that afternoon.

"Bet you didn't think you'd see me again so soon," laughed Brooke. "But we just had to come by for another cuppa."

"Dear lady, twice in one day is an absolute delight," assured Drayton. "Now let me share with you a Castleton estate tea. Still an Indian black tea, just not as buttery as your beloved Goomtee. This one is slightly fruity, but kindly reserve judgment until you've given it a fair shake."

"Who's minding the store?" asked Theodosia, as Drayton went off to prepare the pot of tea.

Aerin waved a hand. "Oh, business was slow, so we just hung a sign on the door. You know, one of those hand-scrawled notes that says, *Back in twenty minutes.*"

Theodosia nodded. It wasn't unusual to see signs like that up and down Church Street and at the little shops throughout the historic district. People were always running out for tea or coffee or a quick visit. It was one of the little quirks that made the neighborhood so charming and fun to be part of.

She was also glad that Brooke and Aerin had just casually dropped by. As Theodosia well knew, repeat customers are the bread and butter of any small business.

The importance of generating repeat business was also one of the main reasons Theodosia tried to maintain a database of all her regular customers' names and addresses. If you mailed out postcards on luncheon specials or invited folks to promotional events like the T-Bath open house they were staging Thursday, customers *would* continue to return.

"Say, Theo," began Brooke. "I was telling Aerin about our little talk this morning. You know, when you asked about people just dropping by Heart's Desire and offering items for sale? She remembered someone acted somewhat strangely while I was away in New York."

"That's right," said Aerin. "It was a woman who came in a few weeks ago with a very pretty brooch."

"There was something unusual about her behavior?" asked Theodosia.

Aerin Linley paused. "She just seemed nervous, a little on edge. I remember thinking it was odd at the time, but then I dismissed it."

"Did you buy the piece from her?" asked Theodosia.

"Yes, we did," said Aerin. "I knew our inventory was low and it was a rather lovely piece. An emerald cut citrine surrounded by ten small diamonds. Not a huge piece, mind you, but fairly tasty. Fine craftsmanship and it definitely had some age on it." She hesitated. "Now, thinking back, I guess *I'm* a little nervous about the entire transaction."

Brooke leaned forward in a conspiratorial manner. "I think you even know the seller, Theo. Claire Kitridge?"

"Claire from the Heritage Society?" asked Theodosia.

Claire? Theodosia thought to herself. *The Claire that always seems so buttoned up and straitlaced? The same Claire that collects antique linens?*

"Ladies," said Haley, arriving with their tea. "May I present Drayton's fabled Castleton estate tea. And one of my blackberry scones for each of you. The blackberries, I might add, are from a recent crop grown on nearby Saint John's Island."

There were oohs and aahs from the two ladies as Haley set teacups, teapot, and accouterments on the table and they began helping themselves.

"Enjoy your teatime," said Theodosia as she slipped away. "I'll chat with you again later." Slightly unnerved, she went to the display shelves and began rearranging the antique teacups she had placed there just yesterday. In her heart, she knew Brooke and Aerin had to be mistaken. Claire Kitridge was above reproach. She'd worked at the Heritage Society for three or four years now. She'd even heard Timothy Neville, in one of his rare instances of magnanimity, praise Claire for her hard work and dedication.

"Oh no," said Haley under her breath. "Not *him.*"

Burt Tidwell had just pushed his way through the door and seated himself at one of the smaller tables.

Theodosia squinted across the room at him. Tidwell didn't usually just show up unannounced unless he had something on his mind. The question was, *What was on the old boy's mind today?*

"Detective Tidwell," said Theodosia, trying her best to manage a lighthearted greeting. "Good afternoon, how can I help you?"

Tidwell arranged his mouth in a reasonable facsimile of a smile, but the vibes weren't particularly warm. "Tea and the prospect of polite conversation have drawn me to your little establishment today."

What a maddening oblique manner he has, she thought to herself. Studied, slightly formal, but still with that cat-and-mouse attitude he was so famous for. *Very well,* she decided, *I'll play along for now.*

Hastily brewing a pot of uva tea, a delicate, slightly lemony Ceylonese tea, she put a stack of madelaines on a plate and carried everything back to Tidwell's table.

"Sit a moment, will you?" he invited. "Join me?"

She turned back to the counter, grabbed the first teacup she could lay her hands on, a Delvaux porcelain. She balanced it atop a Spode muffin plate, another antique piece from her collection, and went back to join Tidwell at his table. Sliding into the chair across from him, she watched as Tidwell poured out a stream of the pale amber tea into her teacup first, then his.

"This is nice," he said with another quick twitch of a smile.

She wasn't sure if Tidwell was referring to her company or the tea. It didn't really matter. The sentiment didn't feel genuine.

"You've been busy," Tidwell began. His large fingers skittered across the plate of madelaines, stopped on one, gathered it up.

This time she knew exactly what he was referring to. And it had nothing to do with the increase in business at her tea shop.

"Saint Anne's Hospital the other night. Not a smart thing to do," he told her. Tidwell cocked a furry eyebrow, waited for a response.

That man can convey reproach with just the quiver of an eyebrow, Theodosia marveled to herself. *How must a true criminal feel when Tidwell focuses his beady-eyed gaze upon them? Nervous, probably. That's when they know the jig is up.*

"I wasn't aware I had to obtain your permission in order to visit people in the hospital," Theodosia told him, her manner deliberately cool.

"Visitation is not what I was referring to," said Tidwell. "Far be it from me to criticize you and your canine friend from bringing cheer to small, needful children. I was referring to the fact that you gave chase to someone." Tidwell took a sip of tea, then gave her yet another look of stern reproach. "I warned you not to get involved."

"I wasn't involved," said Theodosia. "I went into a hospital room to pay a visit. It wasn't my fault someone was lurking there. I wasn't looking for trouble."

Now Tidwell fixed her with a steady gaze. "I get the feeling, Miss Browning, that you don't ever go *looking* for trouble. It comes calling on you." His eyes bore into her. Then, just as quickly, flicked down to scan the plate. His fingers convulsed, but he did not reach for a second madelaine.

"Detective Tidwell," Theodosia began, "have you been able to look into the incident at the Lady Goodwood Inn?

The break-in that led to the death of poor Captain Buchanan?"

"Ah, change of subject," said Tidwell. "Very well, it was done politely. Not the most graceful segue in the world, but adequate." He leaned back in his chair, hunched his shoulders, and crooked his head to the left, as though trying to dislodge a kink from his thick neck.

"I carefully reviewed the investigation report that Officers Gallier and Delehanty filed on the so-called break-in at the Lady Goodwood Inn. They did, in fact, check the roof and the various access points to it for fingerprints as well as signs of a disturbance. None were found." He paused. "I stand corrected—on one of the remaining panes of glass in the ceiling, they found fingerprints belonging to one of the maintenance men. A Mr. Harry Kreider."

Harry Kreider, thought Theodosia. That was the man she'd spoken with that awful night, the one who'd lent her the ladder. He certainly wasn't a viable suspect in her mind.

"So it's a dead end," said Theodosia. Frowning slightly, she reached for one of the madelaines, took a bite, chewed absently.

"It was never going anywhere to begin with," said Tidwell. He gazed at her, saw her apparent distress. "I'm sorry," he added, tempering his tone. "I don't mean to be so rude. It was a game try, you made a good guess."

Theodosia exhaled slowly. No, she decided, it was more than a guess on her part. It was a . . . what was it, exactly? A feeling? A visceral intuition that the two incidents were connected?

Tidwell was watching her closely, trying to get a read on her by using *his* natural instincts. She dropped her voice so Brooke and Aerin, sitting at the nearby table, wouldn't hear her. "Let me ask you about something," said Theodosia. She picked up her teacup, took a deliberate sip.

Tidwell continued to watch her expectantly.

"Other thefts in the historic district," she said as she balanced her cup on the muffin plate. "Have you heard of any?"

"Nearly half a dozen."

A loud crash sounded at her feet. Startled, Theodosia looked down to see the teacup and plate she'd been holding just moments earlier lying in smithereens on the floor. Without thinking, she bent down to pick up one of the pieces, immediately came away with a cut.

"Miss Browning," said Tidwell, reaching for her arm, gently pulling it back. "Do be careful." He looked into her eyes, saw what he took to be bewilderment and confusion. "I'm sorry," he said. "I didn't mean to startle or upset you in any way. Please do believe me."

In that same instant, Brooke Carter Crockett had jumped up from her seat at the table and now stood next to Theodosia, surveying the damage. "Oh, no," she mourned, gazing down at the shattered china. "Were they good pieces?"

Theodosia blinked back tears. *Silly,* she thought to herself, *it's only a plate and teacup. Lots more where that came from.* "The teacup, a Delvaux, it . . . was my mother's," she replied. She reached down again, but Haley was suddenly there with a broom and dust pan.

"Careful, Theo," Haley warned. "Those little shards are awfully sharp." She swept the larger pieces into the dust pan, went over the floor again to try to collect the smaller pieces. "These pegged floors are terrible," she complained. "Every little thing gets caught down in the cracks. I'm going to have to bring out the vacuum sweeper."

"Later, Haley, okay?" said Theodosia. She glanced at

her watch. "We'll be closing in an hour or so anyway. Just let it go till then."

Haley, a compulsive cleaner and neat-nik, wasn't pleased with what she viewed as a huge delay in putting things right. But she backed off anyway.

Tidwell rose suddenly from his chair. "Sorry if I caused you any distress," he said. "I just found out about this so-called rash of robberies myself a few hours ago. Very strange."

A half-dozen other robberies, Theodosia thought to herself. *Not good. Not good at all.*

"That's all right," said Theodosia, still feeling slightly distracted. "And this is my treat," she added when she saw him reach into his jacket pocket for his wallet. "Sorry to have been so clumsy." And she hurried off after Haley.

"Are you okay?" asked Drayton. He was ferrying empty teapots and teacups from the various tables. For some reason, the Indigo Tea Shop had cleared out rather suddenly. "You're white as a sheet," he told her.

Theodosia slid in behind the counter. She put a hand to her heart and found it was beating like crazy. "There *have* been other robberies," she hissed at Drayton.

"What?" He stared at her crazily.

"Tidwell just told me. A half-dozen other robberies!"

"Good lord. In the historic district?"

Theodosia nodded.

"Hey," said Haley as she emerged from the kitchen with a cardboard take-out carton in her hands. "What's with you two?"

"Tidwell delivered some fairly earth-shattering news," said Drayton.

"I gathered that," said Haley, glancing over to the spot where she just *knew* some tiny shards were still wedged between the floorboards.

"There have been other thefts," said Drayton in a low voice.

"Holy cow," said Haley. "A lot?" Now he really had her attention.

"A half-dozen or so. Plus Camille's wedding ring and the necklace at the Heritage Society," replied Drayton.

Haley shook her head. "Right under our noses. Imagine that."

"Strange, isn't it?" said Drayton. "I suddenly feel like I've been dumped into a vintage Alfred Hitchcock film. Twists and turns everywhere."

Theodosia nodded her agreement. "Drayton, you just said a mouthful."

CHAPTER 12

FROM THE FIRST day she'd found Earl Grey in her back alley, a shivering, whimpering puppy that some heartless person had abandoned, Theodosia had struggled with his food.

At first, the poor dog had been so starved he gobbled anything and everything she put in front of him, barely pausing to take a breath. She'd fed him a standard dog food with a teaspoon of olive oil poured over it, in hopes of improving his coat. But as Earl Grey had gotten older and started to feel more secure, came to realize he was much loved, and had finally found a permanent home, the dog had become a trifle picky. From gourmand to gourmet.

And so Theodosia began to experiment. Adding cooked vegetables to Earl Grey's food and occasionally boosting his protein intake by giving him a raw turkey neck.

That had seemed to do the trick. The coat that Drayton continued to insist was salt and pepper but Theodosia saw as dappled gray had grown lush and thick, Earl Grey had added muscle tone in his chest area, too, but still remained properly lean so you could gently feel a faint outline of his ribs.

Tonight, Theodosia stirred a mixture of yogurt and steamed broccoli into Earl Grey's food, then heated up a carton of gumbo for herself that she'd pulled from her freezer that morning. Duck and sausage gumbo was a staple all across the South, and no one made it better than her Aunt Libby, who lived out in the low-country. Aunt Libby had prepared gallons of the hearty stew earlier this fall and had given Theodosia at least a dozen cartons. Suffused with smoked sausage, tender breast of duck, okra, rice, celery, onion, hot peppers, herbs, and spices, the gumbo was an aromatic, heartwarming dinner. Especially since Theodosia had grabbed one of Haley's blackberry scones to go along with it.

"What do you think the calorie content of that was?" she asked Earl Grey, who had fixed her with a baleful look as she finished her dinner. "Yes, I know," she told him. "You dined on low-fat yogurt and florets of broccoli while I sated myself with a high-fat, high-carb dinner. Life isn't fair, is it?"

Earl Grey sighed loudly, as if to say, *You're the one who said it, not me.*

"Only one thing to do, big guy," she told him. "Go for a run."

Ah, the magic word. *Run.* Although *walk, jog,* and *out* were big-time favorites in Earl Grey's lexicon, the word *run* seemed to evoke the most joy. For Earl Grey was instantly on his feet and pacing wildly as Theodosia dumped dirty dishes into the sink. He added a low whine to his repertoire as she changed into her running gear, and strained mightily as Theodosia struggled to clip the leash onto the overjoyed dog's collar.

Then they were down the steps and out the door into the dark night.

The historic district on this October night was a thing of

beauty. The atmosphere, heavy and redolent with mist, lent a soft focus to everything. Lights became shimmery, hard edges obscured.

After a fast walk down their alley, Theodosia and Earl Grey picked up the pace. They settled into a good rhythm as they cut across the interior of the peninsula on Broad Street, covering a good eight or nine blocks. Popping out near the Coast Guard station, Theodosia could make out the faint silhouette of bobbing sailboats and towering masts at the Charleston Yacht Club far off to her right.

Jogging down Murray, Theodosia and Earl Grey rounded the tip of the peninsula. For some reason it seemed darker out here. And lonelier. Fog, not just mist, but real cottony, wispy fog, was rolling in now from the Atlantic. Across the parkway, houses and lights that had merely looked soft focus before were suddenly being swallowed up in a wall of gray.

Passing near the Featherbed House, a bed-and-breakfast run by Angie and Mark Congdon, four squat orange pumpkins glowed like beacons from the front steps. Tiny candles flickered inside their carved grins, broadcasting a sinister welcome.

Halloween, thought Theodosia. *It's only a few days away.*

Theodosia and Earl Grey slowed their pace, Theodosia deciding, at the last minute, to head down the Congdons' private alley. It was a narrow cobblestone lane that wound past their garage then connected up with another walkway. That walkway would bring her, in a roundabout manner, back to Tradd Street. It sounded complicated, but wasn't. The historic district was a maze of alleys, walkways, and connecting paths, the result of old carriage drives, servants' entrances, and tradesmen's lanes. Once you had it figured out, you were set.

As Theodosia slipped slowly past the Featherbed House with its second-story bridge that connected the main house with two rooms over the carriage house, Earl Grey gave a low growl. He strained at his leash, jerking Theodosia toward a nearby tree. Then the dog gazed sharply upward on full alert.

What is up there? Theodosia wondered. She hesitated, then approached the tree cautiously. It was an enormous old tree, a live oak, draped in banners of gray-green Spanish moss. It was the kind of tree that was easy to climb. Which meant *anything* could be up there. Squirrel, possum, porcupine, person.

Earl Grey gave a quick sniff at the base as though to once again confirm his suspicions, then rose up on his hind feet and planted his front paws on the base of the gnarled trunk.

Still curious as to what exactly had caught the old boy's attention, she peered up the gnarled base, expecting to see . . . what?

Glinting green eyes peered back at her.

A cat! There was a cat up the tree! Probably one of the old tabbies that lived at the Featherbed House. Angie was a soft touch for strays and always joked about how a network of hobo cats had put the word out on her. *Psst! Come to the Featherbed House for a little R and R. No kitty ever gets turned away.*

Theodosia whistled softly and Earl Grey turned his attention back to her. They continued down the alley past the carriage house and turned right where the alley connected with the back drive of another home, the Ebenezer Stagg House, an Italianate mansion that had once been a private boys' school. The two of them picked their way carefully on glistening cobblestones, taking care where they stepped. The fog really had them surrounded now, London style, and the only thing that kept Theodosia moving forward at a fairly good clip was her firsthand knowledge of these old alleyways.

As they passed behind the Stagg House, Theodosia

could hear footsteps coming from the right. She stopped in her tracks and Earl Grey sat down, a move they'd both practiced during obedience training. But the person, whoever it was, crossed right in front of them without noticing them, and headed down a different alley, an alley that angled back toward King Street.

Who was that? she wondered. *Who else is out creeping around in this fog? Was it Cooper Hobcaw on one of his jogs? Maybe.* But this man, and she was pretty sure it *was* a man, hadn't been jogging. Even though the alley he'd gone down was a nice, even pavement that had been fairly well lit with glowing lamps.

An uneasy feeling began to steal over Theodosia and she shivered under her layers of sweatshirts. Cooper Hobcaw had joked that he went out jogging every night in the historic district. *Does he just prefer the historic district?* she wondered. *Does he drop in on Delaine every night?*

Or is he up to something else?

That last thought stunned her. *Does Cooper Hobcaw have another reason for prowling the historic district at night? Could Cooper Hobcaw be casing the area?*

Theodosia couldn't get home fast enough.

She reeled Earl Grey in close to her and kept to the middle of the pathways until she came upon the familiar lights and sights of Church Street.

So, of course, the phone was ringing as she climbed the back stairway.

"Hello?" she answered, slightly out of breath.

"Theo, it's Jory," came a familiar, upbeat voice.

"Oh, hi there," she answered. "Hang on a minute, will you?" She unclipped Earl Grey's leash, shrugged out of her sweatshirt, kicked off her running shoes. Then she settled down cross-legged on the overstuffed couch, comfy in her T-shirt and sweat pants.

"Okay, I'm back," she told him.

"Good. I called to see if we're still going to the symphony Thursday night. We talked about it, but I'm not sure we ever made it formal."

"The symphony. Thursday. Hmm . . . Thursday's the open house."

"Right," he said. "Your tea bag products."

"T-Bath."

"Exactly. But that'll be over . . . when?"

She considered this. "Maybe four-thirty, five at the latest."

"Excellent," said Jory. "The concert doesn't start until eight. Which should give you ample time to recoup, recover, and get gorgeous."

She laughed. Jory Davis *did* have a way with words. "I suppose you're right," she said.

"Hey," he cajoled, "this is supposed to be fun. We're talking major league date here."

Good heavens, she thought to herself, *I'm acting like an idiot. As Haley would say, this is one cute guy!*

"Sorry," she told him. "An evening at the symphony sounds wonderful. No, better than that . . . fabulous!"

"Over-the-top enthusiasm. That's more like it," he laughed, but a moment later turned sober. "Hey, this thing that happened at the Heritage Society last Saturday night . . . you're not getting all tangled up in Drayton's and Timothy Neville's problems, are you?"

How could she, really? she wondered. She hadn't found a solid clue to go on yet. All she had were hunches. "No," she told him. "Not really. You just caught me at the end of a busy day and a long jog."

"I thought so," he said. "That dog is running you ragged. I told you to get a bulldog or a dachshund. Those guys have little, short legs. Means you'd travel a much shorter distance. But no, you had to go and hook up with a . . . what is he again? A doberarian?"

She giggled. "A dalbrador. Thanks, Jory. Good night."

"'Night, kiddo."

Hanging up the phone, Theodosia decided maybe the better part of valor was to turn in early. She paused, thinking of Jory and their date Thursday night. She was looking forward to spending time with him. As she meandered through her apartment, pulling the draperies across and turning off lights, her mind wandered back to the man she'd seen tonight. Had it been Cooper Hobcaw out loping along in the fog? She'd thought the figure had *looked* a little like him, long legs, slightly haggard frame. But now she wasn't sure. She supposed the fog could make anything a little hazy. Including her memory.

The one thing she *was* sure of, however, was the nagging feeling that something strange was definitely going on. That a cat burglar, or whatever you'd call him, was definitely on the loose out there.

So instead of turning in, Theodosia decided to do a little investigatory work. On the Internet. Surely she'd find *something* about cat burglars. Everything else was there, for goodness' sake.

As it turned out, the Internet search proved very productive. When she typed CAT BURGLAR into one of the search engines, hundreds of hits came up. A few were for a rock band and some for a kind of cat burglar game that sounded similar to the old Dungeons and Dragons-type fantasy game.

But she also found good, solid information, too. Newspaper articles about cat burglars who had struck in places like Malibu, New York, Palm Springs, and Palm Beach.

That chilled her. It was exactly what Burt Tidwell had said. The *migratory* type of cat burglar follows the goods.

There was information posted by different law enforcement agencies, too. And as she scanned the various MOs, one profile seemed to emerge. Cat burglars were bold, even fearless. They were adrenaline junkies who thrived on danger. Apparently, some cat burglars even preferred to ply their trade when a home, hotel room, or shop was *oc-*

cupied. The thrill of someone sitting downstairs, sleeping in the next room, or eating dinner nearby seemed to add an extra touch of danger, an extra dimension to a game they relished. It also appeared that cat burglars often circumvented security systems by scaling buildings or power poles and shutting off electricity.

Shutting off electricity.

That's what happened at the Heritage Society. Or had that been a storm-induced power failure that a thief simply took advantage of? She didn't know.

From everything she read, cat burglars also appeared to be smart. Very smart. One cat burglar, known as the dinner hour burglar, entered homes while the residents were downstairs eating their dinner. Another selected his targets by reading magazines like *Town & Country* and *Architectural Digest.* And still another savvy cat burglar with a predilection for gold and silver carried a test kit along with him. That way he could pass on the candlesticks and platters that were merely gold- or silver-plated and concentrate on stealing only the finer pieces!

Like Camille's wedding ring? Or the silver at the Lady Goodwood Inn? she wondered. *Holy cow.*

Theodosia quickly scanned the rest of the hits. Several law enforcement officials had gone so far as to speculate on the type of person who turns to cat burglary. They tended to be strong and agile, often with gymnast backgrounds, always bold.

She thought about this. Cooper Hobcaw was certainly bold enough. Bold bordering on brash. And as a criminal attorney, he courted danger in a manner of speaking. He could be looking for another outlet from which to get his thrills.

Was Claire Kitridge bold and agile? She wasn't that old, maybe late thirties. And she looked like she was in good shape. Maybe all those weekend jaunts into the countryside looking for antique linens were really . . .

No, not Claire. It couldn't be Claire, could it?

Tired now, eyes stinging from peering at the monitor so intently, Theodosia exited the Internet and shut down her computer.

Enough, she told herself. *Time to turn in.* Earl Grey was already snuggled in his dog bed, snoring softly. It was time she did the same.

But as cozy and comfortable as Theodosia's bedroom was, with the down comforter and the Egyptian cotton sheets, it was a long while before she was able to fall asleep.

CHAPTER 13

LAST EVENING'S FOG, which had grounded planes at Charleston International Airport in North Charleston, had been dissipated overnight by strong winds swooping in from the Atlantic. The sky was a deep cerulean blue with just a few wisps of errant clouds, and the sun shone brightly, gilding the brick facades, wrought iron artistry, and wooden shutters that made the shops of Church Street so very quaint and picturesque.

But as Delaine Dish strode down Church Street, past the Chowder Hound, the Cabbage Patch Needlepoint Shop, the Antiquarian Bookstore, and the Peregrine Building, which housed the newly opened Gallery Margaux, she barely noticed the magnificent day that had dawned in Charleston.

Delaine was a woman on a mission.

She had driven back from Savannah last night with her friend, Celerie Stuart, feeling upset and more than a little helpless. Captain Corey Buchanan's funeral had been a blur. She'd been introduced to a kaleidoscope of solemn-faced, tight-lipped Buchanans, who had all seemed to regard her with the same measure of cool detachment.

After all, it was *her* niece who had been engaged to Captain Buchanan. And the tragic accident had occurred at the engagement party *she* had thrown!

They had looked at her with accusing faces. Did they not know she felt positively tortured by the terrible circumstances? How could she ever forget what had happened? How could anyone forget?

As if the death of Captain Buchanan wasn't enough of a tragedy, the issue of the missing ring had also been a sore point. She'd been informed by one of the Buchanans that they had been in contact with the Charleston Police Department and were awaiting a complete report on the accident.

Thank goodness the entire Buchanan clan seemed to believe the whole thing had been an accident! Delaine thought to herself. A tragic accident that could be chalked up to an old greenhouse and an unfortunate lightning strike.

But the whole time she'd been in Savannah, the conversation she'd had with Drayton and Theodosia had spun hopelessly about in her head, playing like an endless loop on a VCR. She recalled their *hunch,* their *supposition*, that someone *could* have come crashing through the old greenhouse roof and landed squarely atop Captain Buchanan's head.

There were about a million times during the visitation, the funeral service, and the sad reception afterward when she felt she'd simply burst with this knowledge. There were a thousand times when she thought she should just sit down and *share* these terrible suspicions with Captain Buchanan's family.

But then what?

Then she'd have to prove everything. Maybe they'd

even expect her to try to find the person responsible. And bring them to justice!

Delaine touched her right hand to her temple as if the very thought was enough to trigger a migraine.

She couldn't resolve any of this mess. Of course not. There was no *way* she could ever accomplish that type of Herculean task.

But Delaine had the proverbial ace in the hole. Theodosia and Drayton had searched high and low for the missing wedding ring and, in so doing, had become intrigued by the mystery of its disappearance.

Especially Theodosia. She had an adventuresome heart and a fearless soul, Delaine reminded herself. And Theodosia commanded the ear of Burt Tidwell, one of Charleston's finest detectives!

Thank goodness!

Tidwell, bless his snoopy, inquisitive little heart, had stopped by her shop this morning. Early, just after she'd first arrived, before she could even steam the wrinkles from that new line of hand-knit sweater jackets and get them out on the floor. Tidwell had pussyfooted around a bit, asking her this and that. Inquiring whether she remembered anything unusual, asking about any strangers hanging around that terrible night, and did she know the waiters who had worked the party?

Of course she hadn't. But Tidwell's probing had stirred in her a germ of an idea. And given her a ray of hope.

If Theodosia had been guardedly persuasive in her argument about a possible intruder—and now Burt Tidwell was snooping around—then there must be something to it!

Of course, Theodosia was completely convinced that Burt Tidwell hated her. That Tidwell regarded her as a bit of an airhead.

Delaine knew that nothing could be further from the truth. She'd seen the way Burt Tidwell looked at Theodosia Browning.

Not because he had any silly romantic notions. Oh no. Absolutely not. Burt Tidwell was far too professional for that. But Tidwell *did* admire Theodosia, did respect her thoughts and opinions. Valued her keen intelligence and remarkable intuition.

Which meant Burt Tidwell might just go out of his way to help her.

Delaine clutched her buttercup yellow cashmere cardigan around her as though it were protective garb. No, she couldn't venture to dream of getting to the bottom of this all by herself. But if she enlisted Theodosia's aid, really encouraged her to keep investigating, then . . . then she just might have a fighting chance.

"Delaine, you're back from the funeral." Haley stood holding a green Staffordshire teapot, pouring a stream of amber tea into white take-out cups.

Delaine smiled a sad smile, touched a delicately manicured finger to her lips in a gesture that said *shoosh.* Then, choosing the small table closest to the counter, she slid quietly into a chair. "I don't really want to talk about it with everyone in the place," she told Haley. "I'm keeping a low profile for now."

"Theodosia and Drayton have been worried about you," continued Haley. "We all have." *Gee,* Haley thought to herself, *this is one bristly lady when she wants to be. And what's this low-profile stuff? Delaine has never kept a low profile in her life!*

"But I *would* like to speak with Theo and Drayton," she told Haley. Delaine glanced down at the bare wooden table as though she expected to find a teacup, linen napkin, and silverware all set up for her. "Just a cup of black tea this morning, dear. Irish breakfast tea."

"Sure thing," said Haley.

"How was the funeral?" asked Theodosia. Sitting in her

office, she had heard Delaine's voice and immediately come out to speak with her.

Delaine plucked a handkerchief from her leather bag and daubed at her eyes. "Heartbreaking. Captain Buchanan's mother and sisters never stopped crying for one instant."

"Oh, no," said Theodosia as she slipped into the chair across from Delaine.

"At the church, they had poor Captain Corey's casket covered with an American flag and a military honor guard standing by. The service was very somber, of course, and his brother read a poem by Walt Whitman. I think it was *In Paths Untrodden.* Afterwards, the honor guard escorted the casket out of the church to the cemetery. After the minister said his final words, they fired a twenty-one-gun salute. Then a lone bugler played taps. Such a mournful sound."

Theodosia nodded. On the few occasions she'd attended military funerals, the playing of taps at the end had always seemed so sad and lonely. The bugler's haunting notes a signal that the service was over, the deceased committed to the earth for eternity.

"What's Camille going to do now?" asked Haley.

Delaine glanced down at her wrist nervously and Theodosia noticed she wasn't wearing her usual jewel-encrusted Chopard watch. Probably left it at home for the funeral. Too showy.

"She's going to stay in Savannah for a while," said Delaine. "Captain Corey's sister, Lindsey Buchanan, runs a travel agency and Camille is going to work for her."

"That's nice," said Theodosia.

"It will give everyone a chance to heal," said Delaine. "Hopefully." Delaine reached for her teacup, finally took a sip of tea. "So sad," she murmured. "I was going through a few things at my shop late yesterday afternoon, after I got back. And I came across Camille's wedding veil." Tears welled up in Delaine's eyes and threatened to spill down her flawless pink cheeks. "The base of the veil was this tiny little feathery cap, like something a ballerina might wear if she were going to dance *Swan Lake.* So pretty and feminine, with just a bit of dainty lace in front."

"When did you get back from Savannah?" asked Theodosia, eager to guide Delaine to a more neutral and less heart-wrenching subject.

"Yesterday. Early afternoon," said Delaine. "I went to the store because we had a big shipment coming in. But then I couldn't seem to get my head back into it."

"That's understandable," said Theodosia. "You're still in shock. Still in mourning."

"I just let Janine tend to things," explained Delaine. Janine was her sales assistant who'd been with her for quite a few years. "I went out and took a walk. I ended up over at Heart's Desire, talking to Brooke and Aerin."

"Those two were in here yesterday," said Haley. "Very nice ladies."

"You know," said Delaine with careful deliberation, "they *are* saying there's a cat burglar at work."

"Who's they?" asked Theodosia. "Brooke and Aerin?"

"Not exactly," said Delaine evasively. "But everyone up and down the length of Church Street seems to have mentioned it in one way or another. And Brooke and Aerin are both scared to death their shop might be targeted."

"Yes, I know she's concerned," said Theodosia, recalling her conversation with Brooke yesterday.

"You know," Delaine added, "their vault is just *overflowing* with valuable estate jewelry. Brooke confided to me that she just received a shipment of fire opals from Brazil. And she's also a master goldsmith, so she plans to set them in eighteen-karat gold. Won't that make for an absolutely stunning necklace? Fire opals and gold? With matching earrings as well?"

"Delaine, maybe you shouldn't be talking about this," Theodosia cautioned.

"I'm only telling *you,*" replied Delaine peevishly. "It's not like I'm dashing about the entire historic district telling everyone I run into!"

No, Theodosia thought to herself, *but you could let this information slip to someone like Cooper Hobcaw. And that might not be the most prudent thing right now.*

The fax machine on the counter next to them suddenly beeped sharply.

Startled, Delaine jumped at the intrusion, then put a hand to her heart. "What was *that?*" she asked.

"Lunch orders," announced Haley, who headed for the counter, suddenly all business.

"Listen, Theo," said Delaine, now that the two of them were alone. "Remember what we talked about a few days ago? The cat burglar?"

Theodosia nodded.

"Now I am convinced that you were right." Delaine peered at Theodosia, her green eyes sparkling with intensity.

"What changed your mind?" asked Theodosia. She was curious whether Delaine was having an emotional reaction after the funeral or if she'd actually obtained some useful information.

"If there isn't a cat burglar at work, why would everyone be talking about it? And why would Detective Tidwell have been at my shop this morning?" *There,* thought Delaine with satisfaction, *that will certainly throw open this whole mess now.*

"Tidwell came to your shop?" said Theodosia. This *was* an interesting turn of events.

"Indeed, he did," cooed Delaine. "And, I daresay, the ordeal was quite upsetting."

"Why was that, Delaine?" Theodosia tried to manage a note of sympathy even though her curiosity was at a fever pitch.

"Well, Tidwell played it very close to the vest, of course," replied Delaine. "You know how absolutely maddening the man is. He said he wasn't investigating *per se,* merely poking around, looking at things. But I got the very distinct impression that Detective Tidwell shares *your* sentiment. He does *not* view Captain Buchanan's death at the Lady Goodwood as an accident!"

Fascinated, Theodosia waited for Delaine to continue.

"You see," said Delaine, "he inquired about the *waiters.*"

So Tidwell has taken me seriously, thought Theodosia. *But the waiters, that was an angle I hadn't considered.*

"Delaine, what did Detective Tidwell want to know about waiters?" said Theodosia.

"Oh, he wanted to know who I'd hired to work at the reception, serving champagne and such. But of course, I told him the folks at the Lady Goodwood had taken care of all that. They'd hired the waiters."

"Did he ask about specific waiters, Delaine?"

"Not really. He just rattled off some names." Delaine dug in her purse. "I wrote down their names, though. It seemed like the right thing to do." She pulled out a scrawled list on a sheet of Cotton Duck stationery. "I guess not all of the waiters were working at the engagement party, but they were all on the premises that night. There was another function going on in the dining room. A sales meeting or something. For some computer company."

Theodosia scanned the list of names. There wasn't one she recognized.

"Can I keep this list, Delaine?"

"Well . . . I don't suppose it would hurt if you made a *copy* of it."

"Great," said Theodosia. "Be right back."

At the counter she literally bumped into Drayton, who had just let himself into the tea shop via the back door.

"I've got Hattie Boatwright working on the most delightful centerpiece for tomorrow," he told her excitedly. "It's part Japanese ikebana, part Southern luxe. That lady really has exceptional talent. Now if I could just convince her to join our bonsai group, I think she'd be a natural."

"I thought the whole idea of bonsai was that they *weren't* natural," quipped Haley as she emerged from the kitchen. "Stunted trees twisted into bizarre shapes and forced to live in tiny pots. What's natural about that?"

"It's a highly evolved art form," argued Drayton. "One that's been around for more than a thousand years. The style and context of bonsai are highly representational."

"Well, they're cute little things anyway," allowed Haley. She paused to watch Theodosia slide Delaine's list into the fax machine. "Are you trying to make a copy?" she asked.

Theodosia nodded.

"You have to hit the *function* button first, then press *copy*. Here, I'll do it." Haley's slim fingers flew over the keys and the piece of paper began to feed through.

"Tidwell asked Delaine about the waiters who worked at the Lady Goodwood the night of the engagement party," explained Theodosia. "Apparently he shared this list of names with her in the hope that something might pop out."

"You don't say," said Drayton as he watched a grayish page emerge from the bottom of the fax machine and slide into the waiting tray. But as he glanced at the list, his look of mild interest suddenly changed to one of alarm.

"*I* recognize a name on this list," he said quietly so Delaine wouldn't overhear.

"No way," said Haley.

Drayton slid his finger halfway down the list as Theodosia and Haley crowded in closer. "There. Graham Carmody. I think he might have been a waiter at the Heritage Society that night."

"*That* night?" asked Haley excitedly. "You mean last Saturday night when that fancy necklace disappeared?"

Drayton nodded gravely.

"You really think so?" said Theodosia. She was a little surprised that something had even come of Tidwell's list.

"I'm positive it was this fellow," said Drayton. "In fact, I think he was the one I asked to fetch a drink for Delaine."

"Did she ever get her drink?" asked Theodosia.

Drayton scratched his head. "I honestly don't recall."

Lunch was a rush again. They had a full house, then a gaggle of tourists who'd just been dropped off by one of the sightseeing jitneys came pouring in right in the middle of things. Because there weren't enough tables available, Haley had to pack up box lunches for the dozen or so tourists to carry to nearby White Point Gardens.

Delaine hung around for a while, looking alternately morose and sweetly sad, then finally wandered off after consuming a luncheon plate of chicken salad and marinated cucumbers.

And all the while Theodosia fretted. As if Cooper Hobcaw and Claire Kitridge didn't look suspicious enough, what about this waiter, Graham Carmody? He'd attended both functions! The engagement party and the Heritage Society's member's-only party. Well, not *attended* as a guest, but he'd been working there. Which gave him far more freedom and latitude than an ordinary guest. After all, a waiter could slip in and out and no one would really pay him any undue attention. Waiters were even *supposed* to be a trifle surreptitious, she decided.

In the early afternoon, the antique secretary that Drayton had ordered from Tom Wigley's antique shop was delivered and everyone crowded around to ooh and aah. It was a handsome piece, just as Drayton had promised. Hand-crafted of a lovely burled walnut with a fine array of shelves, nooks, and cubby holes. Theodosia decided it *would* make a perfect display case for the T-Bath products.

"And it doesn't take up a lot of space," said Haley, pleased with their new acquisition. "I won't be bumping my keester every time I lug a tray of tea to somebody's table."

"Haley," said Drayton, "if your attitude is such that you're merely *lugging* trays of tea, perhaps the time has come to investigate a new career path."

"All right, smarty, you know what I mean," she shot back. "I just meant that the secretary was an *economical* piece of furniture. It doesn't stick way out into the room." She gave an exaggerated frown and shook her finger at Drayton. She knew that *he* knew *exactly* what she meant.

"Oh, my goodness," said Miss Dimple as she arrived with an armload of ledger books. "Every time I stop by, you folks have something new going on."

"Hey there, Miss Dimple," called Haley. "I've got one plate of chicken salad left. It's got your name on it."

"Thank you, Haley," said the small, rotund woman. "Chicken salad sounds delightful."

"And maybe a muffin to go along?" tempted Haley. "We've got cranberry and orange blossom today."

"Orange blossom," announced Miss Dimple.

"Oh, Miss Dimple," said Theodosia, "you're going to have to sit out here today. My office is not only crammed with boxes, we're going to have to start unpacking and hauling things out."

"That's right," said Miss Dimple, settling herself down at a vacant table. "Your T-Bath products. I've heard so much about these products, I can't wait to try them for myself. There's nothing more rewarding for the soul than a good soak."

"You're coming tomorrow, right?" asked Haley as she set the chicken salad and muffin down in front of her.

"Wouldn't miss it," she said. "Jessica Sheldon from Pinckney's Gifts is planning to stop by, too."

"Good," said Theodosia. She gazed at the ledgers. "So everything's tallied and balanced?"

Miss Dimple put a chubby hand on one of the ledgers

as she chewed a bite of chicken salad. She swallowed, cleared her throat, was suddenly all business. "Shipshape," she told Theodosia. "Profits are up and the only debt you're carrying is for the manufacture and production of the T-Bath products. As we've seen, they did extremely well when you test-marketed them on your web site, so there's no reason to believe they won't do just as well in a retail setting." And with that bit of good news delivered, Miss Dimple dove back into her chicken salad.

"Hey, guys," said Theodosia to Haley and Drayton. "Can you unpack those boxes without me? I've got to make a phone call, then step out for a bit."

Drayton glanced about the tea shop. Besides Miss Dimple, only one other table was occupied at the moment. "I don't know why not," he said.

"So . . . just stick the T-Bath products on shelves and stuff a few baskets?" asked Haley.

"Haley," said Drayton, "you make it sound so *artless.*"

"In that case, my dear Drayton," said Haley, laying on her best boarding school accent, "we shall *artfully* stack products on shelves and *artfully* stuff baskets. How does that sound?"

"Much better, Haley, much better."

Theodosia looked up the number for St. Anne's Hospital, dialed the phone.

"St. Anne's, how may I direct your call?" came the receptionist's voice.

"I'm trying to get ahold of Cecile Randolph, one of the nurses who works on your second floor," said Theodosia.

"One minute," said the voice. There was a click and a buzz and Theodosia was on hold.

"This is Cecile," said a pleasant voice.

"Cecile? This is Theodosia Browning. We met the other night when my dog and I chased the intruder from Mr. Wilson's room?"

"Oh, yes," said Cecile, recognition dawning in her voice. "How are you?"

"Fine," said Theodosia, "but I'm more concerned about Mr. Wilson."

"He's been released," said Cecile.

"That's very good news," said Theodosia. "So he's at home now?"

There was a pause. "I think he's staying with a relative for now," said Cecile. "I'm not sure how much I'm allowed to say, but since you were directly involved in the incident of the other night, I think it's okay to tell you that the police suggested Mr. Wilson not go home for a while."

"But he's feeling better?" asked Theodosia. *This is interesting. Now Harlan Wilson is in hiding. Well, maybe not in hiding, but certainly incognito.*

"He was fine when he walked out," said Cecile. "Just fine."

CHAPTER 14

THE *LADY GOODWOOD* Inn was operating at about half-capacity. The hotel staff was at the ready, with desk clerks and concierge ready to check guests in, bell hops and chamber maids all available to tend to their needs. And in the kitchen, cooks, sous-chefs, prep workers, and waiters were ready to spring into action at a moment's notice. The two women who handled bookings for parties and event catering were waiting for the phone to ring. But it didn't. Business had slowed considerably since that fateful evening when the glass ceiling of the Lady Goodwood's Garden Room had collapsed atop Captain Corey Buchanan.

Frederick Welborne, the man who'd proudly served as general manager at the Lady Goodwood Inn for the better part of two decades, gazed about the empty lobby and sighed. This was not the venerable old inn's finest hour.

Tall and angular, balding and long of face, Frederick Welborne, a man who already appeared slightly burdened, now bore a look of perpetual sadness. The Lady Goodwood Inn was in a state of disrepair. And when the good lady was ailing, *he* was ailing, too.

In the past few days, yards of wet carpeting had been hauled from the ruined Garden Room. And despite the scented candles that had been burned, air fresheners that had been sprayed, windows left open, and contract cleaners who'd been brought in to work their magic with potions and sprays and ion machines, there still remained the unmistakable trace of mildewy odor.

Guests had grimaced at the sight of the wreckage. Two large dumpsters were hunkered down in the parking lot, the repository for all that ruined carpet and glass.

And the question still remained: what would be done about the old greenhouse, the Garden Room? The owners, descendants of the original Goodwoods who didn't even live in the area anymore, wanted it repaired. The inn was, after all, a continuing source of revenue for them, what with the many wedding receptions, business meetings, club functions, and private parties that were booked there, to say nothing of the tourists who stayed in the guest rooms.

One of the contractors who'd been brought in to survey the damage had just shaken his head and recommended the Garden Room be torn down completely.

Now a second contractor had been brought in at the specific request of the absentee owners.

Frederick Welborne wouldn't be a bit surprised if that contractor recommended patching it up.

"Mr. Welborne, do you have a moment?"

Frederick Welborne turned with a slow smile to greet Theodosia and shake her outstretched hand.

"Miss Browning," he said, "nice to see you under slightly better circumstances." After that fateful night, Frederick Welborne had instructed his staff to continue searching for the missing wedding ring and had felt badly that no one had been able to recover it.

"I'm afraid I still don't have hopeful news regarding

your friend's wedding ring," he told her. "We've been looking, we've *all* been looking. But alas, no luck."

Theodosia saw the sadness behind his smile, noted the empty corridors of the Lady Goodwood, and knew all was not well. But then again, how could it be?

"You've got quite a cleanup operation going on here," she told him. "I saw dumpsters out in the parking lot."

"The sooner those are gone, the better," Frederick said. "Just a sad reminder."

"Any plans to rebuild the Garden Room?" she asked.

"Still up in the air." Frederick Welborne sighed. "That decision, I'm afraid, is being left to our attorneys, insurance agents, building contractors, and owners." He smiled sadly. "I am, when all is said and done, simply a humble manager, charged with running this establishment." He gazed around. "Such as it is."

"And a fine job you've done," said Theodosia with as much warmth as she could muster, for she and Drayton had catered several engagement teas, a New Year's Eve party, and even a children's teddy bear tea at the Lady Goodwood Inn over the last couple years. And on each occasion, arrangements at the inn had been impeccable.

"May I go in and take a look?" she asked.

Frederick Welborne held up a finger. "Yes, but give me a moment." He retreated quickly to his office, returned with two yellow hard hats.

"You'll have to wear one of these," he told her. "Regulations."

"No problem," said Theodosia as she slipped the hard hat on her head.

Frederick Welborne smiled faintly at the sight of all that auburn hair spilling out from beneath the yellow work hat. "It looks good on you, you're a natural," he told her as he led her into the Magnolia Room, where Camille and Captain Buchanan's cocktail party had been held, then through the doorway into the Garden Room.

"The room looks a bit different, doesn't it," said Frederick Welborne.

Theodosia gazed about. The Garden Room had looked awful the night the roof collapsed, but now it was barely recognizable. Carpet had been torn up and metal scaffolding crowded the room. The ceiling, which had formerly been a glass arch, had been rebuilt as a temporary flat ceiling of plywood.

"What's going to happen to this room?" asked Theodosia. She gave a little shudder. Now that she'd returned to the scene of Captain Buchanan's death, she was struck by the full magnitude of what had really happened here. *Or is it the scene of a crime?* she wondered.

"Mr. Welborne? Telephone." A bell hop in a burgundy uniform with matching cap stood at Frederick Welborne's elbow. They turned and followed the bell hop out into the hall.

"Joey here went through all the carpeting after it was torn up," Frederick told her. "Looking for the ring. But he didn't find anything."

"No, sir," said Joey with what seemed like genuine regret. "And I *really* did look."

"I believe you," said Theodosia. "Thank you, thank you both," she said, smiling at the two of them.

"We'll stay in touch," said Frederick as he scurried off down the hall to take his phone call.

"I take it business has been slow?" Theodosia said to Joey, noting that despite his youthful name, Joey wasn't exactly a kid. In fact, Joey looked like he might be in his early sixties.

"Glacial. I've been here twenty-six years and never seen anything like it. We had two big wedding parties cancel out on us. And then, yesterday, a ladies luncheon group just turned on their pointy little heels and left. Guess they got spooked because the workers were taking the roof down."

"The roof came off yesterday?" asked Theodosia.

Joey nodded. "What was left of it. That's what that second dumpster's for. The metal struts and such. Got to separate stuff these days. Even landfills are getting particular. Or maybe it's because they recycle it, I don't know."

"Joey," said Theodosia, "is there a way for people to know about the events that go on here?"

Joey cocked an eye at her. "What do you mean?"

"When the Lady Goodwood has receptions and parties and such, is that information published? Or posted somewhere?"

Joey scratched his chin, thinking. "We have a newsletter," he told her.

"A newsletter," repeated Theodosia. "And your mailing list would be . . . how large?"

Joey shrugged. "I don't know, maybe a couple thousand." He stared at her intently, then his lined face seemed to light up as another idea dawned. He snapped his fingers. "We have a web site, too," he told her proudly. "That probably reaches a whole lot more folks."

I'm sure it does, thought Theodosia with grim determination. *Maybe even the person who came here that night and left with a diamond ring in his pocket instead.* "Thanks, Joey," Theodosia told him.

Joey touched his hand to the short brim of his cap. "No problem."

Walking across the parking lot to her Jeep, Theodosia found that her gaze was once again drawn to the two large brown metal dumpsters. Jingling her car keys in her hand, she walked across the parking lot to the side of the building where the dumpsters sat. One was piled high with glass and remnants of old carpet. The other, for all practical purposes, looked empty.

Intrigued, she walked up to that dumpster, stood on tiptoes, and peered in. It wasn't empty at all. Joey had been right. This dumpster was half-filled with metal struts and rails. The bones of the greenhouse roof, she thought to herself. The skeleton.

As she gazed at the twisted metal, Theodosia recalled the strange oval-shaped metal ring she'd seen attached to one of the ceiling struts. She hadn't given the metal ring a lot of thought. After all, she'd been balancing precariously on a monumentally tall ladder just moments after Captain Buchanan had been buried in rubble. More than a few things had been occupying her mind.

But as she stood with her hand on the rough edge of this heavy metal dumpster, something prickled at Theodosia's thoughts.

If someone had crashed through the roof, had actually descended inside the Garden Room, then how did they get back up again?

How exactly did one manage an acrobatic feat like that?

She supposed you could use a pulley of some kind. Or something akin to the high-tech "spider" apparatus that filmmakers loved to feature in spy films like *Mission Impossible.*

Could the ordinary person just *buy* that type of equipment right off the shelf? Better yet, could an ordinary person even *negotiate* that type of equipment?

Did Cooper Hobcaw have the strength and flexibility to manipulate a spiderman rig like that? she wondered. Maybe. He was a runner. Or at least he claimed to be a runner.

Could Claire Kitridge? She looked fairly lithe and limber.

And what of this Graham Carmody? Was he agile, too? Or didn't he have to be. Did he just show up as a waiter and then work his angle?

The questions burned in her mind like wildfire.

CHAPTER 15

GRAHAM CARMODY SAT at his Dell computer scanning the Internet auction site. This was the best part, he told himself. This was what made it all worthwhile.

Oh, finding the objects was exciting, he couldn't deny that. There was the thrill of the hunt, which always set his pulse to racing. But once the object was digitally photographed and put up on the web site, then things *really* got interesting. Because that's when he started making money.

Graham loved checking and rechecking the bids, especially when one of his choice items was reaching its final days. It was exciting to note when his reserve price had been met, even better when bidding heated up and competitors from all over the world began to play a cat-and-mouse game with each other, sneaking in new bids at three in the morning!

What a marvel the Internet was. And what a brilliant way to move merchandise. So fast, so inexpensive, and so highly anonymous. Whoever had *really* invented the Internet (and he was quite sure it hadn't been Al Gore, more likely a bunch of brainy military tech weinies) should be awarded a gold medal. Because the Internet had become the repository for all of civilization's accumulated knowledge. And an international marketplace for all of civilization's goods.

Graham Carmody stretched his long legs, scratched at the scruff of ginger-colored beard that sprouted on his face. He'd have to can it in a little while, get his shit ready for tomorrow. Starting tomorrow noon he'd be working nonstop for the next couple days. A docents' luncheon at the art museum, then the gig at Symphony Hall. Friday and Saturday evenings were booked solid, too. Working as a temp for Butler's Express didn't leave a lot of room for extracurricular activities, but it certainly got him into lots of interesting places. Oh well, hit it hard now, retire early . . .

Reaching for a cigarette, Graham Carmody stood up suddenly, letting his computer chair snap back. He glanced at the walls of his study, at the tasty antiques and oddities that occupied the wooden shelves. He didn't even remember where he'd picked up that pre-Columbian statue. Or that silver tray. Oh well. Didn't matter.

Overcome by fatigue now from too many hours spent staring at the computer screen, he paced the length of the room, glancing out the window into the back garden of the small single house he rented. What luck he'd had in finding this place. Mrs. Gerritsen, an older lady and recent widow, had been looking for a young man to rent the downstairs from her. Give her a sense of security, she'd told him. He gazed at his rumpled reflection in the window. Security. Him. Sure. You bet, Mrs. Gerritsen. Anything you say, babe.

A sudden movement outside caught his eye. He stepped closer to the window, cupped his hands to the glass, and tried to peer outside.

Is someone out there? Moving around in the alley?

He darted through the doorway into the kitchen and threw open the back door.

Hey! he called, leaping down the back steps, intent on throwing a good scare into whoever was sneaking around out back.

But all he saw were shadows. All he heard was the whisper of the wind through Mrs. Gerritsen's dead flower stalks.

Graham Carmody stood on the sidewalk in his bare feet. *Nothing,* he finally told himself. *Probably just a stray cat trying to paw its way into the garbage bag I set out earlier.* He'd seen the damn things around before, thought maybe Mrs. Gerritsen secretly put out food for them.

You're just feeling jumpy, kid. Time to log some serious sack time.

Graham Carmody turned and went back inside his house.

Graham Carmody, Graham Carmody. The name had played like a litany in Theodosia's head. He'd been one of the waiters at Delaine's party; he'd also worked at the Heritage Society the night the Blue Kashmir necklace disappeared. Coincidence or convenience?

And so it wasn't any surprise that at nine o'clock that night Theodosia pulled out the Charleston phone directory, paged through the *C*'s, and ran her finger down the index of names until she actually found the name, *Graham Carmody.*

Over on Bogard Street. Not all that far from here.

She'd stood in her hallway, gazing at her reflection in the mirror, debating how she could pull this off. Go for a jog and take Earl Grey along in case she needed a convincing ruse? Or just drive there and snoop?

In the end she jumped in her Jeep and drove there. Parked a block or so away. Flipped the switch that killed the dome light, then slipped quietly out the door.

Theodosia had scouted the house from the street first. It was your typical Charleston single house. Long and narrow, one room wide, butted up against the street. Charleston folklore held that residences had once been taxed according to how much street frontage they occupied. Hence the evolution of the conservatively narrow Charleston single house.

This one was clapboard, though many single houses were far grander and built of brick or stucco. Graham Carmody's house looked fairly well kept for its age, Theodosia decided. It had probably been built just before the turn of the century. The previous century.

And look, next to the front door. Two mailboxes. The house had obviously been turned into a duplex of sorts. *Is Graham Carmody the landlord or the renter?* she wondered.

Going around to the back of the house, walking down the alley, she'd seen him through the window, working on his computer.

Graham Carmody was surprisingly pleasant looking. Young, probably late twenties. A trifle scruffy, but still the kind of guy Haley would find attractive. Would call hunky.

Theodosia had been staring in at him from outside, drawn unconsciously forward, when the tip of her shoe had struck something.

A black vinyl garbage bag.

Was it his? she'd wondered. *Should she look inside? Better yet, should she take it?*

Feeling a trifle foolish, but still curious, she'd snatched up the black bag and slung it over her shoulder.

That's when the man in the window had reacted. Had bolted out of the room in a flash.

Theodosia had known he was coming after her. He'd seen something, her movement or shadow when she grabbed the bag, and was rushing out to check!

But she was down the alley and around the corner before Graham Carmody ever hit the flower beds. Then she crouched behind a huge clump of magnolias, trying to control her breathing, knowing Graham Carmody hadn't been wearing shoes, but praying he wouldn't run down the alley after her anyway.

He hadn't.

Theodosia waited a full five minutes, during which time she felt like a surreptitious Santa with a bag of who-knows-what thrown across his back.

She took a roundabout route back to her Jeep, unlocked the door, slid into the driver's seat.

Keeping one eye on the rearview mirror, she drove a circuitous route back to her apartment above the Indigo Tea Shop. Finally, when her breathing had returned to normal and she'd parallel parked in the spot behind her shop, she turned her attention to the black garbage bag that rested beside her on the passenger seat.

Digging a fingernail into the soft plastic, she ripped the bag open. But instead of the orange juice cartons, candy bar wrappers, and empty cereal boxes she'd expected to see, there were printouts. Computer printouts. Mounds of them.

Frowning, Theodosia snapped the Jeep's dome light on and stared at the sheets of paper.

They were activity printouts from an Internet auction site. Dates and times of bids. Amounts of bids.

She sat stock-still and stared out the front window of the Jeep. *If Graham Carmody is a cat burglar, what better way to fence his stolen goods than on an Internet auction site! It would be a way to draw millions of buyers from all over the world and still remain anonymous!*

Yes, she decided, this definitely bore looking into. And the sooner the better.

CHAPTER 16

TIMOTHY NEVILLE HAD weathered many crises in his eighty years and many problems during his tenure as president of the Heritage Society. But neither he nor any of his people had ever come under such merciless scrutiny before.

He fairly shook with indignation as he strode down Church Street. Dressed in a double-breasted camel hair blazer and cocoa brown slacks, Timothy was the picture of style. His jacket with its nipped-in waist, his paisley yellow ascot, his highly polished shoes, had been chosen with great care this morning. But after the events of this morning, and his infuriating phone conversation with Vance Bernard, the chairman of the Heritage Society's executive advisory committee, Timothy Neville was beyond caring. In fact, he was positively livid. And when Nell Chappel of the Chowder Hound Restaurant waved hello to him as she collected her morning mail and headed into the kitchen to set a nice pot of she-crab soup to simmering, Timothy didn't even take notice.

"Drayton. A moment of your time, please," said Timothy as he strode into the Indigo Tea Shop like a martinet, ramrod stiff and utterly devoid of any extraneous pleasantries.

"Timothy . . . oh, of course," said Drayton. Clutching a teapot in each hand, his tortoiseshell half-glasses sliding down his aquiline nose, Drayton was completely taken by surprise. "Give me a minute," he told Timothy. "Take that table over there," he said, pointing with his chin, "and I'll be right with you."

Timothy strode over to the table, sat down. Even though he sat perfectly erect, with one leg crossed over the other, his pleated slacks falling elegantly, his face was a thundercloud.

"Timothy," said Theodosia as she rounded the corner from the kitchen. "Good morning, this *is* a surprise." Stopping in her tracks, she suddenly took a good look at him. "What's wrong?"

"Everything," he snapped. "I don't even know where to begin."

"Simply start at the beginning," said Drayton as he arrived at Timothy's table, somewhat breathless. "Haley," he called, "can you get a plate of scones for table three and another pot of Darjeeling for table two?"

She nodded.

"Now tell us," said Drayton. "What's happened to put you in such a state?"

"The Charleston Police came to the Heritage Society some forty minutes ago, that's what happened," said Timothy. "Apparently they received an anonymous tip that Claire Kitridge was somehow involved in the recent thefts that have plagued our neighborhood."

"That's absurd," said Drayton while Theodosia inwardly cringed.

Timothy held up a gnarled finger. "Wait," he cautioned, "it gets much worse. Because of the recent death and apparent theft at the Lady Goodwood and the theft of the Blue Kashmir necklace, the police took this tip rather seriously. Claire, on the other hand, did not take the police seriously." Timothy grimaced. "That was her mistake."

"What happened?" asked Theodosia, a sick feeling suddenly gripping her.

"Oh, they asked Claire a few routine questions. Where do you live? How long have you worked at the Heritage Society? That type of thing. Then they wanted to know if they could have a look inside her desk. Claire said yes, knowing she had nothing to hide."

"I still don't see the problem," said Drayton. "Didn't you tell them the notion of Claire as sneak thief was utterly ridiculous?"

"Of course I did," sputtered Timothy. "Until they rifled through the bottom drawer of Claire's desk and found Delaine Dish's missing watch."

"What!" said Drayton. Now it was his turn to sputter.

"You know, that fancy Chopard with all the diamonds," said Timothy.

"But Claire didn't steal it . . . wouldn't steal it," fumbled Drayton.

"Of course she wouldn't, she's above reproach. *You* know that and *I* know that, but the police . . ." Timothy shrugged. "Well, it isn't good. Obviously, the discovery of Delaine's expensive watch is very incriminating."

"They came looking for a watch without benefit of a search warrant," said Theodosia slowly, "and the whole thing's based on an anonymous tip? I'd say that's awfully fishy."

"So fishy it stinks!" declared Drayton.

"Doesn't it," said Timothy, his voice brimming with bitterness. "And now our illustrious executive advisory committee wants Claire Kitridge fired. Of course, they're calling it a temporary leave of absence, but it's just a matter of time before it becomes a formal disciplinary firing.

Unless, of course, we *somehow* find the person responsible . . ." Timothy's voice faltered and he gazed at Theodosia in despair.

"This is awful!" howled Drayton, gazing at Theodosia with an equal degree of unhappiness.

Timothy reached for his handkerchief, blew his nose, cleared his throat. "Claire . . ." he began, "is a very *good* person. She's been with the Heritage Society for almost four years. In that time I've seen her diligence and kindness shine through." Timothy's voice faltered again. "I've seen Claire go out of her way to make people feel welcome and appreciated. People who've donated things to the Heritage Society, little things like an old letter or a small antique . . . they receive the same heartfelt thank-you letter from her as a million-dollar donor would. Claire is just that kind of person."

Theodosia stared at the two men unhappily. She couldn't help but remember Brooke and Aerin's conversation about Claire bringing in a citrine and diamond broach for sale. Was it possible Claire Kitridge *wasn't* what she appeared to be? That she was, instead, a sly fox in the weeds who took careful advantage of her position at the Heritage Society? Could she have heard about Camille's wedding ring through the grapevine or via Delaine's bragging and gone after it? Because Claire had inside access at the Heritage Society, could she also have snatched the Blue Kashmir necklace? Was she responsible for the other art thefts? The Tiffany vases, the half-dozen other thefts Tidwell had mentioned?

The thought of Claire Kitridge as a cat burglar was sickening to contemplate.

On the other hand, someone very wily and clever could have maneuvered to set Claire up. Someone who needed to deflect blame from themselves. Someone who had access to the Lady Goodwood Inn and the Heritage

Society. Someone with a working knowledge of the historic district and all its wealthy residents.

Someone like Cooper Hobcaw or Graham Carmody.

The rest of the morning was a whirlwind at the Indigo Tea Shop. Customers had to be served, finishing touches put on the T-Bath display, sweet-grass baskets had to be stuffed to the brim with T-Bath products and stacked on the counter. And all the while, they worried about Timothy and Claire.

Drayton had decided they should close the Indigo Tea Shop at one o'clock in order to prepare for the afternoon's open house. And just as soon as Haley returned from Gallagher's Food Service, their favorite restaurant supply house, with ingredients for the California rolls, they'd push three of the tables together to form the head table for the buffet. Then, of course, they'd have to set everything up and decorate the rest of the tables with Drayton's bonsai.

"Drayton," said Theodosia, "I know this isn't a good time to ask, but when is Hattie bringing the centerpiece by?"

"Any minute," he said. "And you're right, it isn't a good time. Why does everything have to happen at once? Good things and bad things all mulled together."

She sighed. "Life does seem to unfold that way, doesn't it?"

"We worked so hard on these T-Bath products and looked forward to this day and now it . . ." He searched for the right word. "It feels *tainted.*"

"I know," said Theodosia. "The good shoulder to shoulder with the bad. Maybe it's a test of fortitude."

"Makes us stronger?" he asked.

"That's what my mother believed," said Theodosia. Her mother had passed away when she was eight, but she could always remember her saying something to the effect that problems can't be solved, but only outgrown.

"Hey, you guys!" The door flew open as Haley rushed in, her long hair streaming behind her, her arms filled with bundles.

"Good heavens, Haley," said Drayton. "You're a regular beast of burden with all those bags. Here, let me give you a hand."

"Thank you, Drayton," said Haley as she handed over her packages. "Hey, Theo, guess what? When I was on my way back from Gallagher's, I came back past Heart's Desire. Guess who I saw in there? Standing at the counter?"

"Claire Kitridge?" said Theodosia. For some reason the name just popped into her head and she blurted it out.

"Nope. Cooper Hobcaw."

"Really?" said Drayton with a frown.

"Oh, yeah," said Haley. "He was leaning across the counter, kind of flirting with that woman, Aerin, who works for Brooke. At least I think he was flirting. They had their heads together, talking awfully close." Haley paused. "I thought Cooper Hobcaw was sweet on Delaine."

"So did I," said Theodosia. She turned toward Drayton, raised her eyebrows as if to say *what's up?* But he appeared equally surprised.

"As far as I know, Cooper Hobcaw has been squiring Delaine around to various social functions," said Drayton. "They were at an art opening last week for that new painter who's showing at the Wren Gallery. And of course, Coop was her guest at the engagement party and the ill-fated Heritage Society members' party."

"So you don't think he'd two-time her?" said Haley.

"Honestly, Haley," said Drayton, "I don't know what to think anymore."

It wasn't until Theodosia was in her office later, unpacking the last of the T-Bath products, that she realized how heartsick she suddenly felt for Delaine. If her hunch or odd feeling or whatever it was about Cooper Hobcaw proved true and he *did* turn out to be a thief, it would be a devastating blow to Delaine. And if Cooper Hobcaw was merely getting cozy with Aerin Linley in anticipation of possibly dumping Delaine, she'd be equally traumatized.

Theodosia propped her elbows on her desk and rested her head in her hands, thinking. Cooper Hobcaw, the lanky, soft-spoken fellow who jogged through the historic district late at night, was a strange duck. Had he charmed Delaine in order to get closer to people and places of wealth in the historic district?

Was he flirting with Aerin at Heart's Desire because she might be a way to unload expensive merchandise? As one of Charleston's top attorneys, he wouldn't be viewed with suspicion if he waltzed into Heart's desire with expensive jewelry. It would just be assumed they were old family pieces.

Theodosia rubbed her eyes tiredly. Okay, what about all those printouts she'd grabbed from Graham Carmody's back alley last night? She hadn't even mentioned them to Drayton and Haley yet. But she'd have to. In fact, she wanted to. She'd lay out what she knew, what she suspected, what appeared to be evidence, and get their opinions. After all, three heads were better than one!

CHAPTER 17

"DON'T GET THE seaweed wet!" warned Drayton. "If you do, the entire California roll will be soggy and completely inedible. And be sure to wrap cellophane around them so you can roll them snugly. Otherwise the darn things just crumble apart on you."

"I'm not going to blow the California rolls," scoffed Haley. "And stop being so futsy." She slapped the back of Drayton's hand as he reached over to poke an avocado and check its ripeness. "The rice has been cooked perfectly, the crab is delightfully pink and fresh, and the avocados are ripe. And by the way, Mr. Conneley, who appointed *you* chief cook and bottle washer in *my* kitchen? Theodosia!" Haley called at the top of her lungs. "Will you *pleeease* put Drayton to work somewhere else? He's making me crazy!"

"Drayton," said Theodosia, "I really could use your help out here." She scanned the room, noting the positions of the tables.

"What?" he said grumpily, emerging from between the green velvet curtains.

"What with all the moving about of tables, the proportions seem a little out of whack," she said. "Can you work some of your magic?"

Somewhat mollified by her request, Drayton scanned the room with an appraising eye. "Well, there's your problem right there," he told her. "You've got two tables absolutely *jammed* against the fireplace." He threaded his way through the mazes of tables, pulled two of them away from the fireplace. Then he looked about the room and made a few more adjustments. Tables were angled, chairs pushed in, the head table also angled slightly.

"Now for the bonsai," he said as he bent down and pulled bonsai trees from the two large black plastic trays he'd used to transport them. "Let's place the small Japanese junipers and dwarf birches on the smaller tables." He quickly began arranging pots of bonsai. "And the larger bonsai, like this elm forest and this taller tamarack, on the larger tables."

"It looks wonderful," said Theodosia once he'd finished his arrangement.

"What time do the guests arrive?" Drayton asked for about the fiftieth time.

"The invitations specified three. Of course, some folks always arrive a little earlier; a few will dash in late as usual. If we plan on serving our Japanese tea and goodies from about two-thirty to four, we should be right on."

"Maybe I should check on Haley again," said Drayton.

"Oh look," said Theodosia as the door to the shop swung open, "here's Hattie with your ikebana centerpiece."

And as Drayton rushed to greet her, Theodosia breathed a sigh of relief and thought to herself, *Saved by the bell.*

By three-fifteen, the reception was in full swing. Delaine had been the first to arrive, bringing with her Cordette Jordan, the woman who owned Griffon Antiques over on King Street.

Brooke Carter Crockett and Aerin Linley followed on

their heels, and shortly thereafter, Miss Dimple and Jessica Sheldon from Pinckney's Gift Shop came rushing in.

There was about a five-minute lull and then a second influx of guests poured in. Angie Congdon from the Featherbed House, Lillith Gardner, one of the partners at Antiquarian Booksellers, Nell Chappel from the Chowder Hound Restaurant, and at least two dozen more friends from in and around the historic district.

Drayton was in his element, alternately pouring tea, answering questions about bonsai, and doing a major amount of schmoozing.

Theodosia stayed near the front door, where she could serve as official greeter, and Haley was kept busy restocking tidbits of sushi and kushiyaki on the main buffet table, in between dashing to the cash register to ring up sales on their new T-Bath products.

The din of conversation rose, as did the clink of cups and the squeal of voices.

"Did you really design this cunning packaging?" asked Nell Chappel. She held up a package of T-Bath Green Tea Soak with its elegant celadon green wrapper and typography done in a Japanese dry-brush style. "It's so elegant and Zen-like," she exclaimed.

Then, just when it looked as though they couldn't squeeze one more person into the Indigo tea Shop, an entire jitney packed full of tourists stopped in front of the shop and a dozen women came tumbling in for tea.

Theodosia met them at the door. "I'm sorry, but we're having a reception here today."

They crowded around her, peering curiously over her shoulder.

"We were looking forward to a spot of tea," said one lady with a pouf of blue hair.

"Of course you're welcome to come in and help yourself to tea," Theodosia said, "but I'm not sure I can offer you a table and a quiet respite today."

"What's your reception for?" asked another lady and Theodosia quickly explained the concept of the T-Bath products.

There were cries of *How wonderful!* and *Can we buy, too?* and the ladies came pouring in to join the ranks of the already jostling throng.

"Theo!" cried Delaine. She waved frantically from across the room as she clutched a sweetgrass basket filled with T-Bath products. "I simply *adore* your new products," she said, making extravagant mouth gestures as she pushed her way through the crowd.

"Thanks, Delaine," said Theodosia. "Your praise is much appreciated." She hadn't been able to speak privately with Delaine earlier and decided to take the opportunity now. It was funny, she thought, sometimes conversations could be the most private when you were surrounded by a crowd of people who were busy paying attention to something else.

"Lavender Luxury Lotion," exclaimed Delaine, digging into her basket of products. "And Green Tea Feet Treat. Marvelous! You know, I wouldn't be averse to stocking a few of your T-Bath items in my shop."

"I appreciate the offer," said Theodosia, "but let's talk about it later, shall we?"

"Of course, Theo," said Delaine. "If you're too *busy* to discuss it now."

"Delaine," began Theodosia, "Timothy Neville tells me that your diamond watch was found in Claire Kitridge's desk at the Heritage Society."

Delaine knit her perfectly plucked brows together. "Yes," she said, "the police called me earlier about that. I meant to tell you. Isn't it strange? And all the time I've been volunteering there, I considered Claire to be an extremely honest and trustworthy person. Salt of the earth, really. It's funny how people can fool you. And disappoint you, too," she added.

"Do you really believe Claire stole your watch?" asked Theodosia.

Delaine was suddenly reluctant to meet Theodosia's gaze. "Well, *someone* did," she said vaguely. "Along with everything else."

By *everything else,* Theodosia knew Delaine was still stewing mightily about the missing wedding ring.

"When did you first decide your watch was missing?" asked Theodosia.

Delaine shrugged. "I don't know. Maybe before I went to Savannah for the funeral. Maybe the day I got back. I'm not exactly sure. It's all a little fuzzy. I certainly had *other* things on my mind."

"Is it possible you took your watch off while you were at the Heritage Society?" Theodosia knew that, as a volunteer for the Heritage Society, Delaine spent countless hours there. "Could you simply have misplaced it? If you did, someone might have found your watch and put it in Claire's desk for safekeeping."

"Well . . ." said Delaine, "I *was* there Sunday morning for a while going over the numbers on ticket sales. And things were still in an uproar from the night before." She shrugged again. "I don't know, Theodosia. Don't let's get into it right now, there's so much that's still very painful for me."

"Please realize," said Theodosia, "that the Heritage Society's executive advisory committee wants to fire Claire."

Delaine looked surprised. "I thought she was just suspended."

"Delaine, *think,* please," urged Theodosia. "This is important."

Delaine suddenly turned flashing eyes on Theodosia. "My niece Camille was important, too. And her poor dead fiancé. And their wedding ring. What if Claire Kitridge was somehow involved in that tragedy?"

"You don't really believe Claire is a cat burglar, do you?" Theodosia asked gently.

Delaine pulled a hanky from her small baguette bag and daubed at her perfectly made-up eyes. "I don't know what to think anymore."

"Could someone have come into your house while you were in Savannah for the funeral?" asked Theodosia.

"Just Coop."

"*What,* Delaine?" said Theodosia loudly.

"I gave Cooper Hobcaw the keys to my house."

"Why?"

"Someone had to feed Sasha. I couldn't let my little darling go hungry now, could I?"

Sasha was Delaine's cat, a seal point Siamese that she absolutely adored.

"No, of course not," agreed Theodosia.

"Well then," argued Delaine, "don't you think Coop would have known if someone broke in or not? He's a lawyer." Delaine hesitated, rethinking what she'd just said. "Well . . . what I *meant* to say was that Cooper Hobcaw is extremely observant. He would certainly have noticed if a window was ajar or a door unlocked."

"You're right," said Theodosia. At this point she knew it was easier to agree with Delaine than argue with her. But she *was* mulling over the possibility that Cooper Hobcaw could have lifted Delaine's Chopard watch and somehow planted it at the Heritage Society.

"Theodosia, this is all so splendid," exclaimed Brooke Carter Crockett. Theodosia turned to find that Brooke and Aerin Linley were also loaded down with an assortment of T-Bath products.

"Isn't it just?" agreed Delaine, glad for the diversion. "And do you know, I'm actually *considering* carrying some of these marvelous products in my store?"

"Is she really?" asked Brooke as Delaine scurried off.

"I think we'll probably end up retailing everything here and on our web site," said Theodosia.

"Delaine *is* a bit of a dragon lady, isn't she?" said Aerin Linley with a wry smile.

"But a good customer of ours, too," said Brooke, in a tone that indicated enough had been said about Delaine Dish. "Oh, I almost forgot . . ." Brooke dug in her purse, pulled out a tiny gold box, and handed it to Theodosia. "For you."

"Brooke! What's this?" exclaimed Theodosia as she tentatively accepted the little box.

"Not much, really. Just a fun thing I put together."

"Go ahead, open it," urged Aerin.

Theodosia carefully lifted the lid on the box, then let out a squeak of surprise. "Is it my teacup?"

Brooke nodded. She had taken the colorful shards of Theodosia's shattered teacup of the other day, rimmed them with sterling silver and tiny bits of gold, and hung them on a charm bracelet.

Entranced, Theodosia lifted the bracelet from the box. The results of Brooke's efforts were spectacular. The broken pieces that had looked so sad when they were lying on the floor now gleamed and danced with a whole new life.

"It's spectacular," said Theodosia. She clutched Brooke's hand. "I don't know what to say."

"Don't say anything. Just wear it in good health," said Brooke. "As we shall continue to drink your tea in good health."

"But it must have taken so much time to create," Theodosia protested.

Brooke waved a hand dismissively. "Really, it's not that big a deal. I buy the silver in small, thin strips anyway and it's extremely malleable. It only takes a few minutes to outline each piece, then pinch everything into place. From there on it was just straight ahead soldering and jump rings. Jewelry Making 101."

"Well, it looks like a million bucks," said Theodosia as she watched the colorful teacup pieces dance and jingle in their reincarnation as charms.

"Think of it more as a priceless memory of your mother's china," said Brooke.

"Theo," said Aerin, who had been watching her with a barely contained smile. "I have an interesting proposal for you."

Theodosia turned inquisitive eyes on Aerin.

"I have a dear friend who's the producer for *Windows on Charleston* at Channel 10. She's always looking for interesting guests and I mentioned your name—"

"Oh, I don't think—" began Theodosia.

"And she mentioned that she'd *love* to have you on!" finished Aerin. "She saw the write-up on you and the T-Bath products in the Style Section and was really intrigued."

"Theodosia *would* be perfect, wouldn't she?" interjected Drayton. He'd come up behind the three of them and overheard part of the conversation. "There's been such an enormous resurgence in tea drinking. And of course, the Charleston Tea Plantation, the only tea plantation left in the United States, is practically in our back yard. Their American Classic Tea has been the official White House Tea since 1987 and has also been designated Hospitality Beverage of South Carolina."

Aerin clapped her hands together. "That's so *perfect,* Drayton. Exactly the kind of sound bite they're always looking for. Theodosia could expound on tea lore as well as talk about contemporary tea drinking. Maybe even share recipes."

"It *would* be a fun piece," agreed Brooke.

"We'll look into it," Drayton assured them.

"Be sure to mention my name," said Aerin.

"What are you doing?" Theodosia hissed at Drayton when she had him alone.

"Encouraging you to get a gig," he said with a poker face.

"What if I don't want to get a gig?"

"Think about it, Theo," said Drayton. "What if you could actually land a *segment* on a local TV show? Think what it could do for business!"

Theodosia glowered at him. "You're using a marketing strategy to try to persuade me. That's how I used to handle clients. Persuade them by pointing out the financial upside."

Drayton smiled. "Then you of all people should want to explore this opportunity. See if you can find out any more from Aerin, will you? She's really a great person to know, exceedingly well connected."

"Drayton . . ." Theodosia began. She still hadn't had a chance to tell him about her visit to Graham Carmody's house last night, and her strange discovery of the Internet auction printouts was percolating in her brain.

"Hmm?" he asked as he looked over her shoulder, his face suddenly lighting up. "Well, look who's here! Hellooo!"

"Oh, my gosh," exclaimed Theodosia as her Aunt Libby walked through the door. "What are *you* doing here?"

Libby Revelle squared her narrow shoulders and gave her niece a mildly inquisitive look. "You invited us, don't you remember?"

"Yes, of course. But I never expected you to show up."

Libby turned to Margaret Rose Reese, her companion and housekeeper. "It seems we're a bit of a surprise," she said dryly.

"You're a wonderful surprise!" exclaimed Theodosia as she suddenly threw her arms around Aunt Libby and planted a kiss on her smooth cheek. She released her, then repeated her motions with a slightly embarrassed Margaret Rose.

"Oh, honey," protested Margaret Rose, who struggled

to maintain the stern facade she'd honed to perfection from years spent as a housekeeper for an aging Episcopalian minister, "you don't have to go all gushy. It's just us." But she was pleased anyway.

"We decided to make an evening of it," declared Aunt Libby. "Margaret Rose and I have been stuck out at Cain Ridge for what feels like forever."

Cain Ridge was the former rice plantation out in the low-country where Aunt Libby and Theodosia's father had grown up.

"Our master plan," continued Aunt Libby, "was to drop by your little reception, then treat ourselves to dinner at the Women's Club. Afterwards, we're going to soak up a little culture at the symphony."

Theodosia stared at her. "*I'm* going to the symphony tonight. With Jory Davis."

"Good," declared Aunt Libby with a sly grin. "Then you and your gentleman friend can buy us both a nice Dubonet with a twist during intermission" And with that, Aunt Libby pushed her way into the crowd, eager to get reacquainted with old friends and enjoy a good chat.

CHAPTER 18

THE HAUNTING STRAINS of *Nessum Dorma* from Puccini's opera *Turandot* filled the auditorium as the symphony orchestra played their fourth piece of the night. Normally, the symphony offered three concert series over the course of their season—Chamber Music, Classical, and Pops. But tonight's gala was a special concert, an opera venue that featured a medley of work from such opera greats as Puccini, Verdi, and Rossini.

On the stage, Timothy Neville played first chair in the violin section. In the audience, sitting center stage, fifteen rows back from the orchestra, Theodosia and Jory Davis listened with rapt attention. Off to their left and a few rows down were Aunt Libby and Margaret Rose. Before the auditorium lights had dimmed, Theodosia had spotted Delaine and Cooper Hobcaw over to her right, their heads together, whispering conspiratorially.

The conductor bobbed and wove with the sweetly lyrical music. Then, as the final elegant notes hung in the air, he spun on his heels, his baton held aloft, and bowed deeply. The packed house rose to its feet and thunderous applause flooded the hall.

Jory Davis gazed down at Theodosia. She could see in his eyes that he approved of how she looked tonight. She'd dressed in a short silver sheath and left her auburn hair loose so that it fell over her shoulders.

"Want to stroll down to the lobby for a drink?" Jory asked. "We've got a good twenty minutes before the second half of the concert begins."

Theodosia's shining face smiled up at him. "Love to," she said.

Everyone seemed to have the same idea, and by the time they'd elbowed their way to the small bar, it was six deep in thirsty customers. It seemed that almost every opera lover was also eager for a cold refreshment.

"I've got an idea," said Jory, taking Theodosia's elbow and steering her away from the knot of people. "Let's sit at one of those little tables over by the window. I actually believe there are waiters who'll shuttle drinks to us."

Theodosia followed Jory to a tiny black enamel table and seated herself on an even tinier black enamel folding chair.

"I wonder where Aunt Libby and Margaret Rose are?" said Theodosia, looking around, trying to peer over heads.

"Maybe they didn't come down for intermission after all? Oh, here we go," said Jory as a waiter dropped two white bar napkins on the table. "Theo, what would you like to drink?"

"White wine, please," she said as she continued to scan the crowd.

"Glass of white wine," Jory repeated to the waiter, "and a bourbon and water."

Theodosia glanced up just as the waiter finished making a note of their drink order and turned to leave. Recognition jolted her and she instinctively clutched at Jory Davis's arm. The waiter who'd just taken their drink order was none other than the young man she'd paid a surreptitious visit to last night! Graham Carmody!

Amazing, she thought to herself. *The very same waiter who was working at the Heritage Society the night the Blue Kashmir necklace disappeared and at the Lady Goodwood Inn when Captain Corey Buchanan was killed! And now he's turned up here.*

As Theodosia stared at the retreating back of Graham Carmody, she realized that, if the young man really *was* a cat burglar, his job as a waiter was the perfect ploy to put him in close contact with potential victims! What better way to check out which ladies were wearing diamond earrings or flashing an emerald bracelet or carrying a Judith Leiber jeweled purse? You could spot your mark and then pounce!

"It's perfect," Theodosia uttered aloud, surprised at the simplicity of it all. Because when you thought about it, working as a waiter for an upscale caterer really *was* a clever cover.

Jory Davis smiled at her, apparently assuming her remark referred to their evening together thus far. "Glad you're having a good time," he replied. "You seemed a bit distracted earlier, but I chalked it up to a hectic day."

"Jory," she said, "we need to talk."

Jory gazed at her anxiously. "Okay," he said slowly.

Theodosia saw the worried look on Jory's face and hastily reassured him. "No, this isn't about us. This isn't one of those *We need to talk because I just want to be friends* kind of things."

Exhaling with a mock sigh of relief, Jory suddenly turned sober. "Hey, you're really upset, aren't you?"

She nodded.

"Tell me what's going on," he urged. "Let me help."

"Okay," she agreed, "but let's get our drinks first. And move outside. You'll see why in a moment."

Once their drinks arrived, they carried them out to a

small patio directly off the lobby. The night was cool and the beginnings of a full moon bobbed overhead. *Halloween's in two nights,* Theodosia reminded herself. A haunting night, a night filled with mystery. Then again, she just might have as much mystery and intrigue as she needed right now!

Settling down on a wide bench, Theodosia took a quick sip of wine, then held Jory's hand in hers as she slowly related to him the events of the past week.

She told him about the mysterious intruder she and Earl Grey had chased from Harlan Wilson's hospital room.

She told him about Cooper Hobcaw and his evening runs through the historic district. Explained that just when Cooper Hobcaw was given custody of the key to Delaine's house, her expensive Chopard watch suddenly turned up missing. Then she related how the watch had been discovered in Claire Kitridge's desk at the Heritage Society, thanks to an anonymous tip.

Theodosia's suspicions about the waiter, Graham Carmody, came as a complete surprise to Jory. So much so, in fact, that when the strains of the opening overture came wafting out, he asked Theodosia if she'd rather stay there and keep talking.

"Absolutely I would," she told him.

"You're sure you don't mind missing the second half?" he asked. "They're doing Bizet's *Carmen.*"

"I've got it on CD. Besides, this is more important, don't you think?"

"It's fascinating as hell, I'll give you that much," said Jory. He frowned, set his empty drink glass down next to his feet. "Okay, let's go back to the first event. The engagement party. That's when everything seemed to kick into high gear."

"Right," said Theodosia. "That's when things came to *our* attention. Drayton's and mine. And Haley's and Delaine's, too, I guess. Then we found out that other valuables had been stolen previously." Theodosia took a final sip of her white wine. "Camille's wedding ring was appraised at something like sixty or seventy thousand dollars." She shrugged. "I don't know the value of the other items that have been stolen, but I'd say our cat burglar has been making quite a haul."

"Only the insurance companies know for sure," said Jory. "But let's see what kind of case we can build against Cooper Hobcaw. Do you remember seeing him after the ceiling crashed in at the Lady Goodwood?"

"Yes," replied Theodosia. "And he was absolutely soaked to the bone. Dripping all over the carpet. But he'd ostensibly run out to flag down the ambulance."

"So that's circumstantial evidence," said Jory. "And we know Cooper Hobcaw likes his nightly jaunts through the historic district. But we don't have proof as to whether he's casing homes or just stretching his legs."

Theodosia snuggled against Jory's shoulder. It was comforting knowing he was securely on her side.

"And this waiter . . ." Jory began. "The one that's here tonight."

"Graham Carmody," said Theodosia.

"He's a real wild card. Turns up like a bad penny." Jory Davis rubbed a hand through his curly hair. "Did you get a good look at those computer printouts you lifted?"

"Pages and pages of Internet auction bids."

"And all on the sale of antiques and jewelry," mused Jory. "I'd say that's fairly incriminating." He thought for a minute. "Let me run a check on this Graham Carmody, see what turns up. You never know, he could have an arrest record."

"What about Cooper Hobcaw?" asked Theodosia.

"We won't find anything there. If he had a record, he wouldn't be doing the kind of lawyering he is."

"There's one person we really haven't discussed," said Theodosia.

"The woman from the Heritage Society?"

"Right," said Theodosia. "Claire Kitridge."

"Doesn't feel right," said Jory.

"Doesn't to me, either," agreed Theodosia. "Why would Claire swipe Delaine's watch then plant it in her own desk? That hardly seems logical." On the other hand, Theodosia thought to herself, what was overtly illogical was often discounted by investigators. They often assumed criminals would act in a certain pattern or mode. So Claire could be dumb like a fox.

"Anyway," said Theodosia, "I get the feeling that any one of our suspects had the talent and wherewithal to snatch Delaine's watch and plant it in Claire Kitridge's desk. And the access," she added.

Jory nodded. "They're all clever enough, that's for sure."

"So what's next?" asked Theodosia.

"Not sure," said Jory.

Theodosia gazed up into the night sky. The moon was almost as round and orange as a wheel of cheddar. "If I had to put money on one of them," she mused, "I think I'd pick Graham Carmody."

"Why so?" asked Jory.

"Because of his familiarity with the layout at the Heritage Society. He's worked there several times as a waiter. Knows the kitchen and back hallways and such. Plus people don't usually give waiters a second glance. Especially when they're busy partying and schmoozing it up."

As the moon continued to rise, full and round in the night sky, they talked back and forth, tossing around various theories. Finally, people began spilling out of the concert hall.

"It's over?" said Theodosia. "We missed the entire second half?"

"Looks that way," said Jory.

Good heavens, she thought. *And we aren't any closer to*

finding an answer. But at least I feel better having talked it all over with Jory.

"Isn't that your Aunt Libby over there?" asked Jory. "With her friend?"

Theodosia peered at the spill of people pouring down the steps. "Yup, that's her."

"Want to go say hi?"

Theodosia smoothed her skirt and stood up, took Jory's hand firmly in her own. Together they crossed the plaza toward the oncoming rush of concert goers.

CHAPTER 19

HALEY CAST AN appraising eye at the yellow froth that bubbled in the top pan of her double boiler. It looked good, she decided, was sticking together nicely. Grabbing a wire whisk, she added the last of the sugar and lemon zest, then continued to whisk the mixture as it cooked. Finally, when her concoction began to thicken, she removed the pan from the stove and began to add soft fresh cream butter, feeding it in a little at a time.

"My goodness, Haley," marveled Drayton as he stepped into the kitchen, "it smells absolutely divine in here. What magic are you whipping up this morning?"

She held up the pan for him to see. "Lemon curd. And it *does* smell wonderful, doesn't it?"

"You're making *real* lemon curd?" he asked in amazement.

"Sure. It's a snap, really. Just four simple ingredients. Eggs, lemon, sugar, butter."

"Yes, but you have to know exactly what to *do* with the ingredients. And it's not just proportions, the cooking times are quite exacting, too. And then there's the double boiler thing."

"Are you saying I don't know how to make fresh lemon curd?" Haley demanded with a crooked smile.

"No, I'm just saying it's a tricky proposition at best."

"Proof's in the tasting," said Haley as she held up a wooden spoon with a swirl of yellow gracing the end.

Obediently, Drayton tasted the dollop of lemon curd. "Oh my goodness!" he exclaimed. "This *is* good. Sweet but subtly tart, too. Layers of flavor."

"My grandmother's recipe," explained Haley. "And if it's any consolation to you, those are the same things *she* said. Awfully tricky, got to get the proportions just so, and a double boiler is a must."

"But you mastered it," said Drayton, still impressed.

"Of course."

"And you plan to serve it with . . ." prompted Drayton.

"There's a couple pans of shortbread in the oven," said Haley. "But lemon curd keeps for a good month once it's refrigerated, so when we do cakes for afternoon tea, it'll make a great topping."

"Morning, Theo," Drayton called as he heard the back door click open. "How was the concert last night?"

"Yeah," called Haley, "I bet it was great, huh?"

Theodosia stood in the doorway of the tiny kitchen and nodded enthusiastically. "Wonderful." She didn't have the heart to tell them she'd listened halfheartedly to the first half, then spent the second half outside, trading cat burglar theories with Jory Davis.

"Timothy was playing first violin, I take it?" said Drayton as he grabbed a silver tray and followed Theodosia into the tea shop.

"And doing a masterful job," Theodosia assured him.

"I'm baffled as to how the man does it," said Drayton. "Poor Timothy is worried sick about the public opening of the Treasures Show tomorrow night, yet there he was playing with the symphony," said Drayton. "He's really quite remarkable."

"I agree," said Theodosia as the two copper tea kettles Drayton had put on to boil just minutes earlier began to sing their high-pitched duet. "So what's on tap for this morning?" she asked him.

Drayton reached overhead and pulled down tins and jars of loose tea. "I thought I'd do pots of Earl Grey and Assam, which are nice and mellow and traditional, although this particular Assam *is* a trifle malty. Then I'll mix things up with a couple blends, perhaps a cinnamon spice and a ginseng plum. Of course, if someone has a special request, we'll oblige them as always."

"Wonderful," said Theodosia. She still felt a little discombobulated from last night. After her intense discussion with Jory Davis, she'd had dreams about cat burglars all night long. *Got to get my head in the game,* she told herself as the door swung open and the morning's first customers came drifting in. *Stop worrying about creepy cat burglars.*

"Oh," said Haley as she sped past Theodosia with plates of shortbread topped with her still-warm lemon curd, "I forgot to give you this." She handed over a large brown envelope. "I guess someone must have slipped it under the door. Anyway, it was lying on the floor when I opened up this morning."

Theodosia took the envelope from Haley and glanced at it curiously. The envelope was a number ten, business size, made of brown craft paper. Glued to the front was a white label with a single typed word, *Theodosia.*

"Wonder what it is?" she said.

Haley, who was busy gathering napkins and placing forks on plates, shrugged. "Don't know," she said, unconcerned. "Maybe a thank-you note from someone who attended yesterday afternoon's reception?"

Theodosia grabbed a butter knife, slipped it under the

gummed flap of the envelope to open it. She pulled out a piece of paper and unfurled it. As she began to read, her brows knit together and a frown creased her normally placid face. It was a note all right, but not of the thank-you variety. Instead, a very strange message had been laser-printed on a sheet of plain white paper.

Twinkle, twinkle, little bat
How I wonder where you're at.
Up above the world you fly,
Like a tea-tray in the sky.

"What is it?" asked Haley, suddenly aware that Theodosia had gone silent.

Wordlessly, Theodosia handed the note to Haley and watched as she read it.

Haley's face changed from polite interest to utter confusion. "What the heck . . . ?" she said. "Is this crazy little ditty supposed to mean something?"

"It's a passage from *Alice in Wonderland,*" said Theodosia.

"Yeah, great. Fun kids literature and all that. But why send it to you? And without a signature yet. Is this supposed to be some kind of inside joke?"

"I'm not exactly sure," said Theodosia. "But I get the feeling that it might be . . . it could be . . . some kind of challenge."

"Holy smokes!" exclaimed Haley, realization starting to dawn. "Because you've been poking around . . . Hey, Drayton!" She motioned frantically for Drayton to come over to the counter.

Drayton came hustling over immediately. "What's wrong?" he asked, taking in the very sober looks on both their faces.

Haley thrust the mysterious note into Drayton's hands.

"Take a look. I found it stuck under the door this morning."

"Addressed to Theodosia?" he asked as he reached into his jacket pocket, pulled out his glasses, and slid them onto his nose.

They both nodded.

Drayton studied the note intently. Finally, he looked up and met their gazes. "It's a passage from Lewis Carroll's *Through the Looking Glass,*" he said.

Haley bobbed her head eagerly. "That's what Theodosia said. Gosh, you two are so incredibly well read. Makes me want to change my major back to English lit."

"Haley . . ." warned Drayton with an owlish look. "I don't think this was intended as a lighthearted little note."

"Theodosia called it a challenge," Haley told him.

"Indeed, it could be," said Drayton. "Witness the teatime reference that clearly relates to us."

"And what about the *little bat* business and *up above the world you fly?*" asked Haley.

"I don't know," said Drayton. "It's strange, I'll give you that much. I get the feeling they're slightly left-handed inferences as to what's been going on around here lately. Flying around, looking around, something like that."

"Mm-hm," said Haley, not completely absorbing all of Drayton's words.

"In other words, a taunt," said Drayton, heavily enunciating the *t*'s.

"You mean someone might be *daring* Theo to take them on?" asked Haley. "Someone being this cat burglar guy?"

"I suppose one could interpret it that way," said Drayton.

"Whoooa," said Haley. "Ain't that a kick."

"It means you've struck a nerve," said Drayton, looking directly at Theodosia.

Theodosia managed a thin smile. "Gulp," she said. She meant her remark to be humorous, but nobody laughed.

Drayton refolded the note, handed it to Theodosia. "We'd better talk about this when we're not so busy."

Theodosia was still standing at the counter with the folded note in her hand when Aerin Linley came bustling in a few moments later.

"Hey there," she greeted Theodosia. "Can I get a couple cuppas to go? Anything you've got ready is fine. As long as it's not sweet."

"Absolutely," said Theodosia, sliding the note across the counter and putting a little green Staffordshire teapot on top of it for safekeeping.

"You okay?" asked Aerin.

Theodosia looked up sharply. "Pardon?"

"Oh, you looked a little worried there for a moment. I would think you'd be doing handsprings right about now. Folks really went ga-ga over your T-Bath products yesterday afternoon. I hope you've called in a big reorder to your supplier."

"Don't worry," said Theodosia as she poured streams of freshly made Assam tea into dark blue take-out cups. "That's at the top of my to-do list today." Aerin's good humor was contagious and Theodosia was suddenly caught up in her enthusiasm. "I'm so glad you and Brooke were able to stop by."

"You know, I was perfectly serious about the TV show idea," Aerin said as she cocked her head and smile at Theodosia. In her pink cotton crewneck sweater, khaki slacks, and beige leather slip-on shoes, she looked very sporty, far younger than her thirty-six or thirty-seven years. "You'd be great on-air," Aerin said with encouragement. "You're so pretty and vivacious, I'm sure you could deliver a great segment."

"Actually," said Theodosia, warming up to the idea, "I'd *love* to do a tea segment. A few folks are still under the illusion that tea is the drink of choice for blue-haired ladies in pillbox hats. Nothing wrong with blue-haired ladies in hats, of course, but tea's really come into its own as a contemporary drink."

"You're darned right it has," said Aerin. "When kids are chugging premixed chai like water, you know tea has hit mainstream! Ohh . . ." she exclaimed as Haley rushed by with another tray of short bread and lemon curd. "Is that lemon curd? *Real* lemon curd? The kind you slave over a hot stove for?"

So, of course, Theodosia had to fill a small, square jar with lemon curd for Aerin to take along with her.

Jory Davis didn't call until they were caught up in the whirlwind that was lunch. "Hello?" said Drayton, deftly balancing the phone, a tray stacked with fruit and cheese plates, and a pot of tea.

"Hi, Drayton," said Jory. "Is Theodosia around?"

Drayton peered out over the tearoom and crooked a finger at Theodosia. She caught his meaning and signaled back. "She'll be with you in a second," Drayton told Jory.

Theodosia hurried across the room and snatched the phone up. "Hello?"

"Hey there," said Jory Davis.

"Hey there, yourself," said Theodosia. "You realize everyone here thinks I was soothed by music from *Rigolletto* and *La Traviata* last night."

"Well, you almost were," he said. "And admit it, wasn't snuggling under a full moon better?"

"You'll get no argument from me. Like I said last night, I can always listen to it on CD."

"Say," said Jory, "I know you're busy, heck, we're *both* busy, but I was able to work in some fast investigating this morning."

"Terrific. What did you come up with?" she asked.

Jory Davis sighed. "Nothing."

"Even on Graham Carmody?" Theodosia asked with surprise.

"Nada," said Jory. "No record. The guy's clean as a whistle."

"That's weird. I had a feeling there might be something."

"I couldn't even find an unpaid parking ticket," said Jory. "He's a model citizen."

"Hmm." Theodosia gazed out over the tea shop, noting that every table was filled and that Drayton and Haley were running around like chickens with their heads cut off. "Listen, why don't you come by for dinner tonight." She wanted to clue Jory in about the note that had been slipped under the door this morning, but right now wasn't the best time.

"Great!" said Jory.

"Hold on," said Theodosia. "I'm thinking about inviting Drayton and Haley, too."

"Oh, a *working* dinner," said Jory, with no less enthusiasm.

"When we get this cat burglar thing figured out," said Theodosia, "I promise dinner for two. With a full complement of candlelight and wine."

"And I shall bring the roses," laughed Jory. "Although I think I'll bring wine tonight as well. What time shall I plan to arrive on madame's doorstep?"

"Eight. And since you volunteered to bring wine, kindly make it white."

"I'll spend the rest of my day pondering the merits of a fine Vouvray versus a Chenin Blanc."

"Bye bye," she told him, laughing.

"My gosh," said Drayton, "I must have looked like the juggler in Cirque du Soleil, what with teapots in one hand and fruit and cheese plates in the other. Sometimes I yearn for the good old days when we only served tea."

"Adding a lunch service really has livened things up," agreed Theodosia.

"And contributed nicely to our bottom line," added Drayton.

Theodosia was keenly aware that they had run in the red for more months than she cared to think about. Now, this last year, they had clearly been in the black, with the last six months veering toward very respectable profits.

"Today will be a push from now on," declared Haley. "Friday afternoons are never all that busy. I guess people must take off early or go shopping or something. Anyway," she looked over at the three tables that were still occupied, "they're not here."

"How would the two of you like to join me for dinner tonight?" suggested Theodosia.

"Really?" squealed Haley. "I'd love to. I didn't have anything special planned."

"What about you, Drayton?" asked Theodosia. "I've invited Jory Davis to dinner, too."

"I'd be delighted," he said. "May I bring anything. Or do anything?"

"That goes for me, too," said Haley.

"Drayton, you just get yourself to my place by eight o'clock. Haley, if there's some leftover shortbread and lemon curd, maybe you could package it up and bring it along for dessert."

"Oops," said Haley, cupping a hand to her mouth. "We just served the last piece of shortbread. But there's still tons of lemon curd to use as topping. How about if I pop a cake in the oven?"

"Fine idea," declared Drayton.

"Only if it isn't too much work," said Theodosia. "After all, we're all still recovering from yesterday."

"I'm sure Haley can manage just fine," offered Drayton. "And if I could interject a thought, might I suggest a coconut cake?"

"Haley, can you manage?" asked Theodosia, amused by Drayton's ravenous desire for cake.

"Seeing how much it means to Drayton," she said, assuming an exaggerated hands-on-hips stance, "I'll try."

Detective Tidwell pushed open the door, eased himself into the tearoom. He let the door close behind him, yet made no effort to move to a table, preferring to stand there in an ill-fitting tweed jacket and pork pie hat, surveying the premises with a slightly haughty air.

Haley noticed him first. "Uh-oh," she said under her breath. "That *detective* is here again."

Theodosia looked over and gave a quick wave.

"He looks like he's been shrink-wrapped in tweed," murmured Haley.

"Ssssh," warned Drayton as he tried to stifle a grin and Theodosia hurried forth to greet Tidwell.

"Detective Tidwell, nice to see you again," said Theodosia in her best tea shop hostess patois. "Won't you have a seat?"

Tidwell shuffled to a table, lowered his bulk carefully.

"Can I offer you some tea?" asked Theodosia. *Goodness,* she decided, *in the wake of Tidwell's sullenness, I sound hideously chirpy.*

Tidwell gave a faint nod.

"Do you have a taste for anything in particular?" she asked.

"Surprise me," said Tidwell in an uncharacteristic move.

Theodosia bustled into the kitchen to scrounge a muffin while Drayton busied himself with a fresh pot of tea.

"Surprise him," Drayton muttered under his breath. "I'd like to surprise that fellow, all right."

Tidwell was already sipping his tea when Theodosia came back with a reheated muffin and small pot of peach jam.

"And this tea is . . ." said Tidwell, still not wasting any time on pleasantries.

"Earl Grey," said Theodosia. "Taste the bergamot?"

Tidwell gave a perfunctory nod. "I do. And a hint of something else, too."

"A touch of white tips," said Theodosia. "Just to lighten things up." White tips meant, literally, the white tips or most prized leaf of the plant.

"Excellent," said Tidwell, finally uttering a positive word. "I take it this is one of your own special Indigo Tea Shop blends?"

"Drayton created it. He calls it Shades of Earl Grey."

"Rather pleasant," responded Tidwell.

Theodosia smiled patiently. She was getting used to these strange exchanges with the venerable detective. They so often started out adversarial then veered toward semi-politeness.

Tidwell dribbled a spoonful of jam onto his muffin. "Not that you'd be interested, Miss Browning, but there has been a report of another theft in your neighborhood."

"Is that a fact?" said Theodosia. *Play it cool,* she told herself. *He's bursting to tell you, but if you ask him outright, he'll probably clam up.*

Tidwell shook his jowly head. "A rather expensive collectible disappeared last night from the Hall-Barnett House."

Built in the mid-eighteen-hundreds and located over on Tradd Street, the Hall-Barnett House had first served as a convent and then a private home. Now it was a small museum, a period house, furnished with the trappings of the era and open to the visiting public.

"I only mention it to you," added Tidwell, "because one of the items missing is a tea caddy."

Theodosia stared at him. *The tea caddy from the Hall-Barnett House was missing?*

"Ah," said Tidwell, noting her surprise, "you're familiar with that particular piece?"

"Of course," said Theodosia. "It's a lovely tea caddy

crafted from tortoiseshell and inlaid with ivory. It's probably from the mid-eighteen-hundreds yet still in excellent condition."

"Yes," agreed Tidwell. "Worth quite a pretty penny, I'm told."

Several thousand dollars, Theodosia thought to herself. "And it's disappeared?" she said to Tidwell.

"That's the strange thing," replied Tidwell. "Mrs. Roman, the woman who was guiding the tours yesterday afternoon, swears she saw the tea caddy sitting in its rightful place on the fireplace mantel. Right before she locked up late yesterday."

"Do you believe her?"

"No reason not to."

"Then what do you suppose happened to it?" asked Theodosia.

Tidwell's eyes burned brightly even as his face assumed a hangdog expression. "I suppose, Miss Browning, it could have caught the fancy of your cat burglar."

"The Hall-Barnett House was broken into?"

"Let's just say a window was open upstairs."

Theodosia conjured up a mental picture of the Hall-Barnett House. Built completely of brick, it was tall and stately, fashioned in the Italianate tradition. *Hard to clamber up the side of a brick building, though,* she decided.

"Did the police find a ladder anywhere?" she asked. "Lying in the yard or stashed in the carriage house out back?"

"Nothing," said Tidwell. "If I had to hazard a guess, although I prefer *not* to, I'd say your cat burglar probably scaled a nearby tree then made a rather heroic leap."

"Why do you keep calling him *my* cat burglar?" asked Theodosia, somewhat testily.

"Because you were the first one to put forth the cat burglar theory," said Tidwell. "Pray tell what's wrong? Aren't you pleased? Here I thought for sure that you'd be pleased."

"No, of course I'm not *pleased,*" she cried out, and the frustration that had built up inside her for the past week suddenly began to explode. "Poor Drayton and Timothy Neville are worried sick about the public opening of the Treasures Show tomorrow night. Captain Buchanan was *killed* at the Lady Goodwood Inn . . . probably in an accident caused by this very same cat burglar. And now, because someone, presumably this cat burglar, stole Delaine's watch and stashed it in Claire Kitridge's desk, Claire stands to lose her job! So no, Detective Tidwell, I am in no way pleased. I am angry, frustrated, and worried beyond belief, but the very last thing I am is pleased!"

Drayton, upon hearing Theodosia raise her voice to Tidwell, suddenly grabbed a pot of tea and hustled over to their table.

"Everything okay here?" he asked as he approached.

"Fine," said Tidwell, putting a chubby hand over his teacup. "No need for a refill."

Drayton pointedly ignored Tidwell and focused his lined countenance squarely on Theodosia. "Are *you* okay?" he inquired.

Theodosia shrugged and her voice was slightly tremulous. "Yes. I'm just feeling . . . embroiled . . . in this rapidly unfolding cat burglar mystery."

"I believe Haley needs you in the kitchen," said Drayton. Now he shifted his gaze to Tidwell.

Theodosia waved a hand. "Haley's fine, Drayton. She's doing . . . I don't know . . . the cake. Remember?"

"I am quite certain Haley is in need of your assistance," repeated Drayton. Now his stare turned into a glower and Tidwell seemed to squirm just a bit under Drayton's intense scrutiny.

"What's the problem?" asked Theodosia, still not picking up on his cue.

"There's a dire problem with the coconut," said Drayton. "A question of toasting or not toasting, I believe."

Now it was Tidwell's turn to look mildly disconcerted.

Theodosia rose from her chair suddenly. "Forgive me, Detective Tidwell, but there *is* a pressing business problem I must attend to."

"Very pressing, indeed. I understand," he said and walked out.

"Are you all right?" asked Drayton as he pushed his way into the kitchen. "Because that detective seemed far more annoying than usual."

"I'm fine, Drayton," replied Theodosia. She was sitting on a stool, sipping a cup of tea. "But thanks for the rescue, anyway. I was pretty much at the end of my rope."

"Glad to be of assistance," said Drayton. He reached over and picked up a small plate decorated with purple flowers that was sitting on Haley's small counter. "What's this?" he asked.

"Remember the muffin plate I dropped the other day?" said Theodosia. "Along with the teacup?"

Drayton nodded. As he studied the plate, recognition dawned. "Oh. This is the plate that broke in half!"

"Haley fixed it," said Theodosia.

"I superglued it," volunteered Haley. "I was going to toss the pieces out, but after I saw the charm bracelet Brooke created, and how delighted Theodosia was at her reclaimed treasure, I decided to try a little glue."

"It was very sweet of you, Haley," said Theodosia.

"Not bad," said Drayton, turning the muffin plate over. "You can hardly see the repair."

"Thanks," said Haley. "It turned out to be kind of a fun project."

"We might have to tap your services for the Heritage Society," grinned Drayton. "Put you to work in our restoration department. Maybe your talents run toward restoring old prints and photographs, too."

"Speaking of the Heritage Society," said Haley, "are you-all still going ahead with the opening tomorrow night?"

Drayton grimaced. "Yes, we are. Up until yesterday there were still nasty rumblings from the executive advisory committee about canceling or even delaying the public opening of the Treasures Show. But of course, Timothy Neville fought them tooth and nail. He's quite adamant about adhering to his predetermined schedule. Don't you know, all the invitations have been sent out and all the publicity done. So what else could Timothy do? Plus, he didn't want to look like an alarmist. After all, this cat burglar fellow could have moved on, just like Detective Tidwell suggested."

"He hasn't," spoke up Theodosia. "In fact, it seems there's been another break-in. Tidwell just told me about it. That's the reason I was so upset."

Drayton put a gnarled hand to his head, rubbed his gray hair. "Oh, no. Did he mention where?"

"The Hall-Barnett House," said Theodosia.

"Wow," said Haley. "What was snatched this time?"

"An antique tea caddy," said Theodosia.

Drayton and Haley just stared at her.

"Weird," said Haley finally.

"So, like the shark with his territorial feeding habits, this fellow is still circling the neighborhood," sighed Drayton.

"And it looks like he's making tighter circles," said Theodosia. "The Hall-Barnett House is just a couple blocks from here."

Haley shuddered. "That feels a little *too* close for comfort."

"This new information is absolutely appalling," declared Drayton, fingering his bow tie nervously. "Who else knows about this?"

"I honestly don't know," said Theodosia.

"If Timothy or the executive committee find out, they'll for sure cancel the opening," said Drayton glumly.

"Then don't tell them," piped up Haley.

They were all three silent for a moment.

"What if," said Haley finally, "what if we could concoct some kind of scheme? Something that would trap this guy for good?"

"We already tried that," snapped Drayton, obviously feeling dispirited and dejected.

"Not really," said Haley. "The electronic devices you set up weren't exactly a *trap.* You said yourself they were more of a security precaution."

"Which didn't work," said Drayton with a dispirited air.

"Because the *electricity* went off," offered Haley. "Not because you guys screwed up."

The timer on the oven suddenly emitted a loud *ding*. Startled, Drayton gave a little jump, then watched sheepishly as Haley slipped an oven mitt onto her hand and opened the oven door. The two round cake layers looked perfect. Beautifully golden brown and pocked with tiny bubbles like the surface of a miniature moon. Smiling, Haley pulled the two pans of coconut cake from the oven.

"Perfect," murmured Drayton as he gazed at the cakes.

Haley set the cakes to cool on the scarred wooden table. "You just said a mouthful, Drayton," said Haley. "Because what you need *this* time is the perfect plan."

He stared at her. "I'm sure I don't know what you're jabbering about."

Theodosia, deep in thought, suddenly spoke up. "Tell me, Drayton, what's the most valuable object that the Heritage Society has in their collection?"

Sidetracked by Theodosia now, Drayton scratched his chin thoughtfully. "I don't know. I suppose it would be a silver tray made by Paul Revere. The Calhoun family had it in their possession for ages until they donated it to us two years ago." He threw Theodosia a dubious glance, as though he knew exactly what she was thinking. "But I *hardly* think Timothy's going to allow us to use a valuable such as that for bait. Especially in light of how our efforts failed so miserably at protecting the Blue Kashmir in the European Jewel Collection."

"Exactly," said Theodosia. "Which means we're going to have to pull something out of a hat."

"What?" Drayton's voice rose in a squawk. "What are you talking about?"

"And," said Theodosia, "it's going to have to be a very tasty little item." She gazed at Drayton, her blue eyes sparkling, her enthusiasm suddenly back with a vengeance. "Drayton, your friend still writes the arts column for the *Post & Courier,* doesn't he?"

Drayton nodded. "Sheldon Tibbets? Yes, he's still doing a fine job of it. But I don't see what—"

"Do you think you could persuade Mr. Tibbets to compose a special little blurb for us?" Theodosia said in a rush.

"I suppose I could," said Drayton slowly.

"Excellent," said Theodosia as her energy seemed to increase by leaps and bounds. "Because we're going to take the liberty of *augmenting* the Heritage Society's collection."

Drayton narrowed his eyes. "What exactly do you mean by *augment*?" he asked.

Theodosia suddenly jumped down off her stool. "The three of us are going to come up with a glitzy, glamorous new objet d'art. Something that's utterly irresistible to a professional cat burglar. And as the icing on the proverbial cake, you, my dear Mr. Conneley, are going to persuade your good friend, Sheldon Tibbets, to give our fabulous new collectible a big write-up in tomorrow's paper!"

Drayton stared at her. "You've got to be kidding."

"I couldn't be more serious," said Theodosia. What had Timothy Neville said to her just a few days ago? She racked her brain. *Oh, yes, he said, "There's no guarantee the disaster of last Saturday night won't be repeated."*

"We're going to deliver a guarantee!" exclaimed Theodosia. "A treasure so tasty and utterly irresistible that it's *guaranteed* to attract every salivating cat burglar from here to Palm Beach!"

Drayton was shaking his head and his voice carried a dubious tone. "But what object could possibly do that?" he asked.

Theodosia thought for a moment, recalling an article about so-called investment collectibles that had run not too long ago in *Business Week* magazine. *Let's see,* she thought, *the article mentioned that sports memorabilia were very big today. As well as the ever-popular antiques and artwork. And gold coins. And what else?*

Theodosia suddenly pushed her way through the velvet draperies back into the tea shop. Puzzled, Haley and Drayton followed in her wake.

Theodosia stood poised in the middle of the Indigo Tea Shop, her eyes wandering as her mind struggled to spin out a plausible scenario.

Something rare, she told herself. Intriguing, mysterious, with a huge intrinsic value. As her eyes continued to wander, they fell upon the display of teas that sat on one of the wooden shelves behind the old brass cash register. There was a huge selection. Boxes of loose tea from Higgins & Barrow Tea, as well as from Toby & Sons, and Chelsea and Worther.

Suddenly, her eyes focused on the box of Dunsdale Earl Grey Tea. It bore a delightful label, pale green with a heraldic crest surrounded by elaborate flourishes. In the middle was a silhouette of some nobleman. Perhaps, she surmised, the founding Dunsdale himself.

Inspiration suddenly hit her.

"How about a postage stamp?" suggested Theodosia.

Drayton blinked. Any enthusiasm he seemed to be mustering suddenly drained out of him. "Theodosia, I'm sorry but I've been collecting postage stamps for almost thirty years and the rarest one I have is an 1861 two-cent Andrew Jackson with a double transfer on the top left corner. A delicious specimen, to be sure, but not quite in the lofty realm of rare stamps. Not in the ranks that might attract the attention of a cat burglar, anyway."

Theodosia smiled placidly as Drayton continued.

"And Timothy Neville's been collecting stamps for over *forty* years and the rarest piece in his collection is a block of four 1851 twelve-cent Washingtons." Drayton paused and pursed his lips, thinking. "We'd have to come up with something far, far better than those if we really wanted to tantalize our thief."

"Like what?" asked Haley.

Drayton thought for a moment. "The Pony Express collection is worth a fortune. But I can't imagine where we'd lay our hands on a set."

"What about a one-cent Z grill?" asked Theodosia.

Drayton stared at her. "The 1869 Benjamin Franklin with the Z grill background? Are you kidding?" he snorted. "*Nobody's* got a one-cent Z grill."

"Aunt Libby does," said Theodosia with sudden calm. Aunt Libby had inherited a very fine stamp collection from her grandfather, Theodosia's great-grandfather.

"Really?" squealed Haley. She grabbed for Drayton's arm, ready to do a little dance. "A Z grill!" She hopped up and down, did a quick shuffle, then stopped suddenly. "What's a Z grill?"

"An exceedingly rare philatelic specimen, that's what it is," said Drayton. He peered at Theodosia and cocked his head in disbelief. "Really? Your Aunt Libby has one?" Now he sounded like Haley. Incredulous.

Yes, Theodosia mused to herself, a rare postage stamp

would be perfect. Stamps in general were escalating in value, sometimes even outpacing other collectibles. Besides, rare stamps were portable, easy to hide, and relatively easy to cash in. They were an easy sell to private collectors, who were often compulsive about completing their prized collections. Who knows, a rare stamp might even be the perfect bait to lure a cat burglar.

Drayton was still looking eagerly at her, waiting for an answer. "You're quite sure it's a Franklin Z grill?"

Theodosia nodded and a slow smile spread across Drayton's face. "Yes," he murmured, "that's the ticket, then. A stamp so rare perhaps only a handful of top collectors know about it or have even seen one."

"What's the story?" asked Haley. "Why will it be on display?"

Theodosia thought for a moment. "We'll say it's part of Drayton's collection." She gazed at him, liking the sound of it. "Will that make good enough fodder for a newspaper article?" she asked.

"I'll call Sheldon Tibbets now," Drayton told her.

CHAPTER 20

CHICKEN PERLOO HAS long been a dinner time favorite in Charleston as well as the surrounding low-country. Really a type of pilaf or jambalaya, Chicken Perloo, usually pronounced PER-lo and sometimes spelled pilau, is a homey one-pot meal that combines chicken, onions, celery, butter, tomatoes, thyme, and that ever-popular Carolina staple, white rice.

Simmering and bubbling on the stove in Theodosia's kitchen, the Chicken Perloo emitted enticing aromas as Theodosia, Jory, Drayton, and Haley sat around Theodosia's dining table. First course was a citrus salad topped with sliced strawberries and toasted almonds.

"Are you sure we shouldn't check on the Chicken Perloo?" asked Drayton. He was seated closest to the kitchen door and was the one most tantalized by the flavorful aroma.

"Don't you dare lift the cover on that kettle," warned Theodosia.

Haley shook her head. "Why do men always want to take a peak?" she asked.

"Because that's how men are," said Jory Davis. "It's inherent in our nature. We're compulsive lid-lifters and oven-door openers." He took a sip of wine. "Curiosity is a wonderful thing," he added.

"Not when it causes a cake to fall," said Haley. "Remember that angel food cake I made last month? Drayton just couldn't resist. Had to sneak the oven door open and take a look. And what were the results of his unbridled curiosity? Bam. A nasty mess. The poor thing crashed like the Hindenburg."

"Why blame me, when the true culprit was the humidity," protested Drayton. "Everyone knows you can't bake angel food cake when the air is completely saturated with humidity."

"We hadn't had rain in days," said Haley. She slid out of her chair and began collecting the empty salad plates. "I'll help you serve, okay?" she said to Theodosia.

"Great," said Theodosia. "And if Jory could pour some more wine, I think we're set."

It was a perfect dinner. Morsels of fresh, plump chicken blended with the tomatoes, celery, onions, and moist rice in a rich milieu. Not quite a stew, not quite a gumbo. And with Jory's crisp white wine and a pan of fresh-baked corn muffins, nothing else was needed.

No one spoke of cat burglars or the dilemma at the Heritage Society until dessert, when Haley's cake and lemon curd were served. And then it was Theodosia who began the discussion by bringing Jory Davis up to speed on the strange note they'd received that morning.

"It does seem like a cryptic warning," he said as he held the note in his hands, studying it. "It's tempting to just blow it off or chalk it up to a disgruntled customer, but I don't think that's the case here."

"Neither do we," said Theodosia.

"So you think it's from this cat burglar guy, too?" Haley asked Jory as she began collecting plates.

"It's possible," said Jory. He stared across the table at Theodosia and concern was apparent in his face. "Tell me again about your idea for tomorrow night?"

Earlier in the evening, when Jory Davis had first arrived and she was still chopping celery, she'd mentioned her plan for putting a rare postage stamp on display at the Heritage Society tomorrow night. Now she filled Jory in about how Drayton had convinced his friend, Sheldon Tibbets, to write a short blurb about the Z grill to run in tomorrow's edition.

Jory Davis leaned back in his chair and chuckled. "Sounds good. Although I must say, you three have exceedingly *active* imaginations."

"But do you think it will work?" pressed Drayton.

"Why not," said Jory, suddenly switching to a more serious demeanor. "Of course, not being a stamp collector or . . . what's the technical term?"

"Philatelist," filled in Drayton.

"Not being a dedicated philatelist," said Jory, "the stamp sounds intriguing. But not something I'd risk life and limb for. However . . ."

He gazed across the table at Theodosia, bathed in the glow of pink candlelight.

"I think that professional thieves are probably also knowledgeable connoisseurs," continued Jory. "My guess is they have a fairly good grasp of today's market value for oil paintings and jewelry and stamps and such. That's what drives them." Haley set a dessert down in front of him and Jory immediately helped himself to a bite of cake. "Mmn, good. That might also be your cat burglar's Achilles' heel, by the way."

"What do you mean?" asked Haley, fascinated.

"My guess is their knowledge is their downfall. It's how they eventually get caught. A professional thief *knows* the value of his ill-gotten merchandise, yet often ends up trying to negotiate with fences or unsavory dealers who *don't.* If these dealers get an inkling that something *is* of real value, they could easily flip on their so-called customer, report it to the insurance company, and pocket a nice fat reward."

"And if a cat burglar sells his stolen goods on the Internet?" said Theodosia.

Jory Davis knew she was referring to Graham Carmody. "That's a different story," he said. He looked around the table. "Have you told them about Graham Carmody?" he asked her.

And so Theodosia quickly related her tale of going to Graham Carmody's house, snatching the black plastic garbage bag, and finding it stuffed with computer printouts from various Internet auction sites.

"Theodosia," chided Drayton, "you continue to trample the boundaries of what is prudent and safe. Going to this Graham Carmody's house alone was far too impulsive."

"Yeah," agreed Haley, "you should have asked us to go along with you. Make a real outing of it!"

Drayton glowered at Haley. "That's not what I meant and you know it!"

"But look at the valuable information she picked up," argued Haley. "Up until now, did you think this waiter was a viable suspect?"

Drayton shrugged. "It was anybody's guess," he said.

"Right," said Haley. "And look where we are now." She flashed a lopsided grin at Drayton, who did his best to ignore her.

"Let's talk about tomorrow evening," said Drayton. "I'm exceedingly nervous about pulling this off."

"I think we all are," said Theodosia. "But at least we'll have our whole cast of characters assembled there."

"Graham Carmody is on the list as one of the waiters?" asked Jory.

"His employers at Butler's Express assure me he'll be there," said Drayton.

"Are we keeping an eye on Cooper Hobcaw?" asked Haley. "I'm still suspicious of him after you told me about his nightly runs through the historic district."

"Cooper Hobcaw will be attending with Delaine," said Theodosia. "After all, she's on the committee for ticket sales."

"What if he's cooling off over Delaine and getting interested in Aerin?" asked Haley. "I mean, the two of them really had their heads together when I saw them. It looked fairly intense. Maybe he's up to something?"

"I'll stop by Delaine's store tomorrow morning and have a chat with her," said Theodosia. "See what I can find out."

"So who else needs to be covered?" asked Jory.

"Claire Kitridge," said Theodosia. "She's kind of a wild card in all this."

"Will she be at the opening?" asked Jory.

"Certainly not as an invited guest," said Theodosia.

"I hardly think Claire will be there," replied Drayton, "seeing as how the poor woman's been placed on suspension."

"I'll watch her," volunteered Jory. "I've always wanted to be on a stakeout anyway."

"I'll baby-sit Earl Grey," piped up Haley, "but if anything big happens, you guys better promise to call me."

"So we're set," said Theodosia. "Our bait will be in place, now all we have to do is see if anyone comes sniffing after it."

"To the hunt," said Drayton, raising his glass of wine in a toast.

Theodosia, Jory, and Haley raised their glasses to join him. "To the hunt," they chorused loudly, startling Earl Grey from his bed and prompting a hearty *woof.*

Haley giggled as their wine glasses came together in a mighty *clink.*

Only Theodosia did not join in the laughter. To her, this was no laughing matter.

CHAPTER 21

CLIP CLOP, CLIP CLOP. Two great gray Belgian draft horses dipped their noble heads and shuddered to a halt on Meeting Street. Behind them, sitting in the brightly painted red and yellow carriage, visitors perked up and listened with rapt attention as their guide began a slightly theatrical narration about two of Charleston's so-called "haunted" houses.

Halloween, or All Hallow's Eve, was tomorrow night and the various carriage tours that plied the lanes and cobbled streets of the historic district were making the most of the spooky legends and ghostly sightings that were so much a part of Charleston folklore.

Theodosia was out with Earl Grey this Saturday morning. Together they were enjoying the fine cool weather and stretching their collective legs. Today, however, Theodosia had opted not to jog, but rather to stroll leisurely through the historic district as she pondered what events might possibly transpire tonight at the Heritage Society's public opening of the Treasures Show.

She was both dreading and looking forward to tonight.

Hoping they'd be able to smoke this cat burglar out of his lair, of course, but nervous about the possibility of putting anyone in harm's way.

Cutting through Gateway Walk back to Church Street, Theodosia passed by St. Phillips's Cemetery. Tomorrow night children would dare each other to run through here, she thought. As if these poor departed souls could cause anyone harm. No, she decided, it was the living that threw a wrench into things. It was the living you had to watch out for.

"You be a good boy and wait here," Theodosia told Earl Grey as she clipped his leash to the wrought iron fence next to the building that housed Cotton Duck, Delaine Dish's clothing store. "I'll be back in a couple minutes."

Earl Grey plopped himself down on the sunny sidewalk and gazed up at Theodosia as if to say, *No problem, I could use a break anyway.*

"Well, lookie who's come to call," sang out Delaine as Theodosia entered the store. "Miz Theodosia Browning."

"Hi, Delaine," said Theodosia as she gazed about at the funkiness and opulence that characterized Cotton Duck. Racks overflowed with casual cotton outfits as well as elegant silks. Antique cupboards, their doors flung open, were filled with a luxurious array of cashmere sweaters, silk scarves, beaded bags, and sparkling costume jewelry. Delaine might be a little over the top, Theodosia decided, but she was utterly brilliant when it came to fashion merchandising. On every buying trip that Delaine made, she focused on a specific palette of colors. Sometimes the clothes and accessories she brought back featured brilliant jewel colors such as emerald, purple, and hot pink. Sometimes they were more subdued shades such as persimmon and mulberry and loden green. But whenever you shopped in Delaine's store, you were guaranteed to find fabulous outfits and accessories that matched and blended beautifully. It was quite a talent, Theodosia had to admit.

"I was just reading the *Post & Courier,*" said Delaine. "Sheldon Tibbits gave tonight's Treasures Show another nice write-up."

"Oh, did he?" said Theodosia with as much innocence as she could muster.

"I certainly had no idea Drayton's stamp collection was so . . . elaborate," said Delaine.

Theodosia decided *elaborate* was Delaine's code word for *valuable.*

"Drayton's been collecting for an awfully long time," said Theodosia.

Delaine reached out and straightened a display of leather handbags. "A Z grill stamp. Now that's something you don't see every day. Nice of Drayton to allow it to be shown tonight."

Theodosia turned her attention to a rack of skirts and grabbed a black skirt in an attempt to stifle a giggle. She was quite sure Delaine had never even *heard* of a Z grill stamp until this morning's article.

"Oh, no, not *that* one, dear," Delaine suddenly protested. "A long black skirt is far too somber for someone like you." She hurried to Theodosia's side, snatched the offending black skirt from Theodosia's hands, and pawed hastily through the rest of the rack.

"This is what you need," she declared triumphantly as she held up a long, elegant silver skirt cut from thin crinkley cloth. *"Très elegant?"* she asked.

"It *is* gorgeous," Theodosia admitted as she gazed at the shimmery skirt.

"Perfect for tonight," declared Delaine. "If you pair it with . . ." Her eyes roamed across the stack of sweaters. "Ah, here's the perfect match," she said as she pulled a sweater out. "A perfect pearl gray cashmere. Cool and understated, but still delivering a hearty dose of va-voom."

Theodosia stood back and appraised the outfit. It was gorgeous. Silver and pearl gray. Very ice maidenish. Or

Swarthmore 'sixty-two. She could accent the clothing with what? A colored gemstone pin? Maybe her garnet earrings?

Delaine held the clothes out enticingly. "Want to try them on?" Then, without waiting for an answer, Delaine spun on her heel. "Janine," she shrilled loudly to her perpetually harried assistant. "Put Theodosia in the large dressing room, will you?"

Minutes later Theodosia was out of the dressing room and doing a pirouette in front of the three-way mirror.

"Lovely," declared Delaine.

"Lovely," parroted Janine, who was perennially red-faced from rushing around trying to follow Delaine's often contradictory directives.

Theodosia smiled at herself in the mirror. Never had she once heard poor Janine express an opinion of her own. Then again, Delaine was opinionated enough for an entire room full of people. Oh well. She peered in the mirror again. Hmm . . . the outfit *did* look good. The long silver skirt gave her a nice, lean silhouette and the pearl gray cashmere sweater, which was baby-bunny soft, made her auburn hair shine. Yes, she decided, she'd wear the garnet earrings Aunt Libby had given her. Definitely.

"You'll wear it tonight?" asked Delaine, vastly confident in her recommendation.

"Why not," said Theodosia, throwing up her arms in mock defeat.

"Janine, be sure to let Theo take the skirt on a hanger," Delaine told her. "Don't go folding it or anything," she cautioned.

"Yes, ma'am," said Janine.

"I imagine you're looking forward to tonight as well," said Theodosia, catching Delaine's eyes in the mirror.

"A lot of us have worked very hard on this exhibition," said Delaine who, Theodosia knew, had headed ticket sales. "So yes, I am. As long as there are no *unusual* surprises."

"Coop will be there with you tonight?" asked Theodosia.

"Wouldn't miss it," Delaine declared breezily.

CHAPTER 22

"I HOPE YOU realize," said Timothy Neville as he pulled Drayton aside, "that philatelists all over Charleston are positively drooling!"

Drayton wrung his hands nervously. "This wasn't actually my idea . . ." he began.

Timothy stared back at him with hooded eyes.

"This rare stamp display was Theodosia's brainstorm," explained Drayton. "Honestly. The stamp isn't mine. The Z grill really belongs to her Aunt Libby," he whispered.

Timothy gave a sharp nod, then gazed over at Theodosia, who was busily engaged in conversation with Delaine Dish and Cooper Hobcaw. Suddenly, an uncharacteristic grin split Timothy's ancient, sharp-boned face. "So that's the story, is it? Well good. Now let's just hope her little plan works!" he declared, giving Drayton a firm thump on the back.

"Isn't this fun," drawled Delaine, giving a little shiver as she slid her wrap off her bare shoulders. "Can you believe how many folks have turned out? I knew ticket sales were going well, but this is absolutely splendiferous!"

Cooper Hobcaw gave her an approving grin. "That's my girl," he told her. "Hits a home run every time."

The first night of the Treasures Show looked very much like a rousing success as hundreds of people streamed into the Heritage Society's great stone building. The red-carpeted lobby was thronged with new arrivals making the requested fifteen-dollar donation, and a waiting line of previously ticketed guests had already formed in the hallway that led to the exhibition rooms.

"Theo," said Drayton as he put a hand on her shoulder, "a moment of your time, please."

"You're looking dapper tonight," cooed Delaine as Theodosia turned her attention toward Drayton.

"And you, Miss Dish, are as ravishing as ever," Drayton said to Delaine, favoring her with a genteel half-bow.

"Don't you ever get tired of being obsequious?" Theodosia asked him as they hurried down the corridor together.

"Me? Never," declared Drayton with a sly grin. "Obsequious is my middle name. Drayton Obsequious Conneley. In fact, you can just call me Drayton O."

At the end of the corridor, Drayton steered Theodosia around a corner, slipping past the purple velvet cord that kept visitors in line, and led her into the largest of the two galleries.

It was a sight to behold.

The large gallery, paneled in cypress wood, gleamed with a welcoming glow. Tables and glass cases displayed the finest treasures from the Heritage Society's sizable collection. A collection of antique pewter tankards rested on a Hepplewhite sideboard. Silver candlesticks and gleaming bowls adorned a revolving Sheraton drum table. On a French Empire card table reputed to have once belonged to Napoleon was an antique Japanese Imari bowl.

Entranced, Theodosia's eyes drank in the various displays. Here was a portrait by Alice Ravenel Huger Smith, an eighteenth-century painter who had immortalized many of the old Carolina rice plantations in her moody, sienna-tinged paintings. And here were a dozen original Audubon prints. And hung on the back wall, a half-dozen painted portraits from the mid-seventeen-hundreds done by Charleston artist Jeremiah Theus.

"Oh, my," said Theodosia, "this is very impressive. You and Timothy and the rest of the crew have worked absolute wonders."

"Tasty pickings, no?" said Drayton. "And look over here." He guided Theodosia to a fall-front mahogany Chippendale desk that was lit from above by pinpoint spotlights. On it sat a collection of antique desk ware—a silver inkwell and matching pen, an ornate French clock of gilded bronze, a silver snuffbox. Propped in front of those accouterments was a bound leather stamp album and displayed on a tiny glass pedestal next to it was the one-cent Z grill stamp. In the dim room, with just the lights from above, the blue stamp with the somewhat stern portrait of founding father Benjamin Franklin did look rather tantalizing. Especially in light of the rather boastful write-up it had received.

Theodosia's mouth twitched in a grin. "It's perfect," she declared.

"Does it look like bait?" asked Drayton under his breath.

Theodosia nodded. "I'm itching to grab it myself."

Reaching into the pocket of his gray wool suit, Drayton pulled out an antique pocket watch. "Eight o'clock on the noggin," he said. "So everything is in place for our little game?"

"Jory Davis is stationed outside Claire Kitridge's house even as we speak," said Theodosia. "Jory's got his cell phone, so he'll call and let us know if anything's going on. We don't expect Claire to show up here tonight, but if she does leave her house and heads for the Heritage Society . . . or anywhere, for that matter . . . we'll be the first to know."

"Outstanding," said Drayton. He gazed about the room, let his gray eyes settle once again on the display case that held the rare postage stamp. "Well," he said. "We know that Graham Carmody is here tonight—"

"You've seen him?" interrupted Theodosia. "You're *sure* he's here?"

Drayton nodded. "Last I peeked he was restocking crackers and tidbits of cheese at the buffet table."

"And we know Cooper Hobcaw is here because we just saw him with Delaine."

"Right," said Drayton. "So . . . we've got all our bases covered."

"We *hope* they're covered," said Theodosia as her cell phone beeped from inside her beaded evening bag.

She fished the phone out and pushed the *receive* button. "Hello?"

"It's me," said a voice on the other end of the line.

"It's Jory," Theodosia whispered to Drayton. "You're still at Claire Kitridge's house?" she asked with a shiver of anticipation.

"Not exactly," replied Jory. "Claire came out of her house about twenty minutes ago and jumped in her car."

"She's headed here!" cried Theodosia.

"No," said Jory, chuckling. "I tailed her for a couple miles until she pulled into some church parking lot. The Divine Redeemer, I think it was. Anyway, I think Claire's in there with some women's tatting group."

"You're sure she didn't sneak out the back?" asked Theodosia.

"Her car's still here."

Theodosia suddenly felt deflated. She'd been sure that if Claire was on the move, she'd be heading for the Heritage Society. "You're positive she's still inside?" she asked, disappointment in her voice.

"Yes, I'm sure she's in there," said Jory. "There's lacy stuff spread out all over the place."

Theodosia slid her cell phone back into her purse and looked around for Drayton. He seemed to have disappeared somewhere, but Timothy Neville was standing nearby, giving a glowing history of the Napoleon French Empire card table to a young couple.

"Timothy," she called.

Timothy excused himself and came over to Theodosia.

"Everything looks wonderful," she told him.

"Appearances are so deceptive, are they not?" he said as he pulled a letter from his jacket pocket. "Because things are *not* wonderful in the least."

"Timothy, what's wrong?" asked Theodosia.

"I received an envelope via messenger a few minutes ago. From Claire Kitridge." He handed the envelope to Theodosia. "Perhaps you'd like to see for yourself."

Theodosia flipped open the envelope. Inside a folded letter was a faded photograph, a black-and-white photo of two women standing in front of what looked to be a car from the early sixties. Big hood ornament, fins on the rear fenders. Theodosia continued to study the photo carefully.

"Oh no," she said finally.

"Oh yes," said Timothy.

Theodosia stared into Timothy's old face and saw sadness. "She's wearing the antique brooch," said Theodosia.

"In a photo that appears to have some age on it," added Timothy.

"So this is pretty much proof positive that the brooch *did* belong to Claire Kitridge."

"Read the letter. She states how the brooch has been in her family for quite some time. Passed down from her great-aunt."

"This still doesn't explain why Delaine's watch was found in her desk drawer, but it certainly clears her on the rumor of possibly selling stolen goods," said Theodosia slowly. She bit her lip. Still . . . this was not good. Not good at all. A lot of people had jumped to conclusions and now Claire Kitridge was left to pay the price. Feeling a bit sheepish, she decided she'd have to call Jory immediately and tell him to abandon his vigil at the church.

"I should never have listened to the executive committee," lamented Timothy. "I feel totally responsible for this."

"It's not your fault, really," said Theodosia. "A lot of us jumped to conclusions."

Timothy continued to look unhappy.

"Do you think you could persuade Claire to return to her job at the Heritage Society?" asked Theodosia. "Once this watch business is cleared up?"

Timothy shrugged. "Claire may still be upset and feel that unfair accusations will always be hanging over her head."

"Then what?" asked Theodosia.

"Then it's our profound loss," said Timothy.

Two hours rolled by and still nothing happened. Graham Carmody and the rest of the waiters began packing up all the dirty serving platters and leftover food and carried everything out to a white caterer's van that said BUTLER'S EXPRESS on the side. Now, as Theodosia and Drayton peered out the window at Graham Carmody, he was standing in a puddle of light with two other waiters, smoking a cigarette.

Theodosia made a quick appraisal of him. His tie was loosened, his shock of ginger-colored hair slightly disheveled, and he seemed tired. In fact, Graham Carmody didn't look at all like a professional cat burglar who was biding his time, poised to strike. He looked like a slightly pooped waiter who was about to go home, put his feet up, and catch the late-night headlines on CNN.

"You think he's going to make a move?" asked Drayton hopefully.

"Are you kidding? The man looks like he's barely *able* to move," said Theodosia.

Drayton yawned. "I know the feeling."

"What a washout," said Theodosia. "I was sure something was going to pop tonight."

"Let's go back and check the two galleries," said Drayton. "Make sure."

"Okay," agreed Theodosia.

On their way back through the kitchen and down the hallway, they ran into Delaine and Cooper Hobcaw. Delaine was still flitting about like a social butterfly, chitchatting with guests, bragging about ticket sales, but Cooper Hobcaw looked as if he was ready to pack it in for the evening.

"Having fun?" Theodosia asked him.

Cooper Hobcaw stifled a yawn. "I'm out on my feet and Delaine here is still going strong."

"No jogging tonight?" said Theodosia.

"No nothing tonight," he told her.

Timothy was suddenly at Theodosia's side, touching her arm. Pulling her aside, he cast a glance about. When he was sure no one would overhear their conversation, he spoke.

"That waiter you had suspicions about?" said Timothy. "I spoke with him just a few moments ago. He was telling me how much he enjoyed the Treasures Show. It seems he's an amateur antique dealer himself. Spends every free moment scouring estate sales and flea markets for various items."

"Yes . . ." said Theodosia, waiting for the other shoe to drop.

"Then he sells them on the Internet," said Timothy.

"Graham Carmody told you this?" asked Theodosia.

"Yes," said Timothy. "He mentioned that he used to

have a booth in one of the North Charleston antique malls, but now he does far better selling his finds on the Internet auction sites."

Oh, lord, thought Theodosia. *Did we leap to conclusions about Graham Carmody, too?*

"Did you mention this to Drayton?"

Timothy nodded. "Yes, I just spoke to him." He cast a quick glance over Theodosia's shoulder. "Here he is now."

"So Timothy's told you?" asked Drayton. "About Graham Carmody?"

"Afraid so," said Theodosia.

The three of them drew deep breaths and stared at each other for a few moments.

"Let's look at the positive side," said Theodosia. "We've just eliminated Claire Kitridge and Graham Carmody as suspects."

"At least for tonight," added Drayton. "I suppose any one of them could *still* be our thief." If anyone could sound down but still hopeful, it was Drayton.

"What about this Cooper Hobcaw fellow?" asked Timothy. "You were so suspicious of his late-night jogs."

"Cooper Hobcaw didn't even seem to *notice* any of the objects," said Drayton. "He just followed Delaine around with a slightly morose look on his face." Drayton looked about quickly. "If you ask me, Hobcaw's not as charmed by Delaine as he once was."

"Maybe, just maybe," said Theodosia, "our cat burglar decided it was far too risky to hit the Heritage Society a second time."

"Maybe," said Drayton, but his heart wasn't in it.

"Thank God," said Timothy, relief apparent on his face.

Theodosia reached for the old man's hand. "Timothy," she said, "thank you for letting us set this up tonight. I know you took a terrible risk."

"Theodosia," Timothy replied, his eyes bright with intensity, "if you can do anything, and I do mean *anything* to help get the Blue Kashmir necklace returned, I will be forever grateful."

It was eleven o'clock by the time Theodosia made her way upstairs to her apartment above the Indigo Tea Shop. She'd talked with Jory Davis on her cell phone one last time, thanked him profusely for keeping tabs on Claire Kitridge, then bid him good night.

She unlocked the door at the top of the stairs and pushed her way into her kitchen before realization dawned that she'd forgotten to swing by Haley's apartment to pick up Earl Grey.

"Oh rats," she said out loud, then stopped suddenly in her tracks.

Did I leave the light on in the dining room?

She thought she'd turned everything off except for the little light over the kitchen sink. That light was still on, winking at her. But there was a definite glow coming from beneath the door that led to the dining room.

Okay, then. Maybe Haley already let Earl Grey in. And he's in there now, curled up on his bed. Or on the couch. That hadn't been part of their plan, but with Haley, who knew what could happen? She was like a miniature sidewinder, always going off in different directions.

Well, decided Theodosia, *only one way to find out.*

Her heart pounding mildly, she pushed open the swinging door that led from the kitchen to her dining room and stepped gingerly into the room.

Every light in the dining room and adjacent living room was on! The cut glass chandelier hanging above the polished oak dining table blazed brightly.

And there, in the dead center of her dining room table, sat a tea caddy!

Theodosia stared at it, barely daring to breathe. The mild pounding in her chest suddenly accelerated to double time.

Is that the tea caddy that was stolen two days ago from the Hall-Barnett House? she wondered. She stared at the highly polished tortoiseshell. *Has to be.*

What is it doing here? Better yet, how did it get here?

Figure all that out later, her brain suddenly flashed. Just get out! And get out now!

Theodosia whipped down the stairway, made a mad dash across the cobble stone alley, and pounded on the door of Haley's small garden apartment. Theodosia could see that a light was still on and she could hear faint music.

"Haley, let me in!" Theodosia called.

"Is that you, Theo?" came Haley's voice from the other side of the door.

"It's me," Theodosia answered. "Open up. Hurry!"

"Oh, hi," called Haley as the lock was unlatched and the chain unhooked from the door. The door swung open inward and Haley appeared, dressed in pajamas and fluffy slippers. "Come for your good dog, I suppose . . ." began Haley. Then she stopped, her smile frozen in place as she caught the look of fear and utter confusion on her dear friend and employer's face.

"Theodosia," she said. "What's wrong?"

"Remember that sleepover we talked about?"

Haley nodded.

"This is it. Someone's been inside my apartment."

"They broke in?" Haley asked, horrified, as she grabbed Theodosia by the arm and pulled her quickly inside.

"I . . . I think maybe the lock might have been picked," said Theodosia.

"Oh my god, we've got to call the police!" exclaimed Haley as she threw her apartment door closed, quickly turned the dead bolt, and scrambled to refasten the chain.

Theodosia watched as Haley dove for the phone. *I'm in a mild state of shock,* Theodosia decided. *Things seem a little hazy and it feels like everything's happening in slow motion.* She shook her head, tried to clear her brain.

"Do you remember the note that someone left yesterday morning?" Theodosia finally asked Haley.

"The *twinkle twinkle little bat* note?" said Haley. She stood, poised, ready to dial 911.

"I think it might have been the same person," said Theodosia. "Only this time they didn't leave a note. They left a tea caddy."

"What?" exclaimed Haley. She put a hand to her forehead in a gesture of incredulousness. "The one that . . . ?"

Theodosia pumped her head in agreement. "I think it's the *exact* same tea caddy that was stolen from the Hall-Barnett House."

"Wow," breathed Haley and her eyes were round as saucers. "This whole thing is getting very, very weird."

CHAPTER 23

THE KNOB RATTLED, then pounding sounded on the door of the Indigo Tea Shop. "Are you open?" called a voice from outside. "Can we come in for tea?"

Drayton went to the door, peered through the leaded pane at the little group of visitors that stood on the doorstep.

"I'm sorry," he told them. "We're closed today." He glanced over at Theodosia, who sat sprawled at the table nearest the little stone fireplace. The lights were on, a tea kettle was whistling and bubbling, but they were most definitely closed. He also had the distinct feeling that if these strange events didn't come to a head sometime soon, they might be closed for a few *more* days.

Last night had been a nightmare for Theodosia. The police had shown up and scouted through her apartment looking for signs of a forced entry. They had found none.

They'd been equally puzzled over the mysteriously appearing tea caddy that sat on her dining room table. Half-heartedly accepting Theodosia's story that it had been stolen earlier, they'd checked back with headquarters at her urging and confirmed that, yes, indeed, a tea caddy fitting that same general description *had* disappeared some two days earlier from the historic Hall-Barnett House.

Theodosia had been at a loss to explain the sudden appearance of the tea caddy in her home and the police hadn't pressed her for details. Just took the tea caddy into their possession and requested that she sign a receipt acknowledging their removing it as evidence.

She and Earl Grey had spent a restless night at Haley's. And first thing this morning, Theodosia had given Drayton a call. It had been his suggestion that they meet at the Indigo Tea Shop and try to figure out a next step.

"Did you call Jory about this?" Drayton demanded as he poured a cup of Assam for Theodosia.

"No, I didn't want to worry him," said Theodosia.

"That's precisely why you *should* call him," responded Drayton. "Because he will undoubtedly be very worried about you."

"I know," she said, taking a sip of the hot tea, letting the sweet, slightly malty flavor refresh and revive her. "Gosh, this is good. Really hits the spot."

"Towkok Estate," Drayton told her. "I thought we deserved to treat ourselves, today of all days."

Drayton knelt down, constructed a little pile of kindling in the fireplace, struck a match to it, and fanned the flames briskly. Once the kindling was crackling nicely, he added a couple of medium-sized logs to the fire.

"Drayton," said Theodosia, "I think that tea caddy was meant as another taunt."

He stood up, looking remarkably poised, and pocketed the matches. "I'm sure it was."

Theodosia peered at him anxiously. "Is it someone close to us?"

Drayton frowned. "Hard to say," he said, staring into the fireplace. "Maybe we miscalculated with the stamp," he said finally.

"What do you mean?" asked Theodosia.

Drayton rocked back on his heels, stuck his hands in his pants pockets, jingled his change. "Not enough of a lure?" He pulled his hands from his pockets, fidgeted some more. "To be perfectly honest, this whole charade made me extremely nervous. And people *did* ask a lot more questions than I thought they would last night. I felt like I had to keep *explaining* things."

Theodosia's brows knit together upon hearing this. "What do you mean, Drayton? What did you *tell* them?"

"Exactly what we rehearsed. The Z grill stamp, issued in eighteen sixty-nine, Benjamin Franklin, blah, blah, blah." He grimaced slightly. "But I still felt like a fraud, seeing as how it's not really part of my collection."

"Did you tell people the stamp was staying on display?" Theodosia asked.

"Heavens no," exclaimed Drayton. "I made it quite clear that this was a one-time event. That I was returning the stamp to my personal collection the very next day." He shook his head. "I really *hated* saying that."

Theodosia stared at him. "That's what you told people? Really?"

"Awful, isn't it? I feel like such a liar when it's not even my stamp. What happens if a bunch of reputable collectors ever ask to see it? I'm cooked." He sat down at the table across from Theodosia, stared at his tea.

A smile suddenly formed on Theodosia's face. Her blue eyes began to twinkle. "Drayton, you're a genius."

He looked up from his tea sharply. "What?"

"You heard me. A genius."

"I am?" He looked pleased yet befuddled, quite unsure as to what his great brain power status was being attributed.

"Don't you see?" began Theodosia excitedly. "Knowing it was on display for one night only, the thief might decide to come looking at *your* house."

Drayton's face suddenly dissolved into worry. "Oh no. That's not good at all. Especially when it won't even be there."

"Are you kidding?" said Theodosia. "This is a terrific break!" She grinned. Yes, she thought to herself, it suddenly made perfect sense. The bait had been there for the taking last night. But then Drayton, in all his nervousness about the stamp, had related his little story about the stamp being on loan just for the opening night. That it would soon be returned to his own private collection. So, if the thief had truly been intrigued by the Z grill stamp, he had to figure it would be much easier to break into Drayton's house than risk a second attempt at the Heritage Society!

Theodosia looked at her watch. "I'd say we've got some serious planning to do."

Drayton gave her a skeptical look. "For what, pray tell?"

"We've got to be ready in case that cat burglar decides to break into your house tonight."

"My house? Tonight?" His voice rose in protest. "Oh, no. I don't think so." He crossed his arms resolutely and shook his head.

"Oh yes," urged Theodosia. "This could be our big chance."

"I'd feel far more confident if we called the police," Drayton argued.

"I did that last night. They didn't seem to have any brilliant suggestions."

Drayton considered this. "True," he allowed.

"In fact, they seemed to have no clue as to how the cat burglar even got in my house," said Theodosia.

Drayton frowned. "I thought you said the locks had been picked."

"Actually, I think our cat burglar came across a series of rooftops, jumped a five-foot span, and snuck in through the dormer in my bedroom."

Drayton stared at her. "Have you suddenly gone psychic? Whatever made you compose *that* elaborate scenario?"

"There's a tiny scuff on my window ledge," said Theodosia. And indeed, there had been. Just the tiniest, minutest scuff. Nothing you'd really notice, unless you'd just dusted a couple days before and were quite sure it hadn't been there then.

Drayton continued to stare in surprise. "A scuff. You base your theory on a scuff?"

"And a hunch," said Theodosia. "A very weird hunch. Trust me on this, Drayton. There's someone out there who adores playing games. Leaving notes, planting clues, playing both sides. And I think there's a very distinct possibility they're going to show up tonight."

"Halloween night," he said. "Why on earth would they choose Halloween night to appear?"

Theodosia considered Drayton's question. "I think," she said, "it would appeal to their sense of play. Now . . . are you in or not?"

Drayton rolled his eyes, plucked nervously at his bow tie. "Of course I'm in," he replied finally. "After everything that's happened, how could I not be?"

CHAPTER 24

THE MOON, STILL a fat round globe with barely a scant wedge missing from it, slid into the night sky above Charleston and shone down through skeletal tree branches. On most every step, stoop, and piazza of the elegant homes in the historic district, fat, orange pumpkins squatted, their innards replaced with flickering candles. Trick-or-treaters in fluttering capes and costumes ran wildly down cobblestone lanes, drinking in the excitement and magic that was All Hallows' Eve.

At exactly seven o'clock, Drayton exited his house, a one-hundred-sixty-year-old brick and wood home that had once been owned by John Underwood, a Civil War surgeon. He made a big production of locking his front door, then stepped jauntily down Montagu Street toward the Heritage Society. Two of his friends, Tom Wigley and Clark Dickerson, would be waiting for him there. He'd phoned them earlier and arranged to hold an elaborately staged meeting that had absolutely nothing to do with Heritage Society business.

The only thing the three men were going to do was talk,

shuffle papers, and sit in one of the meeting rooms with the lights blazing like mad, maintaining the illusion of an important, productive meeting. Anyone peering in from the street would see Drayton participating in this meeting. And know that he was, therefore, not at home.

Theodosia, on the other hand, had been sequestered in the small closet in Drayton's study for the last half-hour or so.

She had assured Drayton that she was going to phone Detective Tidwell on her cell phone, explain exactly what they were up to, and request that he send over a couple of uniformed police officers to keep watch over Drayton's house.

But she hadn't.

Instead, Theodosia was crouched in the confines of the small closet with Earl Grey snuggled beside her, his elegant head resting gently in her lap.

Outside the closet, barely six feet from where she sat, was Drayton's desk where one of his stamp albums lay enticingly open. Rows of plastic-encased stamps that hearkened back to Revolutionary War days filled its pages. This album was propped up against a second leather-bound stamp album. Next to these albums was a smattering of first-day covers, rare stamps that had been postmarked on their first day of issue, and of course, Aunt Libby's Z grill stamp. At the last minute, Drayton had added a few extra props to make it look, as he put it, "not so much like a stage set." A pack of gum, silver letter opener, a leather box filled with paper clips, Haley's bottle of superglue, and a small notepad with some random scribbles on it.

This desk top still life was lit by a single Tiffany lamp that sat on Drayton's desk, which was not really a desk at all but a sturdy old oak library table. The rest of the small twelve-by-fourteen-foot room was lined with bookcases that sagged with all manner of books—fiction, history, poetry, gardening, and cooking. In one corner was an overstuffed leather chair. On the wall opposite the closet where Theodosia sat waiting was a small window that looked out over the back garden.

Theodosia knew that if their cat burglar was going to show tonight, there was a very good chance he'd come in through that window. On the other hand, because Drayton had a prize collection of Japanese bonsai trees, a tall wooden security fence had been constructed around the backyard to make it virtually impenetrable.

So . . . Theodosia told herself, the cat burglar would have to scale the wooden fence, *then* come in through the window. Not exactly a difficult feat for someone who had leapt to her window ledge or climbed the live oak tree outside the Hall-Barnett House or clambered across the glass roof at the Lady Goodwood Inn.

Minutes ticked by slowly as Theodosia sat in the darkness, wondering who, if anyone, might show up.

A few moments ago, there had been knocking at the front door. Small, tentative knocks at first that had escalated into a couple of real whaps. Unhappy trick-or-treaters, no doubt, who'd been hoping for a handout of candy bars or popcorn balls.

Now there was only silence.

Theodosia put her hand to the old brass doorknob on the inside of the closet door, turned it slowly, heard the catch release. Slowly, she pushed the closet door open. An inch at first, then two inches. Now she could see the desk and the little puddle of light that lit the stamp and the stamp albums. Next to it was the office clutter that Drayton had arranged.

Theodosia pushed the door open another two inches. Now she could see part of the window.

Better, she thought as she rested her head against the back wall of the closet and slid a piece of remnant carpet underneath her so the sagging old hickory floor wouldn't be *quite* so hard. Earl Grey, trying to get comfortable himself, had pushed away from her and snuggled himself into the far corner of the closet. Now the dog was curled up in a ball, nose to tail, behind an old leather foot stool that had been shoved in the closet.

Theodosia had sat with her eyes closed for the better part of forty minutes when she heard a faint sound. She watched as the tips of Earl Grey's ears lifted slightly, then relaxed again.

Must be nothing, she told herself.

Scrtch scrtch.

There it was again. A faint scratching.

What is it? She strained to hear. Dry leaves sliding across patio bricks? Kids running down the back alley, their witches capes and superhero costumes rustling in the wind?

Probably.

And yet . . . there it was again. Not really footsteps. But . . . *something.*

Theodosia glanced over at Earl Grey. Now the top of his nose was visible above the foot stool. She held her hand out toward him, palm forward. The hand signal that told him to stay. She could see one of his shiny brown eyes watching her intently.

Then she heard it. A small *creak.* The outside shutter on the window being moved just so? Moved by the wind? She thought not.

Fear suddenly gripped her heart and she had to remind herself that the window was locked. If someone intended to break in, they'd have to break the glass. And if *that* happened, she'd hit 911 on her cell phone.

Now a different sound. Faint, almost imperceptible.

The window in Drayton's office slid up with a low groan.

Ohmygod. Someone must have inserted some kind of tool in the lock and popped it. Probably the same kind of flexible metal bar that police use when you lock your keys in your car!

She hadn't counted on this. Now, any movement in the closet, any dialing of 911, would be immediately detected.

Theodosia held her breath. This was not good, she decided. Not good at all.

She leaned forward slowly, peering through the darkness at the window.

A leg eased itself slowly over the sill and down toward the floor. A leg encased in black lycra. Wearing a shoe of soft brown leather. The kind of shoe that looked very sporty, but could also be worn for rock climbing.

In that instant, Theodosia suddenly understood the identity of the mysterious cat burglar.

It wasn't Cooper Hobcaw, who'd roused her suspicions with his late-night runs through the historic district. And it sure as heck wasn't the waiter, Graham Carmody.

The realization of who had caused Captain Buchanan's death, who had stolen the Blue Kashmir necklace at the Heritage Society, who had been an intruder in her house last night, caused her to inhale sharply. And in that instant, she felt a subtle change in the room.

With a sickening realization, Theodosia knew her cover was blown. Frantically, she grappled for her cell phone, punched the numbers for the Heritage Society, frantically flailed to hit the *send* button. But even as her fingers finally found the button, the closet door was jerked open.

Aerin Linley, eyes hard as ice, peered into the darkness.

Theodosia raised a hand, palm out. Her signal to Earl Grey to stay put, to remain exactly where he was.

Aerin Linley took it as a gesture of surrender and smiled.

Reaching in, she snatched Theodosia's cell phone from her and threw it to the floor. The little black Star Tac smashed into a dozen pieces.

Theodosia stared up into a grim, determined face. *Aerin*

Linley, she thought. *The trusted associate of Brooke Carter Crockett at Heart's Desire. The same woman who'd carefully planted nasty innuendoes against Claire Kitridge. Aerin Linley, who had once made mention of secret drawers and panels in the old homes of Savannah. Aerin Linley, who would have known all the details about the Buchanan family's heirloom ring!*

"Get up," Aerin snarled at Theodosia. Her eyes blazed with a slightly deranged look.

Theodosia rose to her feet. And as she did, a glint of light caught her eye. Aerin Linley had grabbed the letter opener from Drayton's desk and now clutched it menacingly in her hand. Honed from silver, the metal instrument looked extremely sharp.

Can it inflict a serious wound? Theodosia wondered. *Of course it can. No doubt about it.*

"Did you think I was so stupid?" Aerin hissed. "I could smell your pathetic trap a mile away."

Even as Aerin jabbed the letter opener toward Theodosia's throat, she pawed frantically with her other hand, trying to gather up the stamps that lay scattered atop Drayton's desk.

"You goody goody," Aerin sneered at Theodosia. "With your proper little friends and your proper little tea shop." She stuffed the Z grill stamp into the pocket of her black fleece vest, then her hand went back and swooped up the pile of first-day covers. "You really thought you were *investigating,* didn't you? Hah," she barked sharply. "Little Miss Detective. Looks like the joke's on *you.*"

Theodosia stared at her evenly, praying that Earl Grey would continue to obey her command and remain in the closet. In the distance she could hear the shrill of a police siren. Her call *had* gone through. Drayton had known it was her and immediately phoned the police. Thank goodness.

Aerin saw Theodosia register the sound of the siren and

sneered at her. "You think that police car will get here in time? I think not. No one's come close to me yet, no one ever will. I'll be out of here and out of this town so fast it'll make your head swim. And you'll look like a fool." She gave Theodosia the flat, slow-eyed blink of a reptile. A snake about to swallow its prey.

"You were on the roof of the Lady Goodwood Inn . . ." stuttered Theodosia.

"Piece of cake," Aerin sneered at her. "I grew up scaling rocks in the Blue Ridge Mountains. Only gear I needed for that job was an aluminum descender."

Theodosia suddenly recalled the metal ring she'd seen hanging from the strut of the Garden Room's roof. Aerin must have employed the same gear that sport rappellers and police and fire rescue units used.

"Pity the roof gave way," said Aerin in a cold, offhand manner. "And trapped that poor fellow underneath." She shrugged. "You never can tell about those old structures."

"I have to know," said Theodosia. *That's it, keep her talking.* "Did you snatch Delaine's watch and plant it in Claire's desk?"

"Oh please," snapped Aerin, "that was child's play. Delaine's house is a cat burglar's dream and the Heritage Society kindly invited me in on a jewelry appraisal. Convenient, no?" Smug and cold, Aerin's grin was hideous.

She turned suddenly and ripped five rows of plastic-encased stamps from Drayton's album. Still keeping an eye on Theodosia, Aerin backed slowly across the room until her hips connected with the window ledge. Then she sat down and swung one leg over the ledge with ease.

"I'd really love to stay and gab," she said. "But I've got far better things to do. My car's just down the block and the trunk's filled with loot . . . including that antique ring you've been so hot and bothered about."

Theodosia waited until Aerin had completely swung around and was about to drop to the ground.

"Earl Grey, attack!" she yelled at the top of her lungs.

Earl Grey came hurtling out of the closet like a silver streak. He rocketed across the room, his front paws barely skimming the windowsill as he sailed through the window frame. As Aerin Linley dropped to her feet, Earl Grey smashed into the back of her like a freight train. Eighty pounds of well-muscled canine heeding the command of his beloved mistress.

Aerin Linley screamed sharply even as she went down like a rock. The letter opener flew from her hand and made a dull *clink* on one of the patio stones.

As Theodosia ran toward the window, her hand instinctively reached out and grabbed the bottle of superglue from Drayton's desk. Then she had one foot on the window ledge and was clambering out herself.

On the ground below, Aerin was struggling mightily with Earl Grey, batting at him furiously, her hands balled into fists.

"Get off, you horrible mutt!" she screamed. "Get off!"

Theodosia dropped to the ground, stumbled forward, felt the sting of gravel cut into her palms and knees. She rolled, scooped up the letter opener that lay gleaming on the patio stones, found the bottle of superglue that she'd dropped, and scrambled over to the struggling mass of dog and woman. Now she pointed her finger at Aerin's neck.

"Hold tight!" she commanded the dog.

Earl Grey promptly clamped his wide jaws around Aerin Linley's neck. He didn't sink his teeth into her flesh, but he held her very, very firmly, just as Theodosia had commanded.

"Get this mangy creature off me!" Aerin Linley was screaming and carrying on like a banshee. Her face was beet red, her words a garbled cry. Her heels beat furiously against the pavement as her body squirmed and thrashed, struggling to throw the dog off.

Popping the top off the tube of superglue, Theodosia aimed the tip at Aerin's hair. She squeezed, watched as a huge dollop of clear glue came squirting out.

Aerin's eyes rolled wildly. "What are you doing, you idiot!" she cried as she continued to battle. "You'll be sorry you . . ." Aerin Linley's head suddenly stopped straining from side to side.

"My hair!" she screamed. "What's wrong with my hair!"

"Ease off," Theodosia commanded Earl Grey.

Panting heavily, pink tongue lolling out the side of his mouth, Earl Grey gazed at Theodosia, hungry for approval.

She reached down, patted him on the head. "Good dog. *Verrry* good dog."

"What'd you do?" wailed Aerin Linley. "I can't move my head! Help me, oh please, you've got to help me!"

The *whoop whoop* of the police siren was much closer now. It sounded a block away. Now it was directly in front of Drayton's house.

"Help!" Theodosia yelled. She ran to the side fence, boosted herself up as best she could, and waved frantically, trying to capture their attention. "We're in back!" she hollered. "Come quickly!"

CHAPTER 25

"*ANY INJURIES?" DETECTIVE* Burt Tidwell cocked an eye at the paramedic in his navy jumpsuit.

The paramedic, whose name tag read BENTLEY, shook his head, but the corners of his mouth kept twitching upward. It was obvious he was trying to remain professional. In other words, not burst out laughing completely.

"Slight puncture wounds," responded Bentley. "Nothing that requires any *serious* medical treatment, even though your perp is complaining bitterly about what she refers to as *dog bites.*"

"The woman does seem quite unhinged," offered Drayton. He had arrived home just minutes after the police cruiser arrived.

The police, at Theodosia's urging, had contacted Detective Tidwell. And Drayton, of course, had immediately phoned Haley, who'd been trying to call Theodosia at home and was frantic to know what was going on. Not one to miss out on excitement, she immediately came dashing over.

Now they were all gathered in a conversational knot on

the front walk of Drayton's house, a few steps from where Burt Tidwell's burgundy-colored Crown Victoria was parked at the curb.

"You say she's unhinged," said Tidwell to Drayton. "What a quaint assessment. So very Dr. Watson."

"Hey," piped up Haley as she stroked Earl Grey's head. "Drayton *is* Dr. Watson. To Theodosia's Sherlock, that is. Haven't you figured that out by now?"

Tidwell smiled tolerantly.

"Your suspect's *hair* condition is what's really causing the problem," continued the paramedic, Bentley. His eyes sought out Theodosia's. "I don't know what you squirted on her, lady, but it sure as heck is permanent. My partner and the other two officers are *still* trying to cut her off the pavement."

Drayton's eyes widened. "*Cut* her?"

"Well, her hair, anyway," explained Bentley as he packed a roll of gauze and bottle of antiseptic back into his bag. "Looks like she's gonna get a whole new look. Kind of patchy and choppy. That glue or whatever it was is pretty mean stuff."

This time Drayton threw back his head and howled. "Don't tell me you superglued Aerin Linley's hair to my patio!" he exclaimed.

"How else could I subdue her?" said Theodosia. "She was thrashing around like a crazy woman. I certainly didn't want to see Earl Grey get hurt."

"God forbid," said Tidwell as he rolled his eyes skyward. "And pray tell, while we're on the subject, why exactly *did* you stage this elaborate little charade without benefit of any backup?"

Theodosia threw him a look that was pure innocence. "But I *did* have backup, Detective Tidwell. I had you. I always have you."

"What she means is it's comforting to know we can always count on our law enforcement professionals," said

Drayton, jumping into the fray and trying to derail Tidwell's anger. "Thank you so very much, Detective Tidwell."

Tidwell shook his head in bewilderment and gazed down at Earl Grey, who was sitting on his haunches and yawning contently, looking as though he'd just been through a typical, uneventful doggy evening. "I'm afraid the mayor doesn't award certificates of appreciation to canines," said Tidwell. "At least he hasn't up until now. We'll have to find some other way to honor the crime-fighting Earl Grey."

"How about a free cup of Earl Grey tea to all our customers this week," piped up Haley. "And we can put up his photo. With a big *thank-you* banner."

"The dog that helped catch a cat burglar," said Tidwell, and even he couldn't resist a snicker.

"I've got a better idea," said Theodosia. "Let's all go in and have a cup of Earl Grey right now, instead of standing around shivering in the dark."

"When you put it that way," said Tidwell, "it sounds very inviting. The night *is* rather chilly."

"Tea *does* sound nice," said the paramedic, Bentley.

"You have Earl Grey in the house, don't you?" Theodosia asked Drayton. "The tea, I mean, not the dog."

"Of course," said Drayton as he started for the door. "And some nice molasses spice cookies, too." He glanced over at Bentley. "Does your partner drink tea?"

"I guess so," said Bentley. "And we *were* due to go on break," he said, suddenly showing genuine enthusiasm.

"By all means invite him in then," said Drayton. "The other officers, too."

"Hey, aren't they still working on Aerin?" asked Haley.

"She's not going anywhere for a while," said Theodosia with a mischievous twinkle in her eye.

"That's right," chuckled Tidwell. "Let her wait. Let her wait."

RECIPES FROM
THE INDIGO TEA SHOP

Chicken Perloo

1 tsp. olive oil
4–5 pieces of chicken, skin removed
2 slices bacon (cut in 1/4″ pieces) or 2 oz. diced salt pork
1 large onion, sliced
1/2 green bell pepper, chopped
1 cup long-grain white rice
1 can chicken broth (1 3/4 cups)
1/4 tsp. salt
1/4 tsp. pepper
2 Tbsp. minced parsley

Heat oil over medium-high heat using nonstick 12-inch fry pan. Add chicken and cook about 8 minutes or until golden, turning over once. Transfer chicken to plate. Reduce heat to medium and add bacon or salt pork, cooking for 4 minutes until browned. Remove bacon or salt pork with slotted spoon to small bowl. Discard all but 2 tsp. bacon fat from skillet.

Add onion and green pepper to same skillet and cook, covered, for 10 minutes, stirring occasionally. Add rice and stir until evenly coated. Stir in bacon, broth, salt, pepper and 1/2 cup water. Return chicken to skillet; heat to boiling over medium-high heat. Reduce heat to medium-low and cook, covered, 10 to 25 minutes. Sprinkle with parsley and serve. Yields 4 servings.

Tea-Marinated Prawns

2 Tbsp. Lapsang Souchong tea
2 cups water
1 Tbsp. lemon juice
1 lb. shrimp or prawns

Steep tea in boiling water to desired strength, then strain. Add lemon juice to the tea. Cool tea to room temperature. Marinate shrimp or prawns in tea for at least 30 minutes, then grill or stir-fry as usual.

Tea Smoothie

2 bags of Apple Cinnamon Tea
2 cups vanilla ice cream or frozen yogurt
1/4 tsp. cinnamon (optional)

Cut open tea bags and mix tea with ice cream and cinnamon in a blender until fully blended. Pour into a tall glass, garnish with whipped cream. Makes 1 serving.

Hot and Sour Green Tea Soup

3 Tbsp. lite soy sauce
1 1/2 Tbsp. rice wine
1 Tbsp. minced fresh ginger
1/2 tsp. sesame oil
3/4 lb. skinless, boneless chicken breasts, cut into thin strips
1/2 lb. soba noodles
3 cups brewed green tea
1/4 lb. snow peas, cut into thin strips
1 medium leek, thinly sliced
2 Tbsp. umeboshi vinegar
2 Tbsp. chopped cilantro

Combine soy sauce, rice wine, ginger, and sesame oil in a medium bowl. Add chicken strips, tossing to coat, and let marinate for 10 minutes. Meanwhile, cook noodles in boiling, salted water in a large saucepan for 10 minutes. Drain, transfer to bowl containing chicken mixture and cover. Using the same saucepan, bring the tea to a simmer. Add the chicken mixture, snow peas, and leek and cook over low heat until the chicken is just cooked through, about 3 minutes. Stir in vinegar and cilantro and ladle into bowls. Yields 4 servings.

Pear and Stilton Tea Sandwiches

4 very thin slices honey-oat bread
1 Tbsp. butter
1 ripe pear, halved and thinly sliced
Lemon juice
2 Tbsp. crumbled Stilton cheese (about 1/2 oz.)

Spread each bread slice with softened butter. Sprinkle pear slices with lemon juice. Place 1/2 of the pear slices in a single layer on one slice of bread. Top with half of the crumbled cheese and the second bread slice. Make a second sandwich the same way. Slice off crusts. Cut each into 4 finger-sized sandwiches. Yields 8 tea sandwiches.

Easy Cream Scones

1/4 cup butter
1 cup flour
3 tsp. baking powder
1/2 tsp. salt
2 Tbsp. sugar
2 beaten eggs
1/2 cup cream

Sift flour, then add baking powder and salt and cut butter into dry mixture. Combine eggs and cream and add to dry mixture. Pat to 3/4-inch thick. Cut in squares or triangles, sprinkle with sugar and bake at 375 degrees until lightly brown, about 20 minutes. Serve hot with jam or preserves.

Haley's Lemon Curd

3 large lemons
5 eggs
1 cup granulated sugar
8 Tbsp. unsalted butter

Grate the lemon rind and set aside. Squeeze the juice and put into a blender or food processor. Add remaining ingredients and process until smooth. Pour the mixture into the top half of a double boiler. Stir in the lemon rind and cook over simmering water for about 10 minutes, until thickened. Stir the mixture with a wire whisk if it appears lumpy. Chill the lemon curd before serving (it thickens as it cools). Spread on scones, crumpets, muffins, or toast.

Green Beans with Garlic and Tea

1 lb. fresh green beans, trimmed
2 cloves garlic, minced
1 tsp. canola oil
2 Tbsp. Keemun tea leaves brewed in 2 cups of spring water
Toasted almond slices

Steam green beans in water. While beans are steaming, sauté minced garlic in canola oil until opaque. Add brewed tea and simmer with garlic for 2 minutes. Remove beans from steamer and put in large bowl. Pour tea marinade over drained beans. Garnish with toasted almond slices, and serve as a side dish.

Stress-Relief Chamomile Tea

1 cup water
1 tsp. dried chamomile flowers
Lemon juice
Honey

Bring water to boil in saucepan. Sprinkle flowers onto water and boil for about 30 seconds with the lid on. Remove from heat and let stand for 1 minute. Serve with honey and lemon juice.

Tub Tea
(For relaxing in the bathtub!)

From your local co-op or herb store, get about 1 cup of each:

Rosemary
Lavender
Chamomile
Peppermint
Rose petals
Calendula petals

Mix together in a large bowl. Sew small squares of muslin or cotton on three sides. Scoop in herb mixture; sew the fourth side closed. Toss a fresh one into your bath each time you want a relaxing soak.

Teatime Entertaining Ideas

You don't have to travel to Charleston and the Indigo Tea Shop in order to enjoy a specialty tea. Simply invite a few friends in and be creative.

Choose a "theme" for your tea.

Try a Garden Tea in the out-of-doors when flowers are blooming and breezes wafting. Serve tiny triangles of chicken salad, cucumber sandwiches, deviled eggs, and date nut bread. For dessert don't forget tarts topped with the season's fresh berries. A Darjeeling is ideal, although on hot days, nothing refreshes like iced tea. Invite all your guests to wear floppy straw hats.

A Valentine Tea is a grand excuse to nibble an assortment of chocolate cookies, bars, truffles, and bonbons. To complement the chocolate, serve teas that offer blends of orange, vanilla, and spices. Put a white lace tablecloth over red fabric for extra punch and dress up the table with roses!

Quiche, blinis with sour cream, Eggs Benedict, or fruit compotes make a Brunch Tea extra special. If you have a chafing dish, this is the time to use it. Assam tea, with its rich, refined flavor is a delightful complement.

A Midnight Christmas Tea is perfect at this most special time of the year. Serve brioche, roasted chestnuts, and crepes in front of the fireplace. Cardamom and cinnamon teas warm the heart.

A Mystery Tea can mean a rousing game of Clue, reading tea leaves, or enjoying a mystery book discussion. Break out the candles, douse the lights, and serve steaming cups of Lapsang Souchong, the traditional tea of mystery.

If you have a group of friends who enjoy doing crafts together, why not have a Quilters Tea or Scrapbookers Tea? Don't bother to match teacups with plates; just jumble all your patterns together for a creative look. Jasmine tea or an Indian chai would be lovely.

Don't Miss the Next Indigo Tea Shop Mystery

The Last English Breakfast

Dawn is about to break at South Carolina's Halliehurst Beach and the members of Charleston's Sea Turtle Protection League are taking part in the annual "turtle crawl." As they help hundreds of tiny green loggerheads tumble safely into the surf, the dedicated volunteers congratulate themselves with a well-earned shore breakfast. But as the tea steeps and the gumbo simmers, a strange mass is spotted floating off-shore. Donning mask and swim fins, Theodosia paddles out to investigate, only to discover a dead body bobbing in the waves. The hapless victim turns out to be Harper Fisk, a prominent Charleston art dealer and passionate collector of Civil War antiquities. Rumors of sunken treasure and gold bullion have abounded, yet nothing has ever been found near Halliehurst Beach. But now Theodosia begins to wonder—did Harper Fisk finally stumble upon something? And was he killed because of it?

Praise for the other books in the Tea Shop Mystery Series

Gunpowder Green

Named an Editor's Choice Exclusive by the Mystery Guild Book Club

Highly Recommended by the Ladies Tea Guild

"Brilliantly weaving suspense and tea knowledge, this is a true gem."

—*In the Library Reviews*

"A charming mystery . . . as brisk and refreshing as any brew!"

—*Romantic Times Magazine*

"There is real gunpowder in the air . . . not just in the name of the tea."

—*Deadly Pleasures*

"Joins the growing trend of cozies that give food depictions and recipes a close second billing to the mysteries."

—iloveamystery.com

"Keeps the reader guessing until the last pages!"

—*The TeaTime Gazette*

Death by Darjeeling

Named a 2001 New Discovery Award Winner by the Mystery Guild Book Club

#1 on the Paperback Bestseller List of the Independent Mystery Bookstores

"Any fan of Agatha Christie would enjoy this as well."

—*Tea Time Worldwide,* Online Newsletter

"We are treated to a behind-the-scenes look at running a tea shop, as well as solid tea information."

—www.theteashop.com

Find out more about the author, her Tea Shop Mystery Series, and her Scrapbook Mystery Series at www.laurachilds.com